T0059316

To Live in the Light

to live in the light

A Life Renewed,
A Faith Restored

tim eichenbrenner

NEW YORK

LONDON • NASHVILLE • MELBOURNE • VANCOUVER

To Live in the Light

A Life Renewed, A Faith Restored

© 2022 Tim Eichenbrenner

All rights reserved. No portion of this book may be reproduced, stored in a retrieval system, or transmitted in any form or by any means—electronic, mechanical, photocopy, recording, scanning, or other—except for brief quotations in critical reviews or articles, without the prior written permission of the publisher.

Published in New York, New York, by Morgan James Publishing. Morgan James is a trademark of Morgan James, LLC. www.MorganJamesPublishing.com

Proudly distributed by Ingram Publisher Services.

Publisher's Note: This novel is a work of fiction. Names, characters, places, and incidents are either products of the author's imagination or used fictitiously. All characters are fictional, and any similarity to people living or dead is purely coincidental

Morgan James BOGO™

A **FREE** ebook edition is available for you or a friend with the purchase of this print book.

CLEARLY SIGN YOUR NAME ABOVE

Instructions to claim your free ebook edition:
1. Visit MorganJamesBOGO.com
2. Sign your name CLEARLY in the space above
3. Complete the form and submit a photo of this entire page
4. You or your friend can download the ebook to your preferred device

ISBN 9781631958588 paperback
ISBN 9781631958595 ebook
Library of Congress Control Number:
2021952428

Cover Design by:
Rachel Lopez
www.r2cdesign.com

Interior Design by:
Christopher Kirk
www.GFSstudio.com

Morgan James PUBLISHING **Builds** with... **Habitat for Humanity** Peninsula and Greater Williamsburg

Morgan James is a proud partner of Habitat for Humanity Peninsula and Greater Williamsburg. Partners in building since 2006.

Get involved today! Visit MorganJamesPublishing.com/giving-back

For my wife, Carolyn, and our daughter, Stephanie.
Thank you for standing by me when I journeyed into the Dark.

Chapter One

November 2018
Carrboro, North Carolina

This is just a guess, but most people don't end their workday thinking it might be their last day on the job. Right?

My long day was interrupted by ugly encounters with two staff members. A verbal dressing down—nothing physical, but in front of their co-workers. Not my finest hour. I knew better, but I just lost it when the staff mismanaged patients. Now, with heavy lids and my chin dropping, I struggled to complete my charting.

"Dr. Wilson. Got a minute?" It was Payne, the senior doctor in the practice who lived up to his last name—and then some.

"Sure," I answered, quickly righting myself.

"The conference room in five minutes. See you there."

The last time August "Gus" Payne and I were in the conference room together was the day I inked the practice's physician contract eight months earlier. He was an intimidating man then, and nothing had changed. As the founder of the practice, he commanded respect from patients, staff, and colleagues.

What could he possibly want? I straightened my necktie and tucked in my shirttail, attempting to look as professional as possible, and walked in with what I hoped was a look of confidence.

"Have a seat, Dr. Wilson—or Jack, I should say."

I slipped into one of the gleaming mahogany chairs that surrounded the matching table, all of it perched on a thick Persian rug. Upscale art hung from the walls, painted an off-white matte—rumor had it—with Farrow and Ball's best.

No expense was spared. The room's décor seemed an attempt to put the best face on the practice, but obviously, it was meant to intimidate, and did it ever. Talk about a rookie glaring into the bright lights of the major leagues!

A third person in the room, the office manager, sat quietly in the corner, partially obscured by the early evening's shadows. Doing my best to force a smile, my slight nod wasn't returned, but at least I wasn't outnumbered—Karen Hite had been my advocate when I returned from the abyss. "So, what's going on here?" I asked.

"We need to talk about you, Jack . . . specifically, about your job performance." He looked over his readers at me the same way he lorded over patients and staff. "Frankly, you're just not working to the ability you promised when we hired you. Today's fiasco is just the latest example."

The room's walls closed in and the shadows deepened. My pulse quickened, and a mist of sweat formed on my brow. "Not my best day today but still getting my work done and taking care of patients. Sure, a few hiccups now and then, but all in all, my medical skills are as good as ever. Today, I just got a little short with a couple of staff members." I shifted in my seat and glanced outside one of the windows, where colleagues and staff quickly made their way to their cars.

"Exactly, and both of them complained to Karen before leaving for the day. Your skill and knowledge aren't the issues, Jack. It's your demeanor—the way you carry yourself with your patients and co-workers. Your relational skills, not the scientific, technical stuff."

"You *would* agree that I've got to be able to trust my staff to do their jobs, right? I won't accept anything less. None of us should, or we're all in trouble." I gripped the arms of the chair tightly, trying my best to conceal any evidence of self-doubt.

"And I'm sure *you'd* agree it could have been handled in a much better way," Payne said. "Look, Jack, we all know it hasn't been easy for you—especially since the whole Annie episode—but I can't have you threatening the office staff, especially in front of their co-workers."

The Annie episode. How dare he bring that up? Has he never experienced heartbreak? My face heated up, and I leaned forward, ready to fire back, when Karen intervened.

"Dr. Payne, let's not bring Annie into the conversation, please. I don't think that's helpful."

"You're right, Karen. I'm sorry, Jack. I didn't mean to sound insensitive. We all know you're still not up to speed, and we get it. This is the perfect opportunity for you to take some time off, relax, and recharge. Since the holidays are coming, no one will be the wiser."

"Dr. Wilson," Karen said to me with a reassuring smile, "the partners can cover your patients easily enough. You won't have to worry about their well-being, although I know you will. Take some time off, and you'll feel better. I have faith in you."

Faith. That word, again. Annie talked about faith and look where it got her. I might feel better after some time off, but I doubt my faith will come into play.

"Thanks for the offer but no time off. Just need to plow through this and let everything get back to normal." In the heat of the moment, it was the best retort I could muster. My neck muscles tightened, and I reached for them reflexively.

Payne shook his head. "Jack, we're not giving you a choice. It's either time off or, as senior partner of the clinic, I'll be compelled to report you to the state medical board's physician impairment committee. That may sound harsh, but we're worried about your ability to withstand the pressures of a medical practice."

I glanced at Karen. She looked away.

"Our only interest is in your well-being. The other partners and I want to give you a second chance."

So, it's come to this. After all it took to get through medical school and residency and then fighting my way back to work after my world spiraled out of control, I'm now being threatened with an official complaint to the medical board? Maybe lose my license? Or at least have it suspended for whatever time the board thinks necessary. Lose everything I've ever worked for, and all I have left that gives my life meaning?

I removed my glasses and massaged my temples. Payne's brusque tone had intimidated me when I joined the practice, but I took that as the senior partner putting the newbie in his place. Now, he was doing it again. Back then, I was confused and annoyed by his coldness, but now his threats were offensive. This guy could wreck my career. Was that his real intention? *Watch your step, Wilson—and your mouth.*

Convinced it was the better option, I said, "Fine, Dr. Payne. I understand. Some time off." The words caught in my throat. *But I'll prove you wrong about this, Payne. I may have been out of line today, but there's nothing wrong with my ability to practice good medicine.*

And with that, I awkwardly pushed back the heavy armchair, stood, and walked out of the room and away from the only thing that mattered to me now.

Chapter Two

November 2016 (Two years earlier)
Chapel Hill, North Carolina

"Plans with Annie tonight?" Pete Bryan asked between bites of ramen noodles, some of which escaped and ran down his chin.

Life with my best friend was nothing if not entertaining.

I looked up from my plate of leftovers. "Nope. Not tonight. Busy day tomorrow—teaching rounds with the interns and then my afternoon continuity care clinic. Plus, charts to review tonight."

"Always working! You've got to allow yourself more free time, dude. How're you ever gonna have a serious relationship when you're married to your stethoscope?" He paused to slurp some wayward noodles. "Annie's a real catch. If you don't watch yourself, she'll slip out of your hands and fall into some other guy's."

"Oh, now you're giving relationship advice, Petey? Your high school sweetheart dumped you, and you never found someone to take her place." I stopped, careful not to be too harsh with Pete.

"That's fair," he said. "My track record does kinda stink." He looked away and shrugged. "But my experience gives me cred. Don't want you to make the same mistakes I made."

We never agreed on who pursued whom. I think it was her. I boarded the university shuttle one afternoon and took the last available seat, without giving the person next to me even a quick glance. Just looking for somewhere to sit. The last thing I wanted was a mindless chat with a stranger, for heaven's sake.

"I'm Annie Monroe."

I looked up from my book to acknowledge the southern twang interruption and did a double-take, struck by her runner's physique, full smile, and lavish auburn hair. "Jack, Jack Wilson." I returned to my reading to keep from staring at her.

Seemingly undeterred, she plowed ahead. "Are you a student here?"

"Resident—in the Family Medicine program. You?" *That was terrible, Wilson. Your small talk skills could use some work.*

"I'm a student nurse."

I nodded. The shuttle rounded a corner, shifting her closer to me.

"I can tell from your accent you aren't from around here."

"Midwest. Missouri, actually." I tried to resume my reading. *What's wrong with you, Wilson? This girl's a looker, and you're treating her like yesterday's news. You're not a kid calling a girl for a first date. Get with it!*

"Well, this is where I get off. Nice to meet you, Jack, Jack Wilson." She grinned as she stood to leave.

I managed a feeble smile when she looked back, catching me staring at her. *Well, that went just great, Wilson, but you'll probably never see her again.*

A few months later, I ran into Annie, sitting on a bench in the campus quad and writing in a notebook. It wasn't exactly accidental, as I'd been looking for her on every walk across campus and each shuttle ride. I approached her hesitantly, embarrassed by my previous behavior. Perhaps the fall season, with its crisp air, clear blue skies, and leaves colored as if dripping off an artist's palette, inspired me. Her beautiful reddish-brown curls and light green eyes didn't exactly hurt, either.

I cleared my throat. She looked up. "Well, hello again. I'm Jack. We met on the bus."

"I remember—Jack, Jack Wilson, right? I'm Annie. Nice to see you as well." Her eyes sparkled, which made them even prettier.

She hurriedly closed her notebook and covered it with crossed arms. Birds in a nearby oak chirped, their songs blending with laughter and chatter from students on the lawn. The pungent odor of musty, fallen leaves filled the air.

"Homework?"

"No. It's nothing important. Just some personal writing—poetry, actually."

"Ah, I knew it. You're a hopeless romantic," I said, perhaps teasing her too soon, given how little we knew each other.

"If you read it, you wouldn't find it too romantic. I was inspired by the Psalms, and now, I just like to write—you know, for my own pleasure."

Dozens of students were taking advantage of the weather—friends tossing footballs and frisbees, couples walking hand in hand, and students with open books, seemingly engaged in serious discussions. The more we talked, however, the more oblivious I, and I think she, became to anyone else's presence. Seriously, a meteor could have landed nearby, and we wouldn't have even noticed.

"Well, I've got a lecture to go to," Annie said, abruptly ending our conversation. "Nice to see you again."

"Yeah! Who would've thought? Maybe we can get together again—you know, for coffee or something."

"I'd like that." Her face turned up. She stored the notebook in her backpack, stood, and walked away.

She was gone before I realized I'd forgotten to get her number.

"A time and place for everything, Pete," I said, returning to our conversation as I stood to clear the table. "Like I said, work to do. What about you?"

"Headed to the Fine Arts building. Have to study some slides on Gothic architecture before my test the end of the week."

Pete's love of art history was as strong as mine for medicine. "Gothic? You mean big, black buildings adorned with skulls and crossbones?"

He laughed. "No, you moron! I mean Gothic in the traditional sense of the word. You know . . . stone buildings, columns, and flying buttresses. You sure you really went to college, bro?"

"Just my opinion, but if you've seen one Notre Dame, you've seen them all. And yes, I went to college. In fact, while you were drooling over slides of artwork and buildings, I was probably in Organic Chemistry lab all day."

"To each his own. Makes the world go 'round. Anyway, Notre Dame actually has Gothic and Romanesque features. In fact, the elevated nave—"

"Petey, just stop! Spare me the details. Go—enjoy your slide show."

Chapter Three

I first met Joni Clark when I was a freshman in nursing school. We bumped into each other walking into Biology 101. Well, I was walking. She was almost running. "Hi, I'm Annie Monroe."

"Well, hey there, Annie. I'm Joni Clark. Nice to run into you—literally!" She extended her hand. "Sorry. Thought I was gonna be late for class."

Joni was a small-town girl from Black Mountain, North Carolina, who thought Chapel Hill was a big city. Overwhelmed by her college curriculum, she lasted one semester. Not wanting to admit defeat and return home, she became a barista at Coffee Grind, where I'd often meet her for girl talk. Bored with mixing specialty coffee drinks, she enrolled in cosmetology school and then took a job at The Body Shop, a hair and nail salon in Chapel Hill. Not only had we remained friends and prayer partners, I considered her my best friend. She was the one person with whom I could discuss anything. But this? Why share something that might mean nothing?

Reluctantly, I picked up my phone and texted her.

> Met a guy, Joni.

Almost immediately, her response chirped.

> whaaaaaat? omgosh! we need to talk.
> wanna hear all about it!!!!

> Can you make it to dinner, my place, tonight at 7?
>
> sister, does the sun set in the west?

Joni arrived early, her usual modus operandi. I trusted her with a house key, as well as my deepest secrets. She barged through the door without a warning knock, also typical for her, and rushed into the kitchen. I had marinated shrimp and mixed vegetables on the stovetop. The yummy odor permeated the room.

I looked at her and laughed. A bundle of energy topped with a bleached mop of hair. "So platinum's the color du jour, huh?" Between her shiny hair, pierced nose, and tank top partially covered by a worn denim jacket, she looked like she could be on her way to an Aerosmith concert. She dressed to suit herself, with no pretension or thought of what others might think.

"You gotta love it, right?" She flicked her hair, pecked me on the cheek, set her shoulder bag on the floor, and plopped onto a bar stool.

Joni's presence never failed to add a healthy dose of energy and humor to a room. "I love everything about you, sweetheart."

She smiled and raised her eyebrows. "Okay, girl. Spill it," she said.

"I met him on a campus shuttle—"

"So romantic." She winked.

"Like I said, we met on a bus, but then we ran into each other again on the quad." I stirred our dinner as it sizzled in the pan. "We started talking and . . . oh, I don't know. Maybe I'm overreading things." That thought had crossed my mind. *Should I have kept this to myself?*

"I don't know, sister. You've never texted or called me about a guy before. Something must be different. Not the typical silly undergrad, I take it?"

"Actually, he's a resident in Family Practice."

She rested her elbows on the island and leaned forward, her mouth wide open. "Resident, as in 'doctor'?"

"Yep."

"Annie, you hit the jackpot. Praise the Lord."

"Slow down. We've only talked—in fact, we haven't even had an official date yet."

"Ha! With my track record, I count any one-on-one conversation with a guy as a date. So what are you waiting for? Your biological clock's ticking, you know."

"I'm only twenty-one, for crying out loud!" I rolled my eyes.

"I know. I'm just messing with you. Hey, that marinade smells delish!"

"Thanks. I think it's ready. Grab the riesling from the fridge for me, please."

As we ate, Joni tried to pry more information from me about Jack: his hobbies, his likes and dislikes, and his faith. The more she asked, the more I realized I didn't know about Jack.

"Good questions, but I can't tell you very much—not yet, at least." I didn't know much about him but knew I wanted to learn more. A *lot* more.

Chapter Four

March 2017
Ocean Isle Beach, North Carolina

"T hings are moving pretty fast, Jack. Think you should slow this train down?"

"What do you mean?" The breeze blew in from the east, carrying salted air laden with the smell of the ocean.

Pete rested his beer in the sun-weathered chair's cupholder and raised his eyebrows. "How does this square with your career? How many times have you told me how you decided on a career in medicine before you were barely out of adolescence—avoiding parties, serious girlfriends, and sports to study more and achieve that goal?"

We were sitting on the deck of his parent's vacation house, staring out at the ocean as the sun, dropping to the west over our shoulders, cast a yellow-orange glow on the waves as they crested and broke, sending those colors to millions of incandescent sparkles. Dusk was my favorite time of the day, especially at the place I'd rather be than anywhere else: the beach, where I also did my best thinking.

Pete's parents were generous enough to let us use their house over spring break, and for the third year in a row, we'd chosen this location over a more raucous time with our classmates and friends at Myrtle Beach. I had long ago decided on a quieter and more studied approach to life. Missing out on meaningless frivolity was, for me, a no-brainer. Yeah, it sounds boring. But med school was a reach for me, requiring the utmost focus to get in and then through it.

I had to admit that my buddy had a point. To me, anything short of having "M.D." after my name would mean my life was a failure, and I was willing to sacrifice everything else to achieve that goal.

"Listen, bro. You spend so much time on academics, no girlfriend has ever lasted."

"That's harsh, man."

He nodded. "Harsh, but true. Take it from me. After all, you know what a loser I am in that category. Anyway, you always said girls would be a distraction, or a—what was the word you used?"

"Probably 'deterrent.' Don't remember for sure, but I get what you're saying. But all of that was before Annie." Seagulls cried in the distance, signaling the end of their day of fishing.

Annie. The very thought of her sent my head spinning, making me forget about the patient records in front of me when I was at work. Medicine gave my life purpose and afforded me a goal—something I could pursue at the exclusion of all extracurricular distractions. No silly fling, much less love or a forever commitment like marriage, would compete with my education. Medicine would serve as a proxy mistress for any real relationship. Nowhere on my radar was there a chance that I would falter and let my journey go off course. Until now.

Five months had passed since we'd first met. What seemed like simple infatuation and a reluctant pursuit of her affection had blossomed into a steady relationship—something I wasn't certain I really wanted. Would a serious romance be too risky?

"I'm as surprised by this as you are, Pete. When we're together, nothing else seems to matter. Of course, we share an interest in medicine, but we also love going on runs together, discussing books we read, and just meeting for a cup of joe at the Coffee Grind. Maybe this is really meant to be." I sighed. "I think she might just be the one for me." *Did I really just say that?*

His response surprised me. "The *one*? You just started seeing her. Slow it down, dude. I'll ask again—what about all of that 'singular pursuit of medicine' hyperbole you spout?"

Pete sounded like he was doing his best to channel his inner Dr. Phil. Although his reality checks kept me grounded, they sometimes got old. I tried not to take offense. He meant well. I assumed his reaction stemmed from our mutually bad experiences with girls, resulting in a resolute commitment to bachelorhood for both of us. Pete had once been in a serious relationship with a girl who was his first and only high school steady. Not knowing what he wanted to do with his life, Pete took a series of odd jobs after graduation while his girlfriend went off to college. Once she got a taste of the upwardly mobile frat boys on campus, and with the encouragement of her upper-middle-class parents, she decided Pete didn't fit into her long-term plans. The "Dear John" letter hit Pete like a ton of bricks, and he still wasn't over it. Considering all of that, his cautious response to my feelings about Annie was probably appropriate.

"You know, Jack, this feels kinda weird. You're always looking after me, and now I'm giving you advice. I need to stay in my lane. I never talk to anyone else like I do to you. Just forget I said anything, bro." He shook his head.

Pete was right on both counts. For some reason, he lacked confidence and often needed my encouragement when he tried to make decisions. I'd never asked why, and he hadn't volunteered. Given his background, it was hard to understand. He was a Virginian by birth, from a strong family that held God, family, and country in the highest esteem, in that order. His life's greatest scandal was choosing to attend Carolina rather than Virginia Tech or James Madison, in part to get some distance from his ex-girlfriend. Although he was a person of color and a southerner, and I was a pale white mid-westerner from Missouri, we'd hit it off immediately when we moved into the same off-campus apartment building. Even found ourselves attending the same church near the campus. He was the little brother I never had.

"No, Pete, hearing your opinion really helps. We've had many important conversations, but our talks regarding Annie mean much more to me than our usual nonsensical banter about sports, money, and success. I need to hear your perspective. It's just that, when Annie and I are together, I forget about patients, charts, and supervising interns. When we're apart, I can't stop thinking about her. But maybe you're right. Maybe this is all happening too fast. After all, I do have my career to consider."

Chapter Five

Chapel Hill

With break passing much too quickly, Pete and I were back on campus to complete the spring semester. After a boring seminar on the treatment of metabolic acidosis in kidney failure, I needed a jolt of caffeine. I ducked into one of the school's cafés to get my fix. And there she was, sitting with a guy—presumably a student, as he had the requisite book-filled backpack resting against the leg of his chair. Not the jolt I was looking for. *Who was this and what did it mean?* Their heads were close to one another as they talked in hushed tones. Her radar failed to sense my presence until she heard my voice.

"Hi, Annie."

"Oh, hi Jack! Good to see you. This is my friend, Spencer. He's in my nursing school class."

Spencer and I shook hands, my brain in overdrive trying to figure out what was going on. *What should I say? Just play it cool, Wilson.* "Just came in for some coffee. Didn't mean to disturb you. Spencer, good to meet you, and Annie, catch up with you later."

I couldn't get my coffee and exit the café fast enough, my heart pounding and the coffee doing a jig in my trembling hand. I thought back to getting tapped out of a dance with my date at the high school prom. She never returned. Humiliating. *If this is an adrenaline surge, is it from jealousy or embarrassment?* I'd never experienced a negative rush like this, and I didn't like it.

Talking with Pete about my relationship with Annie had clarified things. To get serious with Annie before I completed my training would be an about-face on my life's path. Annie swept me off my feet—you know, like a kid who falls for a beautiful actress on the big screen. Now, look at me—jolted out of control of my emotions. What was I thinking? Why risk the pursuit of my dream for a relationship that could derail all I hoped to accomplish?

I walked briskly across campus, burning my hand as coffee sloshed out of the cup, and mulled over my options. I'd get back to the business of medical training and let the flames of whatever fire that burned between Annie and me cool but not extinguish. After all, she was fun to be with, we shared common interests, and a little social life away from the grind of medical residency couldn't hurt. Just no commitment. Right? Maybe she wasn't even reading the same tea leaves about our relationship. This was all new ground for me to plow, and I had to be careful not to get it wrong. *Nice try, Wilson, but you're kidding yourself.* One thing was for sure. I needed to talk to her about Spencer.

———

We met later that same afternoon, seated outside her apartment, after I texted that we needed to see each other as soon as possible. We sat close to stay warm as the last remnants of the winter chill stubbornly held off the onset of warmer weather. The clear skies, brisk air, and first signs of flowers blooming and trees leafing out confirmed the change in seasons when all things seem renewed. Annie was tight-lipped as she stared off. What was she thinking about? Could it be the awkward encounter at the café? *Just cut to the chase, Wilson.*

"Annie, I was surprised to see you with another guy today."

"Spence? We're just classmates and good friends. Nothing more. Actually, we dated a few times our first year of school, but no sparks flew so we parted amicably. But Jack, it sounds like you don't trust me. Who's to say I can't hang out with anyone I choose?"

She had to mention the word 'trust?' "That's fair. I was just caught off guard. Actually, my reaction surprised me. It's just that I've missed you."

Annie had spent the break at her mom's house in Wilmington, feeling obliged to be home with her as much as possible. Her mom had heard the two words no woman wants to hear—breast cancer. Annie had a brother seven years her senior, but he lived out-of-state and was busy with his career and children. Annie's mom was in remission, but Annie and I both understood we never know how much time any of us have. She was not about to waste an opportunity to spend quality time with her mom just to go to the beach. That wasn't Annie. Admirable.

"I missed you, too, Jack, but with my mom's illness, I had to be there. My worry about her served as a distraction from where I could have gone and with whom I could have been."

"Could have gone where? Do you mean with me and Pete at the beach house?"

"Of course! After all, you did offer . . ." She finally smiled.

I sighed. Feeling silly about my jealousy, I laughed. It was good to see a little humor after what had to have been a somber week for her.

"How *is* your mom?"

"She's an eternal optimist, convinced she will beat cancer. Based on her attitude, stubborn streak, and strength, I suspect she's right."

"What about your dad? Did you see him too?" I knew her parents were divorced, but I didn't know why.

Her eyes narrowed. "I don't want to talk about him."

"But did you see him?"

"No, I didn't. I spent all of my time with Mother. She needed me, and I think she appreciated me being there."

"I'm sure she did."

"How was the beach?"

I hesitated. "Uh, it was fine. You know, just hung out with Pete."

Annie leaned closer and frowned. "Jack, is everything okay? Did something happen at the beach?"

"No, Annie. Nothing at all. Why do you ask?"

"You just hesitated to answer me, and you seem so preoccupied."

"Nope. It's all good. Guess I'm just disappointed the break is over and it's back to work. Gotta say, however, it's really good to see you." My arm found her waist.

As we sat and talked, my determination to cool it a bit with Annie evaporated. Being with her was relaxing and seemed to make all things right in my world. Why couldn't I have both—my career and a serious relationship with Annie? *Wilson, your feelings move up and down and back and forth as much as a roller coaster.*

"Uh, Jack, hello—I asked you a question," Annie said as I came back to the conversation. "There you go again, a zillion miles away." She frowned.

"Sorry. What'd you say?"

"I asked you what your plans are for the rest of the day."

"Back to the apartment to do some laundry and then get ready for clinic tomorrow. You?"

"Pretty much the same. I'll do some writing and maybe some studying for the boards if I don't fall asleep first. It was good to spend the week with Mother, but now I realize how exhausting it was."

"You're a good daughter, Annie. And I know your mom appreciated you being there with her."

She shrugged. "You're sweet."

I pulled her closer and felt her shivering.

"Cold?"

"Yes. Can we go inside?"

"Sure." I nodded and grabbed her hand as we stood. She moved into me, and I put my arm around her hunched shoulders.

Once we got inside, we pulled off our coats and Annie wrapped her arms around my neck. "I feel warmer already, Jack. Can you stay awhile?"

My heart leaped, and a spark flickered.

Chapter Six

By the time I got back to my apartment, I knew what I wanted to do but needed to bounce it off Pete first. I didn't really understand what I was about to say. I mean, I knew, but I was confused. I'd kept a shield up in my personal life, protecting myself from any outside influence that would interfere with the pursuit of my goal in life. That included fun, for the most part, and definitely included girls. And now this?

I walked over to his apartment, knocking once as I opened the unlocked door. *Typical Pete—always trusting.* He was slouched on his overstuffed couch, his sockless feet propped on the coffee table. The TV was on—ESPN's *SportsCenter*. Food wrappers and empty soda cans were scattered around him, testimonies to his disregard for neatness. A fried food odor filled the room.

"Glad you're sitting down, big guy. I've got something to tell you."

"What's up?"

"I'm going to ask Annie to marry me!" *Okay, I've said it out loud.*

"You're going to ask Annie to *marry* you?" he repeated, as he sat up straight and raised his eyebrows.

"That's right. Probably sooner rather than later but at some point. We're just right for each other." A reporter opined on the upcoming weekend's Major League Baseball schedule.

"But why marriage? Why now?"

As a sounding board, Pete could sometimes come off as a dull thud. He meant well, though, and wanted to be sure I was making the right decision. "Talk about popping my balloon!" I said.

"Listen, I know your history and your fear of commitment. Just don't rush things. I don't want to see you get hurt, bro."

17

I shook my head. "There you go again. Look, I know you mean well, but this just feels right. Annie's changed my life. It'll work. I'm sure of it. She's finishing school, so she'll be working soon. I've got just over a year left of residency. It'll be perfect. For the time being, we can swing it financially, and more importantly, we'll be together as much as possible. Make sense?"

"Sure. It just seems so sudden, but if you're that sure of it, I'm on board, bro. Congratulations! I can't wait to give Annie a big hug—if she says yes, that is." He laughed.

That's my Pete.

"Let's celebrate. How 'bout some comfort food—burgers and fries, washed down with a few beers . . . for me, that is. You know, really celebrate," Pete said.

He knew I didn't drink but didn't know why, and he hadn't asked. Coke Zero was my addiction. I agreed to go, even though I was preoccupied with thoughts of Annie and how I'd propose to her.

I texted Annie at work the next morning to arrange to meet her for dinner at one of our favorite haunts—a quiet, unassuming Italian restaurant where we could talk.

The restaurant was nearly empty when we arrived. Perfect timing. Seated at a corner table draped in a red and white checkered cloth, I sighed before speaking. "Annie, there's something I need to talk about with you."

"If it's what you and Pete did on break, Jack, I'd love to hear it, just not right now. As soon as we finish dinner, I've got to get ready for clinicals tomorrow."

Maybe now wasn't the best time, but having steeled my nerves for this, I decided to plow ahead. Plus, I had the romantic Italian music, oozing from the wall-mounted speakers, going for me. "It's not about our break. It's about us."

"Is something wrong?"

"No. Not at all." I leaned forward and put both of her hands in mine. "I fell for you not long after we met. To be honest, I didn't see it coming, but somehow, I just knew we were right for each other. I love you, Annie, and don't want to live without you. In fact, the whole time I was at the beach, my thoughts were on you—wondering how you were doing and wishing I could be there with you. Truth is, Annie, I want you to marry me."

The silence was deafening. She knitted her eyebrows and then let her head drop. *Is that good or bad?* When she looked up at me, there were tears in her eyes.

"I love you, too, Jack. I've never said that to anyone before. But marriage? This is just so sudden. You're proposing, and we haven't even discussed something very important."

"Oh? What's that?"

"Faith, Jack. I'm a Christian and can only marry another Christian."

"I *am* a Christian. My grandparents made sure I was in church every Sunday, and Bible school every summer. In fact, I answered the preacher's altar call when I was in sixth grade."

"So you're saying you've checked all the boxes? That's not what being a Christian is all about, sweetie. It's about living a life directed by and focused on God."

"I do that! I'm in church when I can make it—just ask Pete."

"Going to church doesn't make you a person of faith, Jack."

I was getting frustrated. "Can we get back to the proposal, Annie? Maybe you're not ready, or I caught you by surprise. If so, then don't answer now. Think about it—at least overnight. If you say yes, it will have been worth the wait. If the answer is no, then at least I had a night of hoping."

"With Mother's illness and all, I don't know if the timing is right. I'm so overwhelmed by my responsibilities to her, trying to finish school, and looking for a job. Now, this—the most important decision I'll ever make?" She closed her eyes and shook her head. "Besides, I know how important finishing residency and joining a practice are to you. I don't want to be the one to derail your plans."

Don't let her see my disappointment. Annie was throwing me a major league curveball, and I didn't want to whiff. I caught myself rubbing the back of my neck.

"I understand, Annie. I really do, and I appreciate you thinking about my career. Like I said, just think on it, and then let me know. In fact, take as much time as you need."

We punctuated our dinner with small talk, avoiding any further discussion about marriage. After I walked her home, we hugged and then left each other for the night.

Chapter Seven

Needing to relieve tension, I went for a run with Molly, a shaggy, mixed-breed stray Pete had taken in when she started lingering around our apartment building. She was loving, loyal, and never held a grudge, and I considered her mine as much as Pete's. As my feet rhythmically struck the pavement and my breathing became more labored, Molly effortlessly loped along in a way that hardly defined exertion, her brown coat bouncing with each step. But hey, she does have four legs. A chorus of barks greeted her along the way, but she looked and ran straight ahead, undeterred.

I knew I would feel better after running—and think more clearly. *What if Annie turns me down?* What had been self-confidence now turned to something between presumption and despair.

Pete was raiding my fridge—a common occurrence—when Molly and I returned to the apartment.

"Caught in the act again. Slim pickings." I grinned.

"Busted," he said, and then, looking down, "Hey, Molly girl! How was your run?" She licked his outstretched hand.

Biting at his lip, he then turned to me. "Well?"

"Well, what?" Pete looked like a kid waiting to see what was under the Christmas tree.

"Did you pop the question, dude?"

"Yes."

"Awesome. What did she say?" Pete could be as persistent as a hungry dog digging for a bone.

"She said she'll think about it."

He frowned and then smiled brightly. "Well, at least she didn't say no. I guess that's something, right?"

I didn't know what to think. I'd never loved someone so much that I wanted to spend my life with them. Those I'd loved all left me. Maybe things were moving too quickly. Annie made a good point. She did have a lot going on in her life. Maybe she was so bitter over her parents' divorce that she was afraid to commit to a lifelong partnership? Or she struggled with the same issues I worried about. *Why not just ask her?* Pete didn't need to know these thoughts running through my head. At least, not tonight.

"I'm going to take a quick shower. After that, why don't we go over to the Grind? Sure could use a good cup of coffee, and you obviously need something to eat."

"But it's late, Jack."

I'd never known Pete to turn down food. Was he concerned he'd pushed too hard, and he needed to give me some space? "Oh, come on, Petey. At least a cup of coffee? My treat."

"What the heck? Let's go," he said, nodding.

Chapter Eight

I wanted to text Annie after Pete and I got back home but figured the ball was in her court, and it would be better to give her as much time as she needed. *Did she want to talk to me as much as I wanted to talk to her?* I wondered all night long.

The following day, I was in my continuity care clinic—my one sanctuary where I could get my mind off of personal matters. The place was as comfortable as an old overcoat. The clinic was part of the family practice residency, and some of my patients had been with me since my first year in training. They were mostly older and poor. Basic Medicare was their only ticket to health care. The schedule showed the usual smattering of patients with high blood pressure, obesity, and chronic back pain, with a few more interesting problems like Stage II kidney disease and early-onset Alzheimer's thrown in. There was one bright spot on my schedule: Sydney Blanton, an adolescent. Many doctors hated taking care of teens who obsessed over a few pimples or two extra pounds of weight, but I found young people a welcome respite from adults with their self-induced medical problems.

When my medical assistant and I walked into the exam room, Sydney cut her eyes at me but didn't greet me with her usual smile. I feared something was wrong but smiled and casually said, "Hi, Syd. Good to see you. What's going on?"

"Hi, Dr. Jack. Thanks for seeing me. I'm having headaches—you know, like this squeezing of my head all over, making it pound."

We went through the usual headache-specific questions: time of day or night, intensity, associated vomiting or dizziness, relationship to meals, what makes it better or worse. Sydney's responses were vague and unhelpful. Although uncommon in young and otherwise healthy patients, blood pressure was always worth checking. When I pushed up the right-sided sleeve of her gown to wrap the cuff,

I saw bruises that a first-year medical student would recognize as a hand pattern: four linear streaks on the inner aspect of the arm with an opposing bruised, swollen area. Sydney squeezed her eyes closed and gasped as I palpated the area then opened her eyes and looked away when I asked how it happened.

"Oh, that? I was at cheerleading practice and fell as we were in a pyramid formation. One of the girls grabbed me to break my fall."

My assistant and I glanced at each other. I let it go for the time being. After completing the exam, we excused ourselves, allowing Sydney to get dressed before I talked to her.

When I returned, Sydney was pacing the floor and visibly shaking.

"Syd, have a seat. We need to talk. You need to be honest with me about your injury."

"Like I said, I—"

"Syd, I know what you said, and we both know it's not true. Your arm is injured, and it's obviously sore. Had it been an innocent injury, you would have come in for that. You know you can be honest with me."

She looked away, eyes open wide and rivulets of tears running down her cheeks.

"It's my dad, Dr. Jack. He gets drunk, and then he gets violent . . . usually with my mom, but the other day, I just happened to walk in at the wrong time, and he grabbed me by the arm and threw me out of the room. I know he didn't mean to hurt me. He's just not himself when he's drinking. You won't say anything, will you?"

I realized I could lose Sydney's trust but knew my responsibilities to her and the system. "Sydney, first, I'm going to have your arm x-rayed, just to be sure there's no fracture. More importantly, however, I'm going to call social services and have them initiate an investigation."

"No. No, Dr. Jack—you can't do that! My dad will get really mad at me, and he might even leave my mom and me. You've always said I can trust you and what we discuss is confidential. Were you lying?"

"Syd, the law requires me to report any case of possible domestic violence. There's no other option. I'm not trying to betray your trust. My only interest is your well-being. What could happen next time? You can't live like that."

My words bounced back to me like an echo reverberating from a stone façade. She was a mirror, reflecting an image of me as a young boy. My mind reeled: *the drinking . . . why couldn't Daddy just stop . . . it was dark and I was alone . . . death must have been instantaneous . . . they didn't suffer.*

A child's instinct is to unconditionally accept his parents. Even when I wished him dead, I still loved my father.

It was all I could do to get Sydney off to x-ray and compose myself enough to make the phone call.

—————

"Dude, are you alright?" Pete said as he and Molly walked through my apartment door.

I was sitting with my elbows on my knees and my head in my hands in the room's silence and impending darkness as the sun dropped from the sky. "Not really. You know, bad day. It happens. I'll be fine." I looked up and patted Molly. "Hey, girl."

"Well, you don't look *fine*. Let's go get something to eat and talk about it."

There were clusters of students and a few single stragglers in the student union, but it was absent the activity and noise typically present. Pete acknowledged a few of his art classmates who were looking at pictures of nineteenth-century impressionist artwork on their iPads as they consumed cup after cup of coffee. How they and Pete could take such an interest in art history escaped me. Of course, he was equally amazed that I could love the blood and gore of medicine enough that I wanted to make a career of it. Maybe opposites do attract—right brain, left brain type thing.

"Pete, you know my history, kind of."

He narrowed his eyes. "What do you mean by *kind of?*"

As he handed me a plate at the food bar, I noticed his short, uneven fingernails—the result of a habit I'd always known him to have. I hesitated and looked around. My story was for Pete's ears only. Nevertheless, we moved to a corner table where we were safely alone.

I'd never told Pete all of it. How I lost my parents in a car accident after an alcohol-fueled argument between them. A fight I witnessed that first, was just verbal but then became physical. That my father was an alcoholic, and my mom always tried to stop him from driving while drunk, but she could never convince him it was dangerous. I talked about the awful night it got violent. How my last memory of them was her chasing him to the car and climbing in, trying to keep him from driving away in a drunken rage. That we think driving drunk was the cause of the accident. How I felt so abandoned and lost; though my grandparents took me in, they basically just offered me room and board without much emotional support. After all, they were struggling with the loss of their daughter. They did provide room and board, made sure I did my homework, and made a point of getting me to church. It just wasn't like a real family after that—even an imperfect one.

Pete's mouth was wide open, but no words came out until finally, "So does all of this have anything to do with your decision to focus on academics?"

"Absolutely. My life had been turned upside down, and I was unhappy. I still had a few friends, but most of them treated me differently once I was orphaned. It was hard to have true friends."

Then, I told him about Tommy, a kid my age with interests similar to mine, who was the only exception. We were in school together and attended the same church. He was actually the only connection I still had to Sedalia, my hometown. A real estate agent. We texted each other on birthdays and holidays, but that was about it. Of course, Pete knew my history with girls, so we didn't even go there. Basically, I was a loner, but I was a decent student so, with few friends and no social life, I devoted all my time to schoolwork. Once I realized how much I loved science, I set my sights on becoming a doctor and slowly left my memories of Sedalia behind.

"You never mention your grandparents. Are they still living?" Pete asked.

"No. Grandmother died of a stroke when I was an undergrad. Two months later, my granddad never woke up. I guess a heart twice-broken can only take so much."

"Man," Pete said, leaning back in his chair and slowly shaking his head. "It all makes sense now. Sorry you went through that. Your dad's drinking—is that why you don't drink?"

"Precisely. Not wanting to risk any chance that his alcoholism might be inheritable, I decided a long time ago to just avoid all alcohol."

"I'm glad you told me, but what's all of this got to do with today?"

Being careful not to violate any HIPPA regulations, I recounted the visit with Sydney. How everything came flashing back to me—a drunken father, violence, trauma. To top it off, I had to report it, so now my patient no longer trusted me, and heaven only knows what would happen to her family if and when charges are filed.

We took our trays to the belt, discarded our trash, and walked outside. The skies had darkened, and a light mist was beginning to fall.

Pete seemed lost in thought, silently looking into the distance. Suddenly, he took me by the elbow.

"Well, the way I see it, bro, you didn't get to choose your parents, and you had no control over your father's drinking. You were a victim of a very dysfunctional parent, just as this kid must be. But what you did get to choose is what you did today, and that could be the best thing that could happen to her."

I nodded, but I thought "best thing" didn't belong in any description about what had taken place with Sydney.

Chapter Nine

Annie

> Meet me at the Grind after work today?
> Gotta talk.

Joni answered immediately.

> sure. see ya soon.

Walking in, I heard "Annie" and then saw Joni waving me over to her table.

"Hey, sister! I've already ordered for you. So how ya doing?" she said.

"Okay, I guess . . . actually, that's why I wanted to see you."

She set her usual iced vanilla soy latte on the table and leaned forward, brushing her now fire engine red hair out of her eyes. "What's up?"

"It's Jack."

Her eyebrows raised. "Uh oh. Problems?"

"He proposed to me. I told him I'd think about it. I'm just not sure." I heard my name called and jumped up to grab my coffee at the counter.

"Girl, do ya think your bar might be set a little too high? A handsome, blond-haired hunk who's already a doctor? Money, smarts, and good looks . . . all wrapped up in a Christian. What more could a girl want?" she said before I'd even returned to my seat.

I glanced around. None of the few late afternoon patrons seemed to be within earshot, but I didn't want to take any chances. "Shush! Not so loud, Joni." I looked around again to see if we were being eyed. "It's just that I'm so busy with school and my mom's health issues—"

"Annie, do you love him?"

"Well, yeah. I do."

"Then what's the problem?" She tilted her head and pursed her lips. Then, her eyes widened. "It's the high school thing, right? What was his name? Chet?"

"No. Chip. But I really don't want to talk about him."

"Have you told Jack about him?"

"No," I said, vigorously shaking my head. "Besides my parents, you're the only one who knows. I *really* don't want to talk about him, Joni."

"But is Chip the problem?" Joni was persistent.

"I don't know. Like I said, I'm confused."

"Well, you've seen some of the losers I've gone out with, so I might not be the best judge, but Jack seems pretty terrific to me."

"I know." I sighed. "And I know he's a catch physically-speaking, but actually, there is a church thing."

"Church thing?"

I unloaded my concerns about Jack: his insistence that he was a Christian but his infrequent church attendance and his failure to discuss faith unless I brought it up first. Jack was my first true love. The fling I'd had with Chip in high school was a teenage mistake, but also a lesson in how important it was for me to date, let alone marry, a believer. Just thinking about Chip was unnerving.

"Then bring it up, sister. Be bold! Annie, are you listening?"

"I do and I am . . . sorry. I got distracted. I also miss church when I'm working, Joni, so I get what he's saying."

"Annie, is Jack pressuring you?"

"No. He said to take as much time as I need."

"Well, there you go. Take your time and think about it. And keep working on the 'church thing,' as you put it."

"Yeah, I will. Thanks. So how are things with you?"

"Oh, you know, hair and nails, all day every day—living the dream. Work keeps me busy, but I'm not complaining. And I'm never too busy to talk to you, girlfriend. So call me later, okay?"

"Okay. Thanks, Joni. You're a sweetheart."

"Oh, yeah. Bible study tonight. Be there?"

Our Bible study was another connection between the two of us. Most of the other women who attended were older women, but Joni and I still enjoyed being there and learning more about Scripture.

"Wouldn't miss it. Sometimes, I think the Word is the only thing I can count on."

We finished our coffee and tossed the cups in the trash on the way out the door. As I made my way back to my apartment, I couldn't get one question Joni had asked out of my head: "Annie, do you love him?"

I had my answer and knew what I had to do.

Chapter Ten

The next day in clinic I re-read Sydney's x-ray report. No fracture. I called her mom to check on Sydney, and she informed me they had moved in with extended family once her husband's investigation started. I was still upset over having to report what happened, but I was happy to know Sydney was safe.

My schedule that morning was uneventful until my cell rang during lunch. Annie. *This can't be good. She never calls me at work.*

I answered, fearful of what she'd say.

"I need to see you, Jack."

No hello—just cut to the chase. My worst fears confirmed. My worry about balancing my career with a marriage was probably all for nothing.

"Of course, Annie. I'll be there after I finish my clinic this afternoon—dinner maybe?"

"Fine. Just come to my place first. We need to talk."

Okay. Stay cool, Wilson. "Will do. Soon as clinic's over."

———

I knocked tentatively, unsure of what to expect. To my surprise, Annie greeted me with a hug and a kiss, and then put her arm in mine as she guided me to her sofa.

"Sweetie, thanks for coming over. This couldn't wait. I don't know what was wrong with me last week, but I didn't want to go another day without talking to you. I love you, Jack, and I want to spend my life with you, so . . . yes, I'll marry you!"

Stars shone brighter, bells rang louder, and music filled the air. At least, that's what it seemed like. I wanted to leap for joy but grabbed and hugged her instead. I released her and looked her in the eye. "But what about everything else? All that's going on in your life? None of that has changed, right?"

"We'll make it work. What can be more important than the fact that we love each other and want to spend our lives together? And one other thing, Jack. I've got to know we're on the same page with our faith. I'm not going through life with a partner who doesn't share my Christian faith."

"Understood, Annie. I know my faith's not as strong as yours, but I'll get there. I promise. Anyway, this is wonderful news. I'm ecstatic. Can't wait to tell Pete, and you need to let your folks know."

"I'll call Mother, but I'm not telling my father."

Trying not to look confused or sound judgmental, I just nodded. But why wouldn't she tell me more about her father? There had to be a reason for her to be so secretive. But what was it?

"And Jack, before you go running off to tell Pete, stay with me for a while," she said and then raised her eyebrows and smiled wickedly.

Chapter Eleven

April 2017
Asheville, North Carolina

Annie sank back against the passenger seat and closed her eyes. "I'm really looking forward to this trip."

Taking advantage of that rare Friday when both of us were off, we left for a long weekend in the Carolina mountains to celebrate our engagement. We were staying at a rustic lodge just outside Asheville, near one of the great old rivers of western North Carolina: the French Broad. It wasn't the beach—our favorite go-to place—but at least it was water. We planned to hike, go kayaking, and relax. We also had some things to discuss.

I glanced over at Annie, put down my travel mug, and placed my hand on her thigh. "Now that we're engaged, Annie, I really want to meet your parents. We've kinda done this out of sync."

She turned her head and opened her left eye, squinting against the sunlight flickering off her face like sun rays dancing on the surface of a crystal-clear lake. "What do you mean?"

"You're engaged to a guy your parents haven't even met, much less given their approval of."

"Yes, that's the second thing Mother said when I called her with the news."

"The second thing? What was the first thing she said?"

"Is that just a rhetorical question, or do you really want to know?"

"Yeah. I want to know."

"She asked if I was completely sure you were the one for me. You know, pointed out that we had only been seeing each other for about six months, and this was a decision that I had to be sure of. Probably just concerned I might make the same mistake—oh, never mind. Just don't worry."

I suspected that Annie's guarded response was rooted in whatever had happened between her parents. Trying not to seem disappointed, I said, "Your mom is right. I do need to meet her so she can be sure you've made the right decision. I'll win her over with my rugged good looks and sense of humor." I winked at Annie. But meeting her mom and gaining her approval was no laughing matter. Truth be told, I was intimidated.

"I'll call and arrange for us to spend our next free weekend with her."

"And your dad?"

"There's no reason for you to meet him, Jack. I neither need nor seek his approval for us to get married. I guess I could locate him if I wanted to, but there's no way will I spend what little time I have with Mother searching for him. He'll hear about the wedding one way or another."

"What about your brother?"

"Eric? Already called him. He was thrilled but just surprised I was getting married at such a young age. Guess he just wants me to be sure—you know, since his own marriage failed. But then he said he can't wait to meet the lucky guy getting to marry his favorite sis. Of course, I'm his only sister!"

"Well, at least I've got one family member on my side." I laughed.

"No. At least two. Count me in too! Now, enough talk about that. I'm starving. I can't wait to get to the lodge and try out their cozy little restaurant. I read the menu online, and it specializes in Carolina barbecue with all the fixin's."

We arrived mid-afternoon, giving us just enough time to check-in and walk the grounds and nearby trails before heading back to eat. Enormous trees lined the trails, their leaves just starting to emerge due to the later spring the mountains experience. Sunlight flickered through branches and warmed us as we hiked.

We ate ravenously, punctuating our bites with animated conversation, even though both of us were fatigued from the cross-state drive and the hiking we'd done. The restaurant was comfortably intimate, with soft mountain music piped in overhead and heavy wooden tables and chairs. A large blaze roared in the centrally located fireplace. I was so content to be spending time alone with Annie, it didn't even bother me when the people at the closest table kept looking over, probably annoyed by the noise we were making.

"I'm beat, Annie. Hate for the night to end, but I've gotta get some sleep," I said as we finished dessert.

"Who says it has to end?" She grinned.

I grabbed Annie's hand as we walked upstairs to our room. Exhausted, I sat on the edge of the bed. But when Annie sat down beside me, I felt a surge of energy, a bolt of desire. We embraced. Her face found the curve of my neck and nestled there. My hands explored areas where they'd not previously been. My heart beat faster, my body warmed.

"Jack."

I ignored it.

"Jack," she repeated. "There's something we need to discuss."

"Now?"

"Yes. Now."

My hands returned to my lap as Annie lifted her head and looked me in the eye.

"What?" I asked.

"I can't go any farther. At least not now, not yet. As a Christian, I want to save it for our wedding night. It has to be that special. I really believe that. Don't be mad at me, please." She looked down, and then her head dropped.

"Mad? I'm not mad. Disappointed maybe, but I'm not mad."

Actually, I was frustrated. But hey, I'm just your typical all-American, twenty-eight-year-old male with the girl of my dreams in my arms. So don't judge.

"I love you, Annie." I reached out and hugged her, holding her until I sensed the steady rhythm of her breathing, indicating sleep. I gently released her to the bed.

I sat beside Annie, consuming the delicious beauty of her features. Thoughts about the prospect of meeting Annie's mom, our conversations earlier that day, and the heat and emotion I felt for her played through my head as sleep settled in.

We were both up early the next morning, enjoying breakfast together in the lodge's café. The sun, as it broke through the Smoky Mountains' haze, illuminated the highest peaks in a way that, to me, was equaled only by the Blue Ridge and, perhaps, the Rockies. Shards of light cascaded down from the ridgeline, burning off a shroud of fog and illuminating the eclectic mix of hardwoods. They finally worked their way to the lodge, shining through the shop's windows and settling on us as we ate.

"About last night—" she said.

I reached out to take her hand. "Last night was wonderful, and I respect you even more now if that's possible."

She smiled. "You're sweet." She suddenly tapped the table's surface with both hands, her big green eyes opening wider. "Hey, let's decide on a weekend to visit Mother. I don't think her calendar is exactly full right now, so most any date should do." Annie sighed. "She's mostly just resting and recuperating. She tends to stay home and take long walks as her energy allows."

"Sounds good," I said, as we both pulled out our phones to check calendars.

We spent the morning enjoying the lodge's many amenities, an indulgence our budgets and time constraints would not afford us again any time soon. I persuaded Annie to go into the game room, where we shot pool and played the pinball machines. She returned the favor by pulling me along as she browsed in the lodge's several clothing and souvenir shops.

After lunch, we went out on the water in kayaks, navigating the twists and turns of the river. By late afternoon, we were hiking the forest, sauntering along trails, bordered by majestic trees rising like arms reaching for the sky and peppered with toe-stubbing roots snaking across the path. By the end of the day, I sensed we were both either exhausted, mesmerized, or some combination of both. Too tired to shower and dress for dinner, we opted for carry-out at a nearby Italian restaurant and sat on a side porch of the lodge as we consumed generously sized pieces of pizza, washed down with Coke Zero for me, sweet tea for Annie. After eating, we sat quietly, enjoying the sun as it dropped from the earth for the night. The coolness of the evening air sent us inside, where we grabbed coffees and went to our room.

I sat in the only chair in our room. Annie walked over and snuggled in my lap, cradling her coffee in both hands.

"What a glorious day," she said.

I nodded and then took the cup from her and placed it on the side table. I wrapped my arms around Annie and brought her to me.

"This is so perfect, Jack. Just smell the crisp mountain air."

We were on one last hike on our final morning. I stared at Annie, caught yet again by her soft features and seductive smile. A variety of birds, awakening for the day, serenaded us as we walked a trail that coursed nearer the water, glimpses of which we saw through breaks in the tree line. Before returning, we rested on a large rock formation at the top of an incline, basking in the morning sun's glory.

Once packed and in the car to head home, I said, "I'm going to take the scenic route on the Parkway for as long as possible and then work our way over to the interstate."

The sunlight flickered through the trees' emerging verdant suits of leaves, casting darts of light into the car. The barrage of light and my ever-present thermos of coffee kept me alert, avoiding any chance of drowsiness at the wheel and assuring us we'd get home safely.

It had been a much-needed weekend off. I was re-energized and ready to get back to work, but I was also filled with terror over the idea of meeting my future mother-in-law.

Chapter Twelve

Chapel Hill

"You're back," Pete said, as I came through the door of my apartment, where he was just as likely to be found as he was in his own place.

"You're a master of the obvious, buddy." Pete stood up from the couch and we shoulder-bumped our greeting. "I see you're housesitting again. Where's Molly?"

"Napping in your bedroom . . . and do I detect a little sarcasm, bro?" He grinned. "Hope that doesn't mean the weekend didn't go so well."

"Just kidding, Pete. You're always welcome here. And actually, we had a great weekend; we relaxed, but made some important plans too."

"Cool! Happy for the two of you." He smiled.

A dog barked in the distance, bringing Molly loping to the window for a look. Seeing nothing, she jumped on the couch and fell back asleep.

Pete had been a huge part of my life since we met on campus, and I wanted that friendship to endure for a lifetime. Most people have a lot of friends but only a handful of really close ones—people who can be called at any time for anything, dropping everything to help out. That was Pete for me. No way did I want him to get lost or forgotten in all the excitement of the engagement.

We went out to the car to unload and lug in my bags. Tired as I was from the drive home, in the spirit of our bromance, I offered to buy him an afternoon "snack."

"Let's grab some pizza, and I'll fill you in on the weekend."

"Sounds good, dude. I never turn down food, especially if you're treating!"

Vintage Petey.

We cut across the school grounds to a pizza joint just off-campus and grabbed the most isolated table we could find. The air hung with smells of pepperoni, sausage, and garlic, all competing for dominance. There seemed to be more adults than students in the shop. Sunday evening was when students typically got caught up on work due the following week or took in a football game on TV.

"The more time I spend with Annie, the more I'm convinced I made the right decision. It feels kind of funny saying this to a guy, but I'm head-over-heels for that girl."

"Given that you're engaged to her, that's probably a good thing!"

Pete's wit again. He often used it as a defense mechanism, but it was one of the things I loved about him.

"We had a great weekend and made plans for our next step."

Pete placed his hands on the table and leaned forward. "What's the 'next step'?"

"Well, we decided it was time for me to meet Annie's mom. Gotta say, my amygdala is in overdrive."

"Your amygda-what? English, please."

"My amygdala, Pete. It's the part of the brain that controls fear and anxiety."

"Okay, you stick to your body parts, and I'll stick to my buildings and artwork." We both laughed. "Anyway, I'm sure I'd be nervous, too, if I was meeting the mother of the girl I'm gonna marry. But you've gotta do this, right? What about her dad?"

I hadn't talked to Pete about the relationship Annie had with her father, or the lack thereof. It wasn't something he had to know about just yet, especially since even I didn't know the full story.

"Well, Annie's parents are divorced, and Annie doesn't communicate with her father—by her own choosing, I might add. She hasn't told me exactly why her parents divorced and what happened subsequently, so that's all I can tell you."

"Sorry to hear that. Must have been hard on her. It really makes me appreciate my family—" Pete stopped mid-sentence, probably realizing that might have hurt, given my history. "Anyway, at least you don't have to ask Annie's dad for permission to marry her. That ought to make it a little easier." He shrugged.

"One thing I know, though, is that I want you to be my best man, buddy. After all, you are my best friend."

Pete jumped up and gave me a bear hug. "I'd be honored. I was actually worried you wouldn't ask. What do I need to do?"

"Nothing now. Just save the date—once it's set, that is."

As we finished our pizza, Pete updated me on his art history studies. He felt confident about his prospects of finishing the semester in good shape. I talked about wrapping up the second year of my residency. I knew my final year would be easier, with fewer nights on call and less of what we called "grunt work"—drawing blood, chasing down lab results, starting IVs when the nurses couldn't find a vein—but with more supervision of the interns and second-year residents. I'd still have my outpatient clinic for my continuity care patients—my favorite aspect of the program, as it most resembled what I'd actually do once I was in private practice.

"Never ceases to amaze me how excited you get talking about medicine, Jack."

"I love medicine because it fascinates me. Billions of cells form structures that coalesce into organs, and those organs all work together in a way that produces the end result: a remarkable human being."

"That simple, huh? Still way over my head, dude!"

"Well, that's the Cliff notes version. And just think: with all the physiologic mechanisms that have to take place and could go wrong, it's amazing humans don't deal with more diseases than they do."

"Must be the work of a higher power. Right, Jack?"

A higher power? I hadn't given that much thought lately. Maybe that was Annie's point. "Yeah. You're right, Pete."

"I'm beat," he said as I paid the bill. "Time to go home and kick back."

"Agreed."

"Hey, thanks for the pizza, bro."

"Of course, and thank you."

"For?"

"Agreeing to be my best man!"

Chapter Thirteen

Early May 2017
Wilmington, North Carolina

"We need a plan, Annie," I said. We were finishing our breakfast at the Grind before leaving for the coast. Simple food in a coffee aroma-filled atmosphere as comfortable as a worn couch.

"A plan?" She wiped the last vestiges of cream cheese from the corner of her mouth.

"Yeah, a plan—you know, for how we're going to handle the weekend with your mom."

"Sweetie, we don't need a plan. We go there, you meet her, and then you just be yourself. It should all be very relaxing."

"But what if she doesn't like me? What if she resents the guy who threatens to take her little girl away from her?"

"Give her more credit than that, Jack. She doesn't think of me as a possession. Anyway, she'll like you. Like I said, just be yourself."

"Do you think that'll work?"

"Well, it did with me, didn't it?" She squeezed my hand.

She did have a point. Our relationship was growing stronger every day. With our busy schedules, we cherished the time we had together, especially when we could get out of town.

We took the interstate until we were almost to the coast and then picked up secondary roads until we got near Annie's hometown, a small bedroom community in Wilmington. As we got closer, beads of sweat formed on my forehead, either from the intensity of the morning sun beaming through the car window or from nervousness . . . or maybe both. Annie texted her mom to give her a heads up that we were almost there. *Come on, Wilson. Just be yourself.*

When we arrived, I was struck by the simple beauty of the house. It was of modest size, one and a half stories and well-maintained, with its off-white clapboard siding gleaming in the brightness of the morning and contrasting with the Williamsburg-green shutters and front door. The house was comfortably sandwiched between houses of similar size, all with well-groomed and landscaped yards. The neighborhood, apparently a community that prided itself on neatness and order, had "Southern Living" written all over it.

"Good morning, children," said a woman at the door who had to be Annie's mom. She swung the screen door wide to greet us before we had barely gotten out of the car. I stretched my legs as the cool morning breeze sharpened my senses, dulled by the three-hour drive.

Virginia Monroe was a strikingly attractive woman: thin and regal, standing with perfect posture. Her prematurely silver hair was perfectly styled and fashionably cut just above her shoulders. Her real beauty, however, was in her smile and her green eyes, sparkling and inviting, as though welcoming one to her presence. Annie's eyes.

Annie bounded up the steps and gave her a big hug and a kiss on the cheek and then turned to introduce us.

"Mother, this is Jack."

"It's truly a pleasure to meet you, Jack," her mom said in her fetching Carolina accent as she clasped my hand in both of hers.

"The pleasure is all mine, Ms. Monroe."

"Oh, please, call me Virginia. I'm getting too old to rest on formalities. But where are my manners? Please, y'all, come in."

The front door opened into a Persian rug-covered foyer, off of which was the formal living room. It was handsomely furnished. Annie's mom took a seat in one of the wingback chairs that bookended what appeared to be an antique sofa. As Annie and I sat, I noticed a picture on a side table of two young children. I knew the little girl was Annie, as I'd recognize that face at any age, and I assumed the little boy was Eric. A stack of books by William Faulkner, Thomas Wolfe, and Pat Conroy sat on the coffee table, pushed aside to make room for a tray of pastries, cookies, a carafe of coffee, and a pitcher of sweet tea, the requisite southern hospitality staple I'd come to love since living in North Carolina. Despite my nervousness, I was famished, so I helped myself to cookies and iced tea, opting out of coffee, as I was already uncomfortably warm.

"Jack, I've really been looking forward to meeting you," Virginia said. "I understand you're completing your medical residency next year."

"Yes, ma'am. That's right. I'm looking forward to finishing and then going into practice."

"A doctor and a nurse—perfect," She smiled.

"How are you doing, Mother?" Annie said.

"I feel great. My doctor says I'm in remission, and I shouldn't worry. I suppose the two of you would know a lot more about that type of thing than me, however. I just trust my doctor."

Music to my ears. I already like this lady.

"Tell me about your plans, please."

"Well, Mother, we haven't made many plans yet. That's one of the reasons we're here. Besides you and Jack meeting, I wanted Jack to see my hometown and the church I attended as a child. As I told you earlier, we plan to get married there."

"Wonderful. I'm sure you'll love it, Jack," she said, looking at me. "Oh, and Eric said you called him with the good news too."

Annie nodded. She'd called him shortly after our engagement to let him know to keep his calendar as free as possible, and that she'd get a date to him as soon as we set our plans.

"And your father?"

Annie spilled some of her coffee as she set her cup down. "No, Mother, he doesn't know about my engagement. You know we don't speak."

"But he's your daddy. Don't you want him involved? Walk you down the aisle?"

"Absolutely not," Annie answered, with a look on her face that I had only seen previously when the subject of her father came up. "He's my father, but he's never been a 'daddy' to me. He hasn't been a part of my life for many, many years, and he's not going to come back into it now."

"But, Annie—"

"I don't want to talk about it anymore," Annie said, looking away as she shook her head.

Virginia furrowed her brow and looked down, and I began to feel more uncomfortable.

"Let's get you two settled in," she said, gesturing toward the staircase. "Jack, you'll sleep in Eric's old room, and Annie, of course, you know where to go."

Sensing an opportunity to diplomatically remove myself from the present conversation, I left to grab the bags from the car and get them upstairs.

Chapter Fourteen

Afer unpacking our bags, we had a nice, casual conversation with Virginia about less stressful things: the neighborhood, old friends, and the weather. She cooked a delicious meal for us, topped off with homemade apple pie and vanilla ice cream.

"That was delicious, Ms. Monroe."

"Virginia! Please."

"Right. Virginia. Anyway, thanks for dinner. I'm stuffed."

"I don't do nearly as many things as I used to, but I can still cook. It's just nice to have someone to cook for," Virginia said.

"It *was* yummy, Mother."

I nodded. "Ladies, I've got to check on some loose ends from the hospital. After that, I'll probably just read a little before going to bed. I'll leave you two to catch up."

The light filtered through the shutters as I woke up the next morning. The crispness of the morning air and the first sound of birds beckoned me to go out for an early run. Not knowing the neighborhood, I made mental notes of landmarks and my turns. After what must have been two or three miles, I turned to retrace my route. As I slowed to a walk near the driveway, a gentleman at the house next door was stooping to retrieve his newspaper.

"Good morning, young man. I'm Tom Barnes. You must be Jack. Virginia told me you and Annie M—that's what I've always called her—would be in town this weekend."

He was a slightly heavy, older man with a shock of silver hair and a pleasant face. Eyeglasses hung from his neck. "Yes, sir, I'm Jack. Pleased to meet you."

"Right back atcha," he said, extending his hand. "I heard talk that you and Annie M are engaged. Let me tell you something—you're one lucky guy. My wife and I have known the Monroe family for years, and Annie M since she was a baby. She's a real sweetheart."

I couldn't argue. "Yes, sir. I agree."

"My wife's going to be so disappointed to miss seeing Annie M and meeting you."

"Is she out of town?"

He shook his head. "She's in the hospital. Some kind of intestinal thing. Flares up at times and causes her so much pain and nausea she stops eating and has to be hospitalized for a few days. Doc says it isn't cancer, which is good, but it sure is a big inconvenience, to say the least. We weren't meant to miss meals, I always say."

"Sorry to hear that." It sounded like some kind of inflammatory bowel disease, *or maybe an ulcer,* I thought. Being in medicine, I was always silently diagnosing problems, even when not asked to do so. That habit was fraught with potential danger, as I'd quietly misdiagnosed a neighbor's case of simple pernicious anemia as leukemia, and I once dialed 911 for an ambulance to help a child in acute respiratory disease from a suspected foreign body aspiration. As it turned out, he had simply had the breath knocked out of him while playing football.

"I just met your next-door neighbor," I said to Annie and her mom, who were in the kitchen having coffee and preparing breakfast.

"Oh! Mr. and Mrs. Barnes?" Annie said.

"No. Just him. Said his wife is in the hospital."

"Another flare-up of her intestinal thing," Virginia said as she nodded.

"Mother, why didn't you tell me?"

"I was going to, dear. Just hadn't gotten around to it."

"Mr. and Mrs. Barnes were like second parents to me," Annie said. "When Mother was at work, Mrs. Barnes would look after me or, when I was older, she made sure I got home safely from school, got a snack, and then started on my homework. Oh my—in the hospital! I have to go see her." Annie drew her eyebrows together and bit at her lower lip. Then, her eyes widened. "I'll stop on the way and get some flowers for her."

"Oh! She'll love that. You go right ahead after breakfast, and please give Ethel my best. Jack and I will be fine. In fact, it'll give us a chance to get to know one another a little better."

"Take my car, Annie," I said. *Alone with Virginia? What will we talk about?*

After breakfast, Annie left for the hospital. She looked back and waved as she left the house.

"That girl does love Tom and Ethel Barnes," Virginia said.

"It's obvious they mean a lot to her, and she thinks you hung the moon, by the way," I said.

"Well, we do have our moments, as you witnessed yesterday. However, we love each other deeply. I know I'm extremely biased, but you've got yourself quite a gal in Annie."

Over coffee on the back porch, Virginia asked me about my family.

I gave her the short version of a long story. "I lost my parents when I was young, and my grandparents raised me. They're both deceased now, so I really don't have any close relatives. It's different, but I've gotten used to it. I must say, however, I'm envious of the relationship you and Annie have."

"Has Annie talked to you about her father?" she asked.

"No." I shook my head. "I've broached the subject, but I always run into a dead end."

"I'm not surprised, Jack. It's complicated, but I think I need to tell you about it. I don't know when, if ever, Annie will be completely forthcoming about their relationship . . . or lack thereof."

I gripped my coffee cup and glanced out at the backyard. *Wilson, should you be hearing this?*

"Annie's father was a hard worker. Matter of fact, he was so dedicated to his job that he was rarely here when the children were growing up. He'd often come home long enough for dinner and then leave to make evening sales calls. It was a different world then. Don't get me wrong; he was a wonderful provider. This house is proof of that, but I'm just referring to material things. He wasn't much in the emotional fulfillment department, if you will. I don't think I ever heard him tell the kids he loved them, although I truly believe he did. Gradually, as he fell more and more in love with his work, or so I thought, he grew distant from the three of us."

"You 'thought'?"

"Well, come to find out, his work wasn't his only mistress."

I fidgeted in my chair and began to rapidly tap my foot. Sweat beads dotted my forehead.

"He began seeing one of his clients, eventually moved in with her, and filed for divorce. Hit me like a Mack truck, and the children were devastated. Not having a father home very often was one thing, but losing him altogether was quite another." She shook her head.

"I am so sorry, Ms. Monroe—"

"Virginia," she insisted.

"Okay. Sorry . . . Virginia." I couldn't imagine why Annie's father would walk out on such a sweet, thoughtful, and attractive woman, especially with two young children. "No wonder Annie won't talk about it."

"That's not all, Jack. Once our divorce was finalized, he married his mistress and then sued for custody of the children. After his lack of involvement in their lives, I couldn't believe it. I really didn't think it could happen. He insisted, so we went to court, and after an ugly legal battle, I was finally granted full custody of the children. He was given visitation rights but never used them. Neither Eric nor Annie really wanted to see him anyway, so they were glad he never came around again. It's hard for a child to lose a parent, but I guess you know that better than most."

I nodded, but I didn't feel my situation was any more tragic than what Eric and Annie went through.

"I know it must be difficult for you to talk about this."

"Not as hard now," she replied. "Time has a way of putting hurt and despair in their proper place. Somehow, hearts do mend. Now that you know, sooner or later you'll have to let Annie know I told you the whole sordid story."

That will not be a pleasant conversation.

Annie returned home after a two-hour stay at the hospital.

"Mrs. Barnes was so glad to see me. It was wonderful to visit with her again, even under those circumstances. Such a sweet lady. She hopes to be discharged in a few days. Did the two of you have a nice chat while I was gone?"

"It was nice," Virginia answered as I nodded.

"What'd you talk about?"

"Just, stuff," I said rather stupidly before Annie's mom could respond. Virginia looked away.

"Stuff?" Annie said.

"Yeah, just stuff."

"Oh, okay." She shrugged. "Well, let's get an early lunch so I can take you through town to show you some places that meant a lot to me when I was growing up."

Chapter Fifteen

"Such a picture-perfect day, Jack."

"Yep," I said as we walked through a town that looked like a scene from a Norman Rockwell painting.

I enjoyed seeing the sparkle in Annie's eyes as we passed by her elementary school, the public library, and the local drug store with its old-fashioned soda shop. Occasionally, we'd pass a local who knew Annie. "Miss Annie," some said as they nodded, "nice to see you back home."

"Annie Monroe, I do declare," others said. All of them seemed to eye me as if gaging my worth to be in a local girl's company. Except one. I noticed a woman we passed who seemed to be glaring at us. She followed us for a few blocks, and Annie quickened her pace as she briefly turned her head in the woman's direction.

"Jack, turn here—it's just around the corner . . . there it is!"

A brick church sat on a handsomely landscaped knoll. It was white; its age betrayed by a copper steeple now turned patina green. Five steps rose to double front doors, stained antique oak and glimmering in their varnish finish. The stained-glass windows were bordered with hinged shutters painted a dark green. On the parking lot side of the church were a sidewalk and a short driveway leading to a porte-cochere at a side entrance.

"Mother made sure we were here every Sunday. Won't this be a beautiful place to be married? With our small families, the church is more than large enough to meet our needs." There was a gleam in her eyes.

"It *is* a beautiful building. Can we take a look inside?"

Walking through the narthex, we entered the sanctuary, where my eyes were drawn to the large wooden cross hanging on the back wall of the chancel. Its stain matched that of the front doors and the pews, the latter divided into two sections by a central aisle. Stained glass side windows refracted sunlight, casting an array of colors throughout the room.

"See? I'm in church!"

"Hilarious."

"I'm just kidding. It looks perfect."

"More than perfect," Annie said in a hushed tone as she put her arm in mine. "This is where I was baptized as a baby and confirmed as a teen. I gave my life to Jesus here."

"That's nice, Annie."

"It's not just nice, sweetie. It's everything. You know, we haven't talked enough about church. We need to do that. You do want to go to church—at least when you're off, right?"

"Well. I'll go, but not religiously." My grin was not met by one from Annie. *Probably the wrong time for humor.*

"You told me you went to church when you lived with your grandparents. What denomination, sweetie? Southerners like to ask that, you know."

I hesitated to answer, but she just stared at me. Finally, "Uh . . . casual?"

"Seriously, Jack? I think you're kidding, but a Christian shouldn't be 'casual.' Christians should be all in."

We turned to see a woman enter, carrying a bouquet of flowers to the altar. *This is your way out, Wilson—at least for now.*

I took Annie by the arm. "Hey, babe. Let's talk about this later, when we have privacy."

"You can bet we will," Annie said.

We made our way back home. The walk down memory lane seemed to have lifted Annie's mood. She excitedly told her mom who and what we saw.

"Jack loved the church."

"That's wonderful, kids," Virginia said. "I'm so glad you got to see our little town, Jack. We're like one big family here."

"I can tell."

"Annie, why don't we take Jack into Wilmington for dinner tonight? My treat."

"That's a great idea. Jack?"

"Sounds good to me," I answered, never one to turn down a meal. "I'll drive."

As we made our way into town, Annie repeated a frequent complaint about my car: its age. She was right. It didn't even have airbags.

"I plan to trade it in as soon as I go into practice."

"Speaking of that, Jack, where do you plan to work?" Virginia asked.

"That will depend on where Annie's working and my finding a practice that needs a new provider. I'd like to stay close to the university, if possible. The idea of practicing in a small town, yet still close enough to the medical center where I can send patients when they need a higher level of care really appeals to me."

We soon entered downtown Wilmington, a port city bound by the Atlantic to the east and the Cape Fear River to the west. We turned down a cobblestone road, arriving at one of the restaurants that front the Cape Fear. Some of Wilmington's historic houses watched over us from their perch on the bluff. We arrived just as the sun began to descend to the west, transforming the greenish-blue water to an orange glow. It was the perfect setting.

"Mother and I have been here many times. We love dining outdoors with a view of the river." Annie grabbed my menu and said, "Let me order for you, Jack. I think you'll be pleasantly surprised."

"You southerners will add grits to anything!" I said after Annie ordered shrimp and grits for me. "This will be a big leap from the burgers, peanut butter, and ramen noodles Pete and I live on."

"Pete?" Virginia said.

"Oh, right. Sorry. Pete's my best friend and practically my roommate, even though he has an apartment next door to mine. He's going to be my best man, so you'll meet him the weekend of the wedding."

Dinner came, and I had to admit the shrimp and grits were great.

"Jack, you know I already feel like you're a part of our family."

I almost choked on a piece of shrimp. No one had ever said anything so nice to me.

"Thank you, Virginia."

"Virginia?"

"Yes, Annie," said her mom. "While you were at the hospital, I simply insisted that Jack call me that."

"Well, that must have been quite a conversation!"

If she only knew.

Fortunately, our conversation turned to less threatening topics as we finished our dinner, topped off with crème brûlée and coffee. Dark clouds hovered over the water and obscured the moon as we walked to the car. Thunder rumbled in the distance, and a cool breeze blew the odor of seaweed and fish our way. I shoved my hands deep into my pockets, and Annie moved close to her mom, wrapping her arm around her waist.

A chilly mist began to fall on our way home, quickly morphing into a steady rain. We ducked our heads as though we could dodge the raindrops and hurried inside,. I plopped down in a chair, kicked off my shoes, and propped my feet on an ottoman. "I'm beat. How about we catch a movie on television?"

"Great idea! I'll find something," Annie said.

Annie found *North by Northwest,* an old Hitchcock movie starring Cary Grant. I didn't ask, but I suspect it was mostly to please her mom. Before the movie ended, I was nodding off to the rhythmic beating of rain peppering the windows. "I'm done for the day, ladies. Going upstairs to read a little before bed. Good night."

Sleep did not come readily, as my mind was racing with the information Annie's mom had shared with me earlier in the day. I felt guilty not letting Annie know I was aware of her family history. I'd have to disclose it to her at an opportune time. I'd have to pick that time carefully.

The next morning, Annie and her mom put together a quick breakfast of Danish, muffins, juice, and coffee before we left. We ate on the screened porch. The rising sun checked the crisp, cool air and dried the grass, still wet from the previous night's rain. Pines, oaks, and maples populated the backyard. In the only clearing sat an eastward-pointing bluebird house, patiently awaiting the arrival of its first inhabitants of the upcoming season.

"Mother, I promise I'll be back in touch soon with wedding details," Annie said into her ear as they embraced, and she rested her head on Virginia's shoulder.

Virginia turned to me. "Jack, it's been a pleasure having you here."

I was struck by the strength of her embrace when we hugged.

As we drove away, I saw Annie's mom mouthing a last goodbye. "Your mom really is a remarkable woman and a gracious hostess. She made me feel right at home. What a great weekend! Oh, by the way, Annie—when we walked through town, did you notice a woman kind of staring at us?"

"I did, but I'm sure it was nothing," Annie said, seemingly preoccupied with something she was not sharing with me.

Chapter Sixteen

Chapel Hill

"Well, how'd it go?" Pete said before I could even get my bags inside. "Give me all the details."

"Annie's mom is a wonderful woman, and we had a great time with her. By the way, why are you in my apartment again?"

"Waiting for you, bro. I heard you drive up. Hard to miss your old ride." He slumped in the chair and frowned, apparently yearning for something juicier than what I'd offered. Pete was my best friend, but hey, guys will be guys, and I think he expected to hear about some tense moments. Of course, the one uncomfortable conversation was about Annie's father, and I wasn't about to discuss it with Pete—at least not until I talked it over with Annie.

"I hope you're not disappointed," I said. "Tell you what, let's go get lunch, and I'll fill you in on all the boring details."

"You buying?"

"Don't I always?"

"Dr. Wilson, the department secretary called and left a message that Dr. Pritchard wants to see you after clinic this morning," my assistant informed me as I arrived at work the next day.

I nodded. As the department head, it was not unusual for Roger Pritchard to call in a resident to discuss clinical or administrative matters. Probably something to do with my senior resident position next year.

"Jack, have a seat, please," Dr. Pritchard said as his secretary left and closed the door. "We need to talk."

"Yes, sir. What's going on?"

"That teenage girl you saw who you thought had been abused by her dad—"

"Sydney?"

"Right. Sydney. Well, it turns out her father—Lou Blanton is his name—and the hospital CEO, Bob Sanders, belong to the same country club and often play golf in the same foursome. He went to Sanders and complained about the incident, and now Sanders wants it fixed."

"'Fixed,' sir? What do you mean?"

"He wants you to apologize to Blanton and make this all go away. He admits the guy sometimes has a little too much to drink on the nineteenth hole but believes he wouldn't lay a hand on his child."

"Apologize? I was just doing my job." The knot forming in my stomach tightened. "Anyway, I'd have to visit him in jail to apologize, and I don't think—"

"No, Jack. That's just the point. He was investigated, but it was basically his word against his daughter's, and the mother wouldn't side with either of them. Everyone's back at home, with the only stipulations being that their situation be monitored and he enters an AA [alcoholics anonymous] program."

My breathing quickened. I wasn't sure if it was from the idea of meeting with Sydney's father, or if it was my concern about her well-being.

"I don't know, Dr. Pritchard. I'm really uncomfortable with the notion of apologizing for protecting my patient. It's not like I did something wrong."

"Nonetheless, Jack, you'll do it. I'll ask my secretary to coordinate your schedules and have the two of you meet at Sanders's office as soon as possible.

"But, Dr. Pritchard—"

"That will be all, Jack."

Chapter Seventeen

Mid-May 2017

Annie and I saw much less of each other as the end of the school year neared. I was focused on my final year of residency and looking at practice opportunities, while she was finishing her clinical rotations and studying for her nursing license exam. Much later, I realized our busyness was a pattern we allowed ourselves to fall into, one I would come to profoundly regret. At the time, however, I selfishly justified it as a necessary means to an end.

I finally mustered the courage to bring up the topic of her dad one night at dinner, several weeks after our visit to her mom's house. We were at my kitchen table, eating takeout from a nearby Mexican restaurant after my pitiful attempt to cook a simple chicken casserole had literally gone up in flames. A charred odor lingered.

"Annie, do you remember when we were at your mom's, and when you came home from visiting Mrs. Barnes, your mom and I were rather vague about what we'd been discussing?"

"Now that you mention it, I do remember. I just assumed it was idle chitchat."

After taking a deep breath, I said, "Actually, it was much more than that. Your mom and I started talking, and suddenly, she was telling me the story of how your father left the family. I wasn't sure I should be hearing it from her, but she just came out with it."

"She what?" Annie said, much louder than usual. "How could she do that?" Her voice was now rising to a yell. She began to stand, but my hand on her shoulder kept her seated and in eye contact with me.

"She thought I should know, Annie, and she wasn't sure when, if ever, you would tell me."

"Mother had no right to talk to you about that, Jack," Annie shouted, her face getting redder by the second. "I was planning to tell you eventually—when the time was right." She pushed my hand away.

At that point, her voice was shaky and her hands were trembling. I'd never seen her like that, and she'd never raised her voice at me.

"Annie—"

"Stop, Jack. Don't talk to me. It's bad enough that someone else told you about my father, but it's even worse that you waited to tell me you knew. Is that what you do, Jack? Keep secrets? I thought I could trust you."

"No! No, of course not. I just didn't know how to handle it."

"I'm going to call Mother when I get home and let her know how upset I am with her."

"Annie, please don't do that. At least, not now. Give yourself a chance to calm down and think about things before you do anything rash. You know how much your mom means to you, and I think you'll regret having a fight with her."

"Just stop talking. I don't want to discuss it any further."

The rest of dinner was picked at in silence, accompanied only by the occasional clinking of utensils on plates. Annie was so upset she hardly ate and then stood and began cleaning dishes and the kitchen counter. Stony silence, until she told me she wanted to go home. I walked her back to her place or, at least, tried to. She stayed ahead of me and said nothing. When we got to her apartment, she told me goodnight and went inside. No eye contact.

Well, that actually went worse than I'd expected. I knew the divorce was hard on Annie, but lots of families go through that and come out just fine. I walked back home. At least it was done but likely not over.

Early the next morning, I texted Annie before she would normally leave for the hospital.

> so sorry. didn't know how to handle
> things once I knew your family's story.
> should have discussed it with you
> right away. please forgive me.

No response.

"Dude, you look awful," Pete said as he walked into my apartment in gym shorts and a sleeveless tee, by all appearances having just rolled out of bed.

I was sitting on the couch with a cup of coffee in my hand, and even in his post-arousal stupor, it was obvious he could tell something was wrong. "Annie and I had a fight last night. It ended badly, and I've got to figure out what to do."

"Call her."

"I just did . . . well, I left a message, but she didn't answer."

"Good. She'll see your message and know you tried. Good start. Want to talk about it?"

"That's really all I have to say." He was the one person with whom I could talk about anything, but not this—at least, not yet. I went to my room to get ready for work. The day could only get better, or so I thought.

⸻

"Hi, Jack. How's it going?"

"Oh. Hi, Van. Good to see you." Van was a surgery resident who started his training the same year I did. An all-around great guy. *We could always use more surgeons with personalities.*

"Glad I ran into you. I've got one of your teenagers on my service—a ruptured spleen and a bruised kidney. She's post-op now and doing fine." He wrinkled his forehead. "Her name's, uh . . . Sydney, Sydney Blanton."

My heart leaped to my throat. "Sydney? Oh no! What happened?"

"Came in with abdominal pain and bloody urine from an accidental fall. While she was in surgery, however, her mom admitted to a nurse that the girl had been pushed by her dad, causing her to fall down the stairs. Seems there's some history there—"

"Yeah, Van, I know all about that. Hey, thanks for letting me know. I'll stop by to see her."

"Better make it soon. She'll probably be discharged in a day or two."

⸻

Sydney was as blanched as her standard-issue hospital sheets. As I approached her bed, her eyes opened weakly. She squinted as the sunlight made its way through the window's mini-blinds.

"Dr. Jack. You came. Thanks."

"Of course, I came, Syd—just as soon as I heard you were here. How are you feeling?"

"Very tired but no pain. They've got me on something for that. Dr. Jack, I'm sorry I got upset with you at your office. Now I realize you were just trying to protect me. I should have trusted you more."

"No need to worry about that. Just focus on getting better." I visualized her falling down the stairs. My face heated and my neck muscles tightened with the thought that her father was living at home again. "I'm going to leave, Syd, so you can get some rest. I'll be back to check on you later." *Wilson, you can't let that man ever hurt her again.*

"Dr. Jack," she said in a barely audible voice, "It wasn't my dad. It was my mom."

Eyes wide and mouth gaping, I'd failed to disguise my shock. Fortunately, she seemed to be drifting off.

I patted her forearm and reassured her. "I'll be back later, Syd."

"I know you will," she said. Her eyes closed and she fell asleep.

Work was difficult that day. I couldn't get Sydney's confusing statement off my mind. Was she telling the truth, or had her post-op medication caused confusion? I knew who I needed to talk to. After calling and texting Annie repeatedly throughout the day, I finally reached her. Her voice was calm, which I took as a good sign. "Annie, I'm sorry."

"Jack, I've thought about it a lot, and I'm afraid I let my feelings for my father color my response to what you told me. I'm sorry too. We need to see each other. I can't stand the way we ended our last conversation."

We made plans to meet at Coffee Grind after work that day.

Chapter Eighteen

Like I said, Jack, I overreacted last night. I'm sorry."

Annie and I were sitting near the end of the counter at the Grind. The wait staff was hustling orders from the kitchen, and the place reeked of freshly brewed coffee—my favorite scent. Once we'd been served our order of coffee and pastries, we were left alone and free to talk privately.

"And I'm sorry, too, Annie. Could have handled it better. Can we just move on?"

"Of course. But no more secrets, right?"

"Right." I nodded.

"But one more thing that's been bothering me, sweetie."

"What?"

"We started talking about faith and church when we were in Wilmington but never finished the conversation. I need to know that you'll work at getting to church more often. We need to go together. It's important in a marriage."

"Sounds good," I said.

"Don't just say that. You have to mean it. Like I said, a Christian needs to be all in."

"Listen, babe. I know I've drifted away from the church. Hey, it happens when you leave home and you're on your own for the first time."

"Well, it didn't happen to me."

"Good point. Okay, I promise I'll work on it." Annie seemed intent on pushing how important a faith-based marriage was to her. I couldn't argue, but with the disappointment I'd experienced in my childhood, and now the busyness of my life, I just hadn't made time for church, or much of anything related to religion. I wasn't about to push back, though.

"Fair enough, Jack. Hey, let's talk about something I know we can agree on—our wedding plans." Annie sat her coffee cup on the countertop, looked up, and took my hands in hers. "I don't need a big wedding. I want to keep it simple, which'll make it easier for us and for Mother. I've only got a few close girlfriends, so having a lot of bridesmaids is out of the question. In fact, I'll ask Joni, my best friend, to be my maid of honor and Mary, my roommate from freshman year, to be my bridesmaid and leave it at that."

Simple certainly worked for me. My family ties were small, having only a few aunts and uncles, none of whom I was close to. They'd probably be surprised to get a wedding invitation from me.

I hesitated but then took a deep breath and said, "Who's going to walk you down the aisle, Annie?"

"Actually, I plan to walk alone. I could ask Mother, but I'd prefer she be seated already."

There it was again. Her disdain for anything related to her father. But I knew better than to argue. "How's your mom, by the way?"

"I forgot to tell you since I've been so busy and, you know, we haven't been talking with each other a lot recently. She called late last week and asked if we'd like to come back to see her for a weekend. I explained that we were both swamped with work, but we'd try to get there as soon as we could. She seemed okay with that, but I sensed a bit of disappointment in her voice."

"I'd love to go back for a visit," I said. Our time with Annie's mom had been so enjoyable. A family atmosphere—something I'd longed for. We'd have to make a point of visiting again, just as soon as we could both free up some time in our schedules.

Sidetracked by talk of wedding plans, I didn't mention to Annie my concerns about Sydney. It just didn't seem like the right time.

The fight with Annie now resolved, I found work the next day to go much easier. No distractions. That afternoon, I left for the hospital to check on Sydney. My surgery buddy had kept me abreast of her progress, and she would likely be discharged the next morning.

"Hey, Syd. Gee, you look great!" Her color was back and she seemed fully alert, although she noticeably tensed when I walked in and spoke to her.

"Hi, Dr. Jack. I'm fine, sort of. I know we need to talk, though." Before I could respond, she said, "I'm sorry I lied and blamed all of this on my dad. I was so confused. He did drink and sometimes got verbally abusive, but he never laid a hand on me, and now that he's in AA, he's not drinking and seems so different—you know, so much nicer. It was my mom both times. She didn't mean it—I think she was just so upset with my dad that she lost her temper and things got out of hand. But it *wasn't* the first time."

"Syd, when you were in surgery, your mom told a nurse your father pushed you down the steps. At the time, I was furious with your father, but now I understand why Social Services absolved him of any wrongdoing and allowed him to return home."

"What's going to happen now? I haven't seen my mom since the surgery."

"I reported what you told me to the authorities, and she's out on bail and awaiting a court date to face charges of child abuse. But she can't be allowed anywhere near you or the house. This is dangerous behavior, Syd, and you have to be protected. When you're discharged, your dad will take you home. Hopefully, the two of you can re-build your lives."

"But I don't want to lose my mom, Dr. Jack. I need her."

"Believe me, Syd. I get it. I've had other cases like this." *Even in my own life.*

———

It had been a difficult day, especially ending it with the visit with Sydney. It seemed that every time I saw her, I had flashbacks to my childhood. Since I was an only child, my parents doted on me, especially my mom. Everything changed when my dad had too much to drink. He would verbally abuse Mom and me, and sometimes, he'd take a swing at her if she tried to talk to him about his drinking. I didn't understand how alcohol could change someone's behavior so quickly, or how addictive it was.

My phone chirped.

> heard you come in. hungry?

Before I could text back, Pete and Molly walked in.

"Hey! I was wondering when you'd get home. Wanna get something to eat?"

"Thanks, but no. Way too much work to do. I'll just grab something here. If you're going out, just let Molly stay with me. She's good company . . . right, Molly?" She pricked her ears at the sound of her name, stood, and put her head in my lap, waiting for her head to be scratched.

"Suit yourself. Headed to the student union. Later, bro." As he walked toward the door, Pete stopped and turned around. "Oh, Jack—I almost forgot. Your department secretary called me because she couldn't reach you. She said an Officer Stanley called and was looking for you. Said it sounded important, so she wanted to get the number to you as quickly as possible. It's on the kitchen table."

Officer Stanley. The name didn't ring a bell. The area code was my hometown's. Not hesitating, I dialed the number.

"Officer Stanley."

"Uh, yes, sir. This is Jack Wilson in Chapel Hill. I had a message to call you."

"Yes, Jack. I'm one of Sedalia's police officers. I'll be traveling through your state this coming weekend on my way to the coast for some deep-sea fishing. I'd like to stop and meet with you, if you'll be around."

"I don't understand. What's this about?"

"It's about your father, Jack. We found him."

"I'm afraid that's not possible. You see, he died years ago."

"No. It was him. I've got details, but I'd prefer to see you face to face. It's kind of complicated. Hold on just a minute." He paused. "Sorry, but I've gotta go—emergency call coming in on the radio. I'll confirm my arrival time with you Saturday as soon as I get to the state."

Just hearing a reference to my father sent my mind racing and my skin crawling. I sat there staring out the window and shaking my head, not sure what to make of what I'd just heard.

Chapter Nineteen

We were at Annie's place the next night, watching an old movie, *The American President*. Yeah, I know; it's a chick flick, but I still love it. The call from Sedalia still bothered me, but I wanted to know more before I talked to Annie about it.

"Jack, are you alright?"

"Sure. Why?"

"You keep staring off and not watching the movie."

"Nope. I'm watching."

"Uh-huh. Tell you what, we'll finish it another night. Anyway, I've got something to talk to you about."

"What's that?"

"We need to set a date for the wedding!"

I laughed. "Yeah, I guess that is somewhat important! Let's not wait too long, especially since our plans are falling into place."

Annie took my hand and leaned closer. "I would love a wedding in early to mid-November. That way, we'd have our first Thanksgiving and Christmas together as husband and wife. Newlyweds at the most wonderful time of the year! Pretty romantic, huh? How about the second Saturday in November?" She looked at me with her beautiful green eyes open wide and eyebrows raised.

"Perfect." Since I assigned work schedules, I knew I could make that weekend and all of the next week work. "What about you? Once you're working, do you think you can get time off so soon?"

"Sure. Shouldn't be a problem. Nurses are always trading weekends and coverage with one another. So, we're set. Right?" Annie was beaming.

"Yep. We're set!" I rested my empty mug on the table. As we stood for me to leave, we stopped to hug and kiss.

"Oh, Jack, I'm so happy—and excited!"

———

Walking into my apartment, I found Pete in the kitchen, looking in my fridge for something to eat. He was in his usual warm-weather attire: short sleeve tee, shorts, and flip-flops. Molly stood at his side, licking her chops.

"Caught in the act again, bro," he said, both arms raised.

"No worries. You know my place is your place. Hey, big news, Petey."

"Oh yeah? What's that?" He handed Molly a few blueberries, and grabbed a bowl of leftover ramen noodles and slipped it into the microwave.

"Annie and I have set the date. I'm telling you first because I need you to be sure you're free the second week of November."

"Jack, I'll be free. You don't have to worry—"

We were interrupted by my cell phone. It was Annie.

"Jack, get over here, please. I need to see you right now."

There was a sense of urgency in her voice. "I'll be over as quickly as possible. Leaving now."

"I've got to go, Pete. Annie needs me . . . don't know why, but it doesn't sound good."

When I got to Annie's place and knocked, she opened the door and threw herself into my arms, sobbing almost uncontrollably.

"Annie, what in the world is wrong? We were both on cloud nine a couple of hours ago."

"It's Mother. I called her as soon as you left to let her know about the wedding date." Her voice caught. "She told me her cancer has spread. I'm sure that's why she asked us to come back to see her so soon after we'd just been there. Now, I feel horrible I put her off."

"Tell me exactly what she said about her cancer."

"She started having some leg pain and shortness of breath, so she went back to see Dr. Parke, our family doctor. He ran some tests and found evidence of cancer in her lungs and the bones of her legs."

Metastases. Not unusual for breast cancer but a bad sign. "But Annie—that's not necessarily a death sentence. There are treatments for this kind of thing. I'm sure her doctor will get her right back to the oncologist to get her enrolled in one of the treatment protocols."

She shook her head. "No. She told him she's not interested in any further treatment. She doesn't want to risk the side effects of chemotherapy or any other kind of treatment, especially with our wedding coming up."

"But without treatment, Annie, you and I both know she may not survive until November."

"I realize that, but I don't think she understands how aggressive and devastating untreated metastatic disease can be. She wants to be as healthy as she can be for the wedding, walking in unassisted and in the best shape possible. I can't believe she's worried about *that* when her own life is on the line."

"Nevertheless, that's her decision, Annie. You've always said your stubbornness comes from her, so I doubt she'll change her mind."

"I know. That's why I'm so upset. What are we going to do, Jack?"

"We'll do what we have to do—the only thing we can do to honor your mom's wishes. We'll move up the date of the wedding. Who knows . . . after the wedding's over, maybe she'll decide to re-start chemo."

Pete had waited for me in my apartment. When I told him we were moving the wedding date and why, he reassured me that he'd make whatever date we chose work.

Pete was only taking one class over the summer and doing some work for the Art History department, but his response was still a relief. That was the only box I had to check for the date change. Annie had the more challenging tasks.

First, she called the church to check on the church calendar and the minister's availability and to make sure the fellowship hall was still available for the reception. The secretary had known Annie since her childhood, so she was more than willing to do anything to help the Monroe family. Annie also had to call her brother Eric, whom I had not yet met, to be sure he and his kids could be there the weekend of the wedding. He, too, was willing to work with us and free up time to get back to Wilmington on the new date.

We had decided on the first Saturday in September. That was just under four months away. Time was going to be critical. Any further delay would only serve to worry Annie about her mom's health and stamina.

Chapter Twenty

Annie

The first time Joni and I walked into an off-campus Bible study, I felt the stares aimed at my best friend. I was certain Joni's avant-garde outfit and hairstyle had to be a topic of discussion for the other ladies, most of whom were older women from the church I attended. Joni didn't care—one of the things I loved about her.

My Bible study kept me connected to the church and often substituted for attendance on Sunday morning worship services when I had to work.

Once, early on in our relationship, when I mentioned faith in passing to Joni, I was surprised to find that she had a strong Christian background. She started attending with me—another bond between the two of us.

After this evening's meeting, we were walking back to campus to catch a shuttle. "Joni, I've got to update you on some news."

"Cool, girlfriend. Hope it's juicy."

"No. It's about the wedding."

"It's not off, is it? Did Jack get cold feet?"

"No—on both counts! But we've moved the date up, and I've got to make sure you can still be my maid of honor."

"Annie, I wouldn't miss this wedding for anything—even if Prince Charming offered me a better option! Plus, I've got my heart set on owning one normal dress." She winked.

I cackled. "Good. You're a good friend, sweetheart."

"But, sister, I've got to ask you something. Why move up the date?" She gasped. "You're not pregnant, are you?"

"No. Of course not!" I said as I shook my head. "C'mon, you know me better than that."

She laughed loudly and gave my shoulder a gentle push. "I was just kidding. But if it were me, with that hunk of a man you've caught, I'd at least consider it!"

"You're terrible! Actually, my mom's taken a turn for the worse, and we need to get married while we know she's healthy enough to attend."

"I'm so sorry. Why didn't you tell me sooner?" She stared at me as the wind caught her purple-tipped hair.

"Well, we just decided yesterday after I heard from Mother. I've been busy today calling Eric and the church to make changes. Knew I'd see you this evening."

"No. Please, don't apologize. I know how private you are, but we do share everything, right?"

I put my arm in hers as we arrived at the stop, leaned close, and said, "Of course, we do."

"How is Jack doing, by the way?"

"He's great. Busy, of course. He spends an awful lot of time on his work."

"Well, I guess that's good. I'd want my doctor to take his work seriously!"

"Agreed. But sometimes, I feel like our relationship plays second fiddle to his work. And another thing: since his teenage years, he's drifted away from the church. I'm not sure his faith is as strong as it should be."

"Well, I know you. You'll get him back to church." Joni pulled my arm tighter to her side. "Don't worry, sister. It'll all get better once you two love birds tie the knot."

The shuttle arrived. "I hope you're right, Joni," I said as we boarded.

Chapter Twenty-One

With my confusion and anticipation seeming to make time pass slowly, Saturday finally arrived. Molly's barking from next door announced someone at the door, even before the bell rang. An older gentleman sporting a Cardinals baseball cap and an Orvis pullover stood there. He had a gray, neatly trimmed mustache and a wrinkled face peppered with age spots.

"Jack Wilson? I'm Carter Stanley." He took off his cap as he spoke, revealing a bald head. "Pleased to meet you."

"Please. Come in," I said, motioning him in the direction of one of the few chairs in my living space. "Have a seat. Coffee?"

"That'd be great. Hot and black, please. Thanks."

We walked into the kitchen. I put on some water and decided to cut to the chase. "Gotta say, your call surprised me. There must be a mistake. See, my dad died in an automobile accident years ago."

He slowly shook his head and sighed. "I know. I was one of the investigating officers. Matter of fact, I was the one who came to the house that night to speak to your grandparents. Based on the extent of the wreckage, we assumed he was killed, Jack, but the accident was still under investigation when I came to your house, and we hadn't recovered the victims' bodies. I was a young cop then and made a rookie mistake. Since then, I've learned not to jump the gun, so to speak."

My mind went back to that awful night as he droned on, explaining that when the wreckage was disentangled, only one body was found, and it was burned beyond recognition. The medical examiner determined it was a female, so they knew my dad had somehow escaped from the vehicle. How they see that all the time—drunks escape serious injury and the innocent aren't so lucky. Once they knew my dad hadn't died in the accident, he contacted my grandparents, who thought it best I not be told. Given my age at the time, it seemed reasonable, but in retrospect, I probably should have been informed once I was a little older and more mature.

I was hot and anxious. My heart was beating out of my chest. "This is crazy—it can't be true. And, if it is, why am I just hearing about it now?" I grabbed the back of my neck, as I felt a sudden ache there.

"Just two weeks ago, an older man's body was found in Dresden, only about ten miles from where you grew up. He lived in a boarding house and, by all reports, was known to just work odd jobs around town. Had no bank account or credit cards—seems he always paid in cash, even for his room and board. No driver's license or anything else that might reveal his identity. He went by J.W., but no one knew anything more about him. To identify him, his prints were taken and run through the database. They matched your dad's prints on file in our precinct—"

"Fingerprints? Why would my dad's prints be on file?"

"A long time back, he'd been accused by one of his drinking buddies of involvement in an old armed bank robbery just outside of your hometown. He was cleared, but his prints stayed in the system. Good thing, I guess."

"Okay, but . . . but, if he was alive, why didn't he reach out to me at some point?"

"Well, he did choose to live close by, probably to be near you. Who knows, maybe he even kept an eye on you. My guess is he knew if he returned, there'd be a litany of charges that would be filed against him: drunk driving, vehicular homicide, and leaving the scene of an accident. On a more emotional level, think about the shame and guilt he must have carried and how hard it would be for him to face you and his dead wife's parents."

Those last words hit me with the impact of a ton of bricks. I was upset, and I had so many questions. *How could this be? Why did he never contact me? What became of his life?*

"What now, officer? Do I need to claim his remains? Bury him?"

"No, Jack. That's already been handled. Seems the town of Dresden has a fund to cover a simple burial for people with no known next of kin. By the time I tracked you down, he was already in the ground."

"Well, I appreciate you taking the time and trouble to let me know. It may take me a while to process all of this."

"Understood, young man." He handed me his card and headed for the front door, turned, and thanked me for the coffee.

So now, I'd experienced the death of my father—twice. Not only did he kill my mom and emotionally abandon me, but he'd also physically abandoned me. I never thought I could be more disgusted by my father, but I was wrong. *I hate him more now than ever.* Tears welled in my eyes.

Chapter Twenty-Two

There was another secret. We were having dinner at Annie's and discussing the upcoming ceremony when she stopped our conversation. "Jack, there's something you need to know."

"Sure, Annie. What's up?"

"You need to know something else about my father—and my past."

"Your past? What's more to know. From everything I've heard, your past—at least in your hometown—was like growing up in Mayberry, except for your father, of course."

"There's more, Jack."

"Go on. I'm listening."

"Well, there was this boy. Chip Edwards. I was a freshman, and he was a senior—on the football team, Homecoming king—all that stuff that seems so silly now, but at the time, I was starstruck. He asked me out, and we started seeing each other on the sly. Mother would have never approved because I was so young. We were getting serious, or so I thought. One night, we were parked, and he forced himself on me. Eventually, I was able to fight him off, but he got really mad—shoved me against the car door and then opened it, pushing me out to the pavement. He had sexually assaulted me, and I was cut and bruised. When I got home, I was so shaken that I told Mother everything. She insisted I go to the hospital to be checked and, you know, to be sure I was completely safe."

I felt my temperature rising as I clenched my fists. I paused, attempting to calm down before speaking. "Annie, I don't know what to say. I'm so angry, but I'm also sorry."

"I don't blame you for being angry with me, Jack. We had a deal—no more secrets." Annie looked away, her hands firmly gripping the chair's arms.

"No, Annie. I'm not mad at you. I'm angry with this kid, Chip. That was an awful thing to do to a girl."

She looked back at me and then threw her arms around my neck. "That's not all, though. Word got out. In a small town, news travels fast. Early one morning, just a few days later, Chip was found behind a store in town, beaten half to death. He lived but had permanent brain damage. Never right again—never even made it back to school. There were no witnesses, but I know who did it."

"How?"

"Because my father came to our house in the middle of that night, drunk and with hands abraded and bloodied. I was in bed asleep, but Mother told me later. He was terribly upset, and he blamed her for letting me go out with an older boy. Said if anything like that ever happened again, he'd take Eric and me, no matter what. Mother felt like I needed to know—to help drive home the lesson as to how dangerous my behavior was, I guess. She never went to the police. She didn't want to bring more embarrassment to the family. As far as I know, it's the only deceitful thing she's ever done."

"That had to be awful. As if rape wasn't terrible enough, you also had to live with the knowledge of what your dad did."

"As crazy as it sounds, I feel guilty. Chip's life must be miserable. And one more thing: that day we walked through town and a woman had her eye on us? That was Chip's mother. First time I'd seen her in years. Somehow, she must have heard I was in town. Seeing her stare like that kind of spooked me. Chip wasn't able to speak well, and he could no longer write, but he must have somehow let his mom know who he thought attacked him. She must, at least, have some suspicion."

"That's her problem, Annie. It was her son who caused it all. I'm glad you told me, but remember, we said there'd be no more secrets."

"No more secrets," she said as she crossed her heart.

When I got home, I did what I always do when I'm uptight: I went for a run. Breaths came in gasps, either from the pace of my run or from my emotions, or maybe both. My head reeled as I tried to process everything that had happened recently: Sydney's case, the revelation about my father's second life, and now this creep who assaulted Annie when she was just a teen. I was a child again, with my world turned upside-down—hurt and not knowing what to believe or whom to trust.

I'd taken solace in the predictability of medicine: the killing efficiency of anti-biotics, blood pressure controlled with anti-hypertensives, and the body's positive response to regular exercise and healthy eating. Love was much different. Don't get me wrong, I wasn't blaming Annie. But would the secrets ever end? Physically and emotionally exhausted, I found myself back at the apartment, still angry and unsure about what to do.

Chapter Twenty-Three

Pete and Molly were in my apartment when I returned. I grabbed a water from the fridge and gave Molly a pat on the head.

Pete looked up from the couch. "Dude, you look whipped."

"Just tired from running. It has been kind of a long day too." I did not really want to delve into recent events. "I'm going to cool off, take a shower, and go to bed. Got an early day tomorrow."

"Sounds good. Oh, by the way—Annie called while you were out. She asked me to have you call her when you got back. She sounded upset."

"Got it. Thanks." One nod and I started to walk away.

"Hey—your phone."

I took the phone to appease him. This was not the right time to return her call. "I'll call her later. Right now, I just want a shower."

"What's going on with you two?"

"Not now, Pete."

After a quick breakfast the next morning, I hurried to the clinic, where I was back in my sanctuary and in control. I noticed that Sydney Blanton was on the schedule, listed as a routine hospital follow-up. Good. I looked forward to seeing her.

Work was therapeutic. I could fix some things, like ear infections and strep throat, but not other more challenging problems, like obesity and stress-induced headaches. Nevertheless, I did my best, and I enjoyed helping my patients. Finally, it was Sydney's appointment. My nurse and I walked in to find her gowned and sitting on the exam table, with her arms wrapped snugly around her chest.

"Hey, Syd. How are you?"

"Hi, Dr. Jack. I'm freezing."

"You know that's not what I meant." I grinned.

"I know. Actually, I'm still a little tired and having some pain if I turn just the wrong way. Is that normal?"

"It is after what you went through, yes. And how are things at home?"

"Sorta okay. It's weird not having Mom there, but Dad's been very supportive and, as far as I can tell, he hasn't had a drop to drink since joining AA. He's actually here today . . . said he'd like to talk to you. I told him how busy you are, and I didn't know if you'd have time—"

I assured Sydney I had the time. I'd see him while she was having her labs drawn. I asked my assistant to bring him in. She returned soon, ushering him into my office. I'd pictured him to be much bigger. His black hair was cut short and neat, set above a face with a delicate nose, thin lips, and eyes that seemed to be searching. He was dressed casually but neatly. He looked up at me and hesitantly extended his hand.

"Dr. Wilson, thanks for seeing me. I know we were supposed to meet and talk, but I figured it would be easier if we did this now, seeing as I'm here anyway with my daughter."

"Of course," I said, motioning for him to take a seat. "I'm sorry how things turned out, what with you getting blamed for Sydney's injuries before the truth came out."

"Well, to get to the point, Doctor, I wasn't happy with you. I know you thought you were doing your job, but I think you jumped the gun. The way one thing led to another, it ended up destroying our family. I still think we could have worked through it. Maybe I could have stopped drinking or at least cut back. My wife wanted to work on her anger issues. In fact, we were scheduled to see a therapist, but all that changed with Sydney's hospitalization."

"I know you and Sydney have been through a lot, and I'm sorry. Thanks for not making her switch doctors—I'd hate to lose her as a patient."

A subtle smile formed. "Switch doctors? I don't think an act of God could get her out of your practice. She still thinks you hung the moon. As for me, at least all of this forced me to join AA and face my addiction. Haven't had a drop of alcohol in weeks."

Sydney walked in with her lab results. As she handed them to me, she glanced at her dad and nodded.

"Looks good, Syd—your hemoglobin is back to the low-normal range. Just keep taking your iron supplement. Your dad and I were just wrapping things up."

"So, uh, everything's good?"

"Yes. Everything's fine, Syd. Now, I want to see you again in a month to re-check your hemoglobin, but after that, you won't need to come back until your next physical. Of course, I'm always here if you need me." I turned to her dad. "Mr. Blanton, thanks for coming in. I'm glad we got a chance to talk."

As I finished my work for the day, my cell vibrated. Annie. I'd been too busy to return her earlier call. "Hi there."

"Hi, Jack. Got time to talk?

"Let's meet for coffee. I'm finishing up here."

Ten minutes later, we were facing each other in a booth at the Grind.

Annie started. "I know last night was hard to hear, and I wanted to make sure we're still good."

"I've thought things over since last night, Annie. We're still good, but I realize we both have a past, and neither of us has been fully honest about things. There's also been other stuff at work going on recently, and I just need to pause and sort of get my head straight. Maybe we should slow down—"

Her eyes widened. "Jack, you're not having second thoughts, are you?"

"No. That's not what I'm saying. Just give me some time, that's all. What's the rush? Worst case scenario, we can always move the date back, right?"

"Maybe not," she said as her chin began to quiver. "Mother called to let me know she's not doing well at all. I'm afraid we're going to lose her sooner than expected. She simply must see her daughter get married. She's earned that right. We can't put off the wedding any longer and take the chance she won't be able to attend or, even worse, won't still be with us." Tears began streaming. She hadn't touched her coffee. "I know you need to think through things, Jack, but now, time is of the essence."

I felt trapped. Like always, just being with Annie heightened my feelings for her and my desire for us to be together. *Being in love is complicated, Wilson.* My preference was to be in no hurry to get married. In fact, extra time could help me resolve the conflicts between my personal and professional lives. But I had to make a tough decision—quickly.

"Jack?"

"We'll move up the date, Annie."

"Are you sure, or are you just appeasing me?"

"I'm sure." *I think.*

Chapter Twenty-Four

June 2017

There was more to my dad's sorry saga. I was at my desk in the clinic, tying up some loose ends: charting, checking lab results, and calling patients back. My assistant, Chris, tapped on my door and stuck her head in my little office. I looked up and over my tablet and a stack of unread medical journals.

"Yes, Chris?"

"Sorry to bother you, Dr. Wilson, but the hospital operator is on the phone. Says there's a Thomas Lawrence on the line, trying to reach you. She wants to know if she can put him through."

Tommy? "Of course. Thanks."

"Long time, no hear, Tommy!"

"Hey, Jack. Yeah, I know. We don't talk often—actually never, except by text. Right? Anyway, have you got a minute?"

"Sure. What's up?"

"I'm calling about your dad—"

"My dad?"

"Yeah. I need to share some stuff with you."

Okay, first the news from Officer Stanley and now my childhood friend who I never hear from calls out of the blue? This just keeps getting weirder. "What about him, Tommy?"

"Well, you know how anything newsworthy makes it big in a small town like Sedalia. Last month, the paper published a story about a man's body found in Dresden, with his identification withheld pending notification of next-of-kin."

"Go on," I said. My foot began tapping the floor rapidly.

"Earlier this week, the authorities released your dad's name after they reported his closest relative had been found and notified."

I could only imagine the stir that piece of gossip must have created as it spread like wildfire in a California summer. Those old enough to remember my parents' wreck, its carnage, and the effect it had on me were probably as shocked as I was to learn that my dad had been alive all these years. Only my grandparents, however, had they been alive, would have been affected anywhere close to how I was.

"Right," I said. "A cop from back home actually stopped by and delivered the news. He explained everything to me."

"But there's more, Jack."

A throbbing in my neck began. "I'm listening."

"I was in Dresden a few months back, actually showing your mom's sister and her husband some real estate. Said they wanted to get back to the Sedalia area. Anyway, your aunt kept looking over her shoulder for some reason. When I asked her if everything was alright, she nodded and said it was weird, but she thought she'd spotted your father, even though she knew that was impossible."

This was getting interesting.

"Well, Jack, I didn't think anything more about it. Then, people in Sedalia who remembered your father started spotting him. I knew your parents were dead, so I ignored it—you know how people love to talk. Figuring it would upset you, I certainly didn't think it was worth letting you know about, at least until now. I guess it must have been him after all."

My mind reeled. My thoughts returned to my childhood. I would hide in my bedroom closet when my dad drank, cringing when I heard him attacking my mom. I felt so helpless and angry—somehow feeling responsible for what my mom had to endure. Her gentility was no match for the beast that came out of that bottle. But I knew I was powerless to protect her. Someday, I thought, I'd stand up to my father or talk my mom into leaving him. I never got that chance. And now, it sounds like he was always nearby, even when I was living in Sedalia. Could he have been looking for me? Did he want to confess? Apologize? Make amends? Or did he want to somehow hurt me again?

"Jack?"

"I'm still here. Sorry. I'm glad you called, Tommy, even though all of this seems so strange to me."

"Yeah, after all this time, I call you with such weird news. I hope I did the right thing."

"Absolutely, man. Thanks. And Tommy?"

"Yeah?"

"Let's keep in touch, and not just on our birthdays."

"You got it, Jack."

I put the receiver back in its cradle and stared out the window, gazing off into the distance at cars emptying from the office lot, not really focusing on anything. I heard Chris again.

"I'm all finished with my work, Dr. Wilson. Okay if I go?"

I continued to stare out the window. "Uh, sure . . . go."

"Is everything okay, Dr. Wilson?"

"Yeah, everything's okay. Just an unexpected call from an old friend. I'll be fine," I said, knowing it was probably a lie.

Chapter Twenty-Five

Late July 2017
Wilmington

❝I'm impressed, bro. You had six weeks to change all the arrangements and get everyone together for the big event." Pete and I were in Wilmington, where we'd stayed at the Hilton Riverfront Hotel the night before the wedding.

Once we rescheduled the wedding date, there was a whirlwind of activity. Annie and Joni shopped for a wedding dress, picked out the bridesmaid dresses, and ordered invitations. Together, we decided the event would be tasteful but not elegant. Annie's mom didn't have to do anything other than buy a new dress. Pete, Eric, and I would all wear summer suits and neckties. Tuxedos would seem too formal and probably be intolerable for a summer wedding in the coastal humidity.

"No other choice, Pete. Annie wouldn't have it any other way. We had to pull off this wedding while her mom was still healthy enough to attend. By the way, what do you think of Mary?" Annie's friend, Mary, had ridden to the coast with Pete.

"Turns out we know each other . . . kinda. Took a class together sophomore year. It was actually good to re-connect with her on the drive down. She's very nice but way out of my league."

Pete and his self-esteem issues again.

We strolled down the riverwalk and found a small café overlooking the Cape Fear River, its morning fog quickly burning off in the warmth of the midsummer morning. We grabbed an outdoor table, took a seat, and ordered. The waitress left us a carafe of coffee.

"Well, Jack, the big day is finally here." Pete slapped me on the back as he squinted against the glare off the water.

"Hard to believe, isn't it? It's all happened so fast. Just like our engagement, things have moved quickly, so it seems meant to be, right?" Our breakfast arrived. "Wow. Speaking of quick, that was fast too!"

"Well, you tell me," he said with a mouthful of his egg and cheese bagel. "You sure you're good with the balance it's going to take juggling your career and a marriage?"

"Yep. It's all good." I couldn't lie and say I never had doubts. Pete would see right through that. But I had thought long and hard about it and realized how lucky I was. Two things I'd longed for—becoming a doctor and finally having someone to love and trust—were both coming true. I was a lucky guy, for sure.

"Enough about me. How's your roommate search going?"

"No longer looking, bro. Even though you won't be next door, and I'll probably get lonely, I'm going to go it alone. Since I only have one year of school left, I think I can swing another year of full rent. Besides, if cash runs low, I know my folks will help out. Molly and I will be just fine. That'll give me plenty of time to start planning my post-college move, whether it's looking for a job or starting grad school. In fact, I need to get on that as my first order of business once senior year starts . . . uh, Jack?"

I guess I looked lost in thought or simply tuned out. Truth was, it was sobering to think of the changes about to occur in my life. Going from a somewhat carefree existence with my best friend to the commitment of marriage was a big leap. *Was I ready?*

"Sorry, Pete. I was just thinking, and maybe it's only natural to have doubts I'm doing the right thing. Maybe I should have put off the wedding until I was settled into my practice."

"What? You have to be sure, bro. You can't serve two masters. You have to decide what's more important in your life—family or work. Think of it like this: When you're on your death bed, do you want Annie by your side, or do you want your medical bag sitting there?"

"Yeah, I guess you're right." I finished the bacon and washed down the last of my muffin with a swallow of coffee. "I'm going to miss all the time we spend hanging out, talking about life, and pondering our future plans."

"Molly's sure going to miss not having you around," Pete said as he downed his last gulp of coffee. "Oh, and *I'll* probably miss you too." He winked.

"Yeah, that's what I'll really miss—you messing with me, Petey. Boy, that breakfast hit the spot."

"Yeah, dude. Sure beats our typical Pop-Tart and coffee breakfast!"

We left the restaurant and made our way back down the riverwalk. Gulls perched on the railing, as though hoping we had some residual crumbs to share with them. A few more industrious ones would spot the day's fresh catch and swoop down to the river's surface, cawing and fighting over their prey. Just as with humans, I guess all notion of harmony ceases when hunger sets in.

It was time. Shortly after arriving at the church, we were joined by Eric and his kids, whom I'd met at the previous evening's rehearsal. Sophie was in a pale lavender, printed sleeveless dress, and Will looked handsome but kept tugging at his navy-blue blazer and English rep tie. His khakis and Bass Weejuns completed his preppy attire, but I wondered what the over and under would be for the time that tie would stay in place.

Virginia Monroe arrived just a bit later with Tom and Ethel Barnes. "Hello, Jack," she said, beaming with pleasure as she hugged me.

She was dressed in a beautiful dark summer dress and wore a colorful hat, as I'd learned southern women were prone to do on special occasions. It framed her head in a way that drew one's eyes to the angular beauty of her face. Her elegance was striking, especially given how sick she was.

Eric escorted Mary, followed by Pete and Joni. The girls were striking in their soft pink dresses highlighted by a touch of fine lace at the necklines. Somehow, Joni's hair was its natural blonde color.

As we took our places, Annie appeared at the back of the church, cued by the organist's music. She wore a simple, brilliant white dress with a veil that dropped down her back to the floor, spilling out several feet. The sunlight streaming through the stained-glass window cast an angelic glow over her as she made her way down the center aisle. Those present who knew the Monroe family story probably had a tear or two in their eyes, after first seeing Virginia and now Annie—two brave women who had endured so much—confidently walking toward the front of the church, each going it alone, just as they'd done in life. Once Annie arrived at her mom's pew, she gave her a quick hug and a kiss on the cheek and then took her place beside me as we turned to face the minister.

The ceremony was a blur. Stunned by Annie's beauty and wondering if this was all too good to be true, I almost missed the minister's prompt for me to say my vows. We exchanged rings, the minister pronounced us man and wife, and we kissed. As we turned and walked back down the aisle to the applause of our guests, it suddenly struck me. *You did it, Wilson. You married the girl of your dreams.*

At the reception, Annie and I danced to Etta James's "At Last," but the deejay had everything from Sinatra and Crosby to ABBA and Bon Jovi, with a little bit of Roy Hamilton and Elvis and a lot of Motown. As I took a turn on the dance floor with Virginia, she whispered in my ear, "Well, Jack, I got to dance at my daughter's wedding. Check that box. Thank you. We've had two marriages in this family fail, but I know this one is forever."

I was at a loss for words, but I managed to smile.

We kept the reception simple and short, as even on the biggest day of her life, Annie's main concern was her mom's stamina. As we drove off for our honeymoon, I saw Virginia waving to us and mouthing, "Goodbye."

"Best day of my life," I said quietly.

"What's that, Jack?"

"I was just thinking how wonderful this day's been, babe—or, should I say, Mrs. Wilson?"

She laughed. "Don't let it go to your head, sweetie. But I agree, and I couldn't be happier. I'm so glad the day went beautifully. Everyone who means anything to me was there, and Mother looked radiant. Thank you again for agreeing to move up the date."

"It really was magical. By the way, did you catch Pete and Mary on the dance floor?"

"I did. They'd make a great couple. Who knows? Maybe that'll happen."

"I know I'm biased, but a girl couldn't do any better than Pete."

"I think I did, Jack." She looked over, smiled, and intertwined her fingers with mine.

Chapter Twenty-Six

The Outer Banks, North Carolina

Moving up the date of the wedding had the added benefit of making a beach trip a great option. We were on the Outer Banks, where beach charm seemed to ooze from every direction, staying at the Beachcomber, an old but well-maintained white brick structure that bordered the line of dunes separating it from the beach. Our French doors opened to an oceanside balcony with steps down to a walkway over the dunes covered in wind-blown sea oats.

On our wedding night, we dined at the nearby Surfside Restaurant. I had the surf 'n turf, while Annie enjoyed a shrimp Caesar salad. As we ate, dusk fell over the ocean, and the gulls grew quiet.

"Annie, I'm going to have an espresso while you finish your wine," I said. "No rush. We can just sit here, relax, and enjoy the view."

"Sounds good, sweetie," she said.

Once finished, we strolled hand-in-hand in the direction of the hotel. "What do you want to do now?" she said as she raised one eyebrow.

"I don't know. Maybe a movie?"

Annie stopped suddenly and looked at me. "Seriously, Jack? On our wedding night?"

"Gotcha!" I laughed and put my arm around her waist as we walked to the hotel.

As we entered the room, I noticed the French doors. "Hey, babe, we left the doors open."

"We did, didn't we?" she said as we walked onto the balcony. The ocean shimmered under the moon, an orb of light in a cloudless sky. "Let's go inside, sweetie."

As we entered our room from the balcony, Annie gave the doors a kick, turned and raised her eyebrows, and then gave herself completely to me.

The next morning, I awoke to two beautiful green eyes gazing at me. I reached over beneath the sheets we were entangled in and brought Annie close to me and kissed her.

"Was it worth the wait, sweetie?"

"Every bit," I said.

———

The week was filled with long beach walks, swimming, bicycling, and sunbathing on the beach. We spent a couple of days kayaking and paddle boarding the Intracoastal Waterway. Nights were private and intimate, filled with a passion new to us both. Time passed much too quickly, and suddenly, it was time to head home that Friday.

———

While we were gone, Pete and some buddies moved all of my personal belongings from my old apartment to Annie's place. Annie and I had combined the best of our furniture, donating the rest to Goodwill. Neither of us being much on disorder, what time off remained before we went back to work was spent getting everything out of boxes and into their proper places.

The following Monday, we both returned to work. I still had my clinic, but as senior resident, most of what I did was administrative work. Overseeing junior residents and interns was like herding cats, as requests for schedule changes and call nights were constantly coming in and then sometimes altered. Not what I wanted to spend my time on, but it was my responsibility. Annie was working as a graduate nurse on the hospital's oncology floor. Having seen what her mom endured, she wanted to work with patients going through cancer treatment. Working on a floor where a higher than usual percentage of patients didn't survive their illness could lead to employee burnout, a risk she was aware of but readily embraced. The oncology service was fortunate to have her.

Now that Annie and I worked in the same facility, we ate together in the hospital cafeteria when our shifts overlapped. Some days, it was the only time we saw each other since we came and went from the house at different times. Our world was hectic again, and the relaxing week we'd spent at the Outer Banks was fading into life's rear-view mirror. In retrospect, our lives intersected at work more than they did during the personal time we made for ourselves.

———

"Chris, call her and find out why she missed, please. That's not like Sydney. I'm worried that something's wrong." I was in clinic, eager to actually practice medicine and get away from my other duties. Sydney Blanton was on the schedule for her two-month follow-up visit but no-showed for her appointment. Not like her.

A short time later, my assistant was back. "I couldn't reach her at home, Dr. Wilson, but she had her grandparents' number listed as the backup, so I called them. Turns out, Sydney's now living with them."

"What?"

"Her grandmother said it's a long story, and she'd rather just talk to you about it. She'd like you to call her when you have time."

This development worried me. "Call her back, Chris. Get the address and ask if I can come by after clinic this afternoon."

I finished the day's schedule of patients but couldn't get Sydney off my mind. I felt some responsibility for her, given the role I'd played in her family's breakup. *What could have happened?* Hurrying through my charting, I finished my day and rushed out of the clinic.

"Hello. I'm Jack Wilson, Annie's doctor."

"Oh, Dr. Wilson. Hi. I'm Bea Mitchell, Sydney's grandmother. Please come in."

Taking a seat on the living room couch, I said, "Well, I was surprised Sydney missed her appointment and even more surprised she's here and not at home. Is everything okay?"

"No, not exactly. Sydney's father was out with friends last week and made the mistake of going to a bar. He had a drink; one drink led to another, and he got drunk. Best I understand, he got into an argument with another patron, and they started fighting. When the police arrived, he refused to cooperate with them— took a swing at one of them, in fact. They charged him with drunk and disorderly conduct as well as resisting arrest. He's still in jail. For some reason, he refuses to post bail, so I reckon he's there until his hearing."

I was stunned. "But I just saw him a few months ago, and he was sober . . . and had been since he and Sydney starting living together without your daughter. He was so proud—"

"But that's what happens," she said. "Being a doctor, I'm sure you know that better than I do. One drink leads to a second and then another, and there you go—down the slippery slope."

"Yes, I understand. Do you mind if I talk to Sydney?"

"Not at all. Let me get her for you. I'll step out and give the two of you some privacy."

Sydney slowly walked in, wearing pajamas and a somber look. We both took a seat.

"Hi, Syd." She looked at me with a tired and anxious gaze.

"Hello, Dr. Wilson."

"Syd, I'm so sorry this happened to you. First, your mom and, now, your dad. You're fortunate to have your grandparents."

"Fortunate?" She gripped the arms of the chair tightly. "There's nothing fortunate about this," she said, her face reddening. "I should have never confided in you about my injuries. If it wasn't for you, I'd still have both my parents at home. Things weren't perfect, but at least we were a family. Even when I hated what my parents did, I still loved them. That might sound crazy to you, but it's true."

"But Sydney—"

"Nothing you can say will change this. You need to leave. Please, just go." She set her mouth in a thin line.

Try as I might, I failed to conceal my emotions. My breathing came in gasps, and I could feel my face getting hotter and my neck muscles tightening. The fights, the drinking, the abandonment, the darkness—all of those painful memories flashed through my brain. Failing to think of anything helpful to say, I responded, "Uh . . . you're, you're right, Sydney. I should go."

I needed to talk to Annie. Now. She answered the call and started talking before I could even say, "hi."

"Jack, I was just getting ready to call you." I could hear the excitement in her voice. "The mail just came. I passed my boards!"

"That's great, not that I ever had any doubts. I'm on my way home. I just need to talk—"

"Let's go out to celebrate, Jack. Nothing fancy," she said.

"Okay. I'll be home soon." Celebration was the last thing I felt like doing, but I owed it to Annie. She'd put in a lot of studying time to ace the boards.

Our night out was at a small, inexpensive, Italian restaurant, DeAngelo's. We ordered chicken penne pasta.

"Jack, I'm going to order a glass of riesling."

"Of course. Hey, it's your night!"

Annie's excitement was apparent as she talked, and I was happy for her to have the floor, as I didn't think I could dampen the moment talking about Sydney—or my past, for that matter.

"I'm so glad that board exam is behind me! Now, I can focus on work, our marriage, and Mother. Speaking of Mother, I called her today to tell her the good news."

"How's she doing?"

"Said she's doing well. She sounded upbeat and, of course, she asked when we were coming back for a visit."

"I guess she gets lonely, huh?"

"No, I don't think it's that. She's lived alone for a long time and has done just fine. I think she just likes to see us."

"Guess we really should visit her. It's just hard to get away for even a long weekend, much less any longer. We'll figure something out, though."

"Oh, Jack, you mentioned on the phone that you needed to talk," Annie said as we left the restaurant. "I've done almost all the talking. What's up?"

I just couldn't bring it up. "Nothing important." I lied again.

Chapter Twenty-Seven

Annie

"Well, Annie Monroe, here we are again. This place is starting to feel like my second home."

"And good morning to you, too, Mrs. Mason," I said, smiling as I entered the hospital room of one of my favorite patients. "It's good to see you again, but I'm sorry you had to come back. How are you feeling?"

"Just tired, dear—tired as a one-armed paper hanger, if you wanna know the truth. I don't know if it's because I don't have much appetite, if it's my low blood count, or both. That chemotherapy is a real pistol, I'll tell you that. I'm hoping to feel better once I get those transfusions. Of course, my numbers will go up, but then, they'll drop again—sorta like an elevator—when they put more of that poison in my IV. I've still got six weeks left on my whatever y'all call it."

Mrs. Mason was a feisty and witty cancer patient. In my mind's eye, I pictured my mother whenever I was assigned to be her nurse. A year earlier, she'd sat at her husband's bedside as he finally succumbed to chronic lung disease, even as her own health hung in the balance. To watch your soulmate gasp for his final breaths of air is a heartbreaking way to part. Despite that, she'd not only survived but thrived. Her physical strength was weakened by the cancer and its treatment, but her spirit remained strong, and I admired her for it. Just my opinion, but every health professional needs at least one patient like her.

"Your protocol, Mrs. Mason, is a treatment plan that is standardized for many, many patients at dozens of cancer treatment centers. Doctors and researchers can then look at the results of patients' treatments and get a good idea if a particular treatment plan is effective or not. Thanks to patients like you, doctors actually learn a lot and many patients benefit as a result."

I'd told her this many times before, but she always seemed to want validation that the treatment wasn't worse than the disease. I was riding high on passing my boards, so I found it easy to be patient as I listened to her treatment complaints.

"Yes, I know . . . or at least, I've been told. The plan, or protocol, or poison—whatever you want to call it—helps me and helps other people too. My family doctor in the clinic, Dr. Wilson, has explained all of this to me before. He's very patient with me. It's just hard for someone my age to understand what doctors say. So much information is thrown at me so fast, and I don't hear like I used to, you know. 'Course, they say your hearing's always the second thing to go, and I don't even want to talk about what goes first, if you catch my drift, young lady! Anyway, doctors always seem ready to leave before they hardly get a foot in the door. But not that Dr. Wilson. He always seems to have all the time in the world for me. He actually sits down and really listens. For my money, he's the best."

She'd told me all of this before, but she was prone to forget. *All the time in the world, and he listens. How I'd love to know her secret. Jack sure doesn't treat our relationship that way. If he can do that for his patients, why can't he do it for me?* Although I could talk to her all day, a glance at my watch told me I needed to get Mrs. Mason settled so I could move on to the next patient.

"You know, he's been taking care of me since he started his residency over two years ago—"

"Yes, I know. Sorry to interrupt. Do you want to stay in the chair, or would you rather get in bed now?"

"I'd like to get in bed, please." But she kept talking. "He was my husband's doctor, too, at least until he died from lung disease, God rest his soul. I used to get on my Jimmy all the time about his smoking, but he said he'd smoked since he was knee-high to a pup, and he wasn't about to stop. Stubborn man. Smoked until he destroyed his lungs and couldn't get enough oxygen to survive. I can't remember what they called it."

"We call it COPD, Mrs. Mason, which stands for chronic obstructive pulmonary disease." *We've been over this before too.* "I'm so sorry the two of you went through that. I know it must have been awful." I double-checked her IV rate to make sure it was right.

"Fancy name for a hideous disease, I'd say, and yes, it was worse than awful. I had to watch him struggle for every breath near the end, blue as a goose. But that

Dr. Wilson, bless his heart, he was with us all the way. He told us he would be, and he was true to his word. If you can count on your fingers, you can count on him, I'm tellin' you that for sure. Didn't really know they still made doctors like that. He did something for us that I will be grateful for 'til the day I die, which might not be long, given how puny I'm feeling. He got my Jimmy home from the hospital so he could spend his final days there, not in the noise and craziness of the hospital." She tried to stand and move to the bed but then sat back down.

"Want the head of your bed flat or about halfway up?"

"Up, please. He even came to the house a few times when he was off, just to check on us, you know, even though Jimmy had hospice care at that point. And get this, Miss Annie, darned if he didn't show up for the funeral. You could have knocked me over with a feather when he came up to me at the visitation. That was a hard time, I'll tell you that. Near put me six feet under too. In fact, I told Dr. Wilson I didn't want to live anymore. Well, he wasn't having none of that. He talked to me time and time again and got me through those dark days."

"He does sound like a very good doctor, one who really cares about his patients, Mrs. Mason." *He'd love to hear us agree on that.*

"You can bet your bottom dollar on that, young lady."

"Well, for now, let's get you comfy in your bed."

I took her vital signs and then helped her up from the chair so she could sit on the edge of the bed. Grabbing her gown, I said, "The lab tech should be here soon to draw some blood so we can update your labs. After that, I'll get you tucked in and comfortable."

"Okay, but it hasn't been that long since my numbers, as you medical folks like to call them, were checked. Why are they always taking blood? I feel like a pin cushion!"

"It's important that the oncologist has up-to-date counts so she'll know exactly how much blood to use in your transfusion." *I was tired of repeating myself.*

"I'm sure she knows what she's doing, but she sure doesn't tell me much. Always seems to be in a hurry. Not at all like Dr. Wilson—he has all the time in the world for me, or at least, that's how he makes me feel."

Mrs. Mason was prone to repeating herself. My mind shifted to the other patients I needed to check on. I quickly glanced at my watch again. *Treat her like you'd want Mother to be treated.*

"All of the oncologists are very busy. They do an excellent job, but they are sub-specialists. Your primary care doctor is interested in your total well-being, not just your cancer. You know, different doctors have different areas of interest and responsibilities. I know you'd rather be at home, so we'll all try our best to get you feeling better and out of here as soon as possible." I smiled.

"I know you will, Annie. You know how much I love having you as my nurse. You're a lot like Dr. Wilson—you take your time to stop and listen. I guess that can be as helpful to a patient as all the drugs in the world, or at least, that's how it seems to me."

Mrs. Mason was much smarter than she liked to let on.

"Well, your attitude does have a lot to do with your health, as well as how you respond to the things done to you when you're sick, whether you're here or in the out-patient clinic."

"I'm ready to get out of my clothes now."

Finally. "Alright, here's your gown. I'll give you a hand with it."

She shook her head. "Pajamas, Annie. I brought my own pajamas from home. They're right there." She pointed to a paper grocery bag by the foot of the bed. "Remember? I don't wear those horrible hospital gowns and risk showing my bum unless I have to! After all, a girl's got to have her dignity. Right?"

Chapter Twenty-Eight

September 2017

I was frustrated. I had things I needed to get out, but it was a struggle. As my wife and a fellow medical professional, Annie would no doubt understand about Sydney, but I'd never shared with her every single detail of my family history. Now, there was even more to tell. My confrontation with Sydney was as anxiety-provoking an encounter as I'd had in my medical career. Not only had I failed her, but in some ways, her predicament mirrored what I'd gone through as a young boy. I could relate to her feelings, but there was no way I could delve into my childhood trauma with a sixteen-year-old patient—or a patient of any age, for that matter. If this was my best effort at handling a physician-patient encounter, perhaps I wasn't the doctor I thought I was. My loss, Sydney's family disruption, and the possibility of losing her as a patient all weighed heavily on me.

I needed Pete. Unlike Annie, Pete didn't know medicine from macaroni, but he did know people, especially me. He was fully clued-in on my personal history, so it would be easier to open up to him, at least until I told Annie more about my past. *Secrets.*

———

We met at one of our favorite burger joints, where the smell of grease hung heavy in the air and the wait staff hustled from one table to the next filling orders.

"Have you found a practice yet?" Pete asked.

"Still looking," I said. "Fortunately, I've got some options, whether I want to stay in this area or go to another part of the state. But leaning toward staying close, as Annie loves her job, and it doesn't seem fair to ask her to pick up and re-locate. But Pete . . ." I leaned forward and said, "There's something else I really need to get off my chest." We stopped long enough to place our orders.

"That sounds serious, bro. What's up?"

"It's about one of my young patients. Her life has spiraled out of control, and I feel partially to blame for it."

Pete shook his head. "I can't believe that's true, Jack. I know you better than to think you'd do something wrong."

"I did what I was obligated to do, but it resulted in a series of events for her that reminds me of some stuff I went through as a child, and I'm not handling it very well."

"Why am I not surprised?"

"What does that mean?" I said, feeling that same tension in my neck I felt when I was with Sydney earlier. We paused as our burgers, fries, and soft drinks arrived.

"Jack, when I'm with you after you've had a tough day at work, you seem to take on the weight of the world. Everything becomes personal for you. You get trapped in the sadness and loss of your childhood." He shook his head. "You've got to stop that, dude."

This was not the reaction I'd expected and it wasn't helpful, but he wasn't finished.

"I know your history better than anyone, but it's just that—history. You'll never be content if you relate everything in your professional life to what happened years ago. It'll destroy any chance for happiness in your work. Same goes for your marriage."

My eyes narrowed as they locked on Pete's. My mind was racing as his words pierced my heart. What was his point, and could he be right? I'd expected consolation from Pete, not confrontation. If Pete felt this way, how would Annie feel? "What's my marriage got to do with anything?"

"Hopefully, nothing. I know you love Annie, but I also remember how reluctant you were to commit to a long-term relationship. The first time you and Annie have a big argument, I'm afraid you'll think you're going to lose her. Man, if that happens, and you're also unhappy about your work, what's left?"

With my brow furrowed, I stared at Pete. "Forget it—just forget I even said anything." I stood, threw a twenty on the table, and stormed out of the restaurant.

Yeah, I know, childish behavior, but I didn't feel like arguing, and I was upset. I'm only human.

—————

I resolved to sit down with Annie that same night and talk about my childhood. Why I'd not done so sooner was beyond me. We were family now, and she deserved to know my story just as much as I deserved to know hers. I didn't want to go on without full disclosure. *Just do it, Wilson. You know she'll understand.*

Annie walked into the apartment that night and, without saying a word, started straightening books on the shelves and then began dusting. A burst of activity was never a good sign with her.

"Annie, what's wrong?" I asked, setting down my tablet and getting up from the chair.

"It's Mother. She called on my way home. Her fatigue and shortness of breath increased, so she saw Dr. Parke. Her tests showed more lung involvement and anemia."

"Nothing that can't be addressed, Annie. You know that."

She picked up my empty coffee cup from the end table and set it on a coaster.

"That's just it. She is refusing treatment—even a simple blood transfusion to get some strength back. Dr. Parke tried to talk her out of her decision, but she wouldn't listen. She's afraid she'll get to the hospital and, one thing will lead to another, she won't ever get home. She prefers to deal with it on her own terms and at home, where she's in charge, not at a hospital. She has people she wants to see—at her house or theirs and not from a hospital bed. She mentioned being at peace with her fate, or some such nonsense." She looked away and shook her head.

"You're thinking like a daughter, Annie, not a nurse. You know—"

"I am a daughter, Jack . . . her daughter, and I don't want her to give up! Don't you get that?" She gripped the dust cloth tightly with both hands and her voice got louder and more rushed. "Dr. Parke even told her about other treatment options, but she insists she's finished with hospitals, treatments, and the side effects from therapy. Why is she being so stubborn and independent? What can we do to change her mind?" Annie began to pace, the dust cloth flapping in the air like a flag blowing in the wind.

I stopped her, put my hands on her shoulders, and looked her in the eye. "We both know it's her prerogative. At some point, every patient with a terminal illness has to come to grips with the fact that further treatment is probably useless. We can go see her, Annie, but not to change her mind—that's not our job. She needs to know we support her decision."

She threw the dust cloth on the coffee table, crossed her arms, and leaned against my chair. "Mother's always been there for me. If she's gone, what will I do? I'm going to visit her."

I followed Annie as she ran to the bedroom. I wrapped my arms around her and held her tightly. "It'll be okay, babe," I whispered.

My story would have to wait . . . again.

Chapter Twenty-Nine

Annie

I'd gotten used to driving to Wilmington with Jack, so this trip seemed different and lonely. During the morning drive, I mulled over what I would say to Mother and considered the advice Jack had given me about her right to make her own decisions. I knew he was right, but I didn't like seeing my mother give up.

"Mother?" I called out as I entered the house.

"Back here, dear. In the kitchen."

I found her arranging cut flowers in a vase on the kitchen table. Sun streamed through the window over the sink. She turned to me, wiped her hands on a towel, and gave me a gentle hug.

"So good to see you, Annie. And I'm sorry Jack couldn't visit, but I understand."

"He sends his love . . . oh, look at the flowers. So beautiful!"

"Just trying to keep this place cheery. Please, let's sit and have some tea. I just steeped some Bigelow Green. I hope it's still your favorite."

"Yes, and it sounds yummy," I said as I took the cup and cradled it in both hands. The tea and being back home were warmly comfortable, as I was where I belonged and the place I would always love.

"Tell me, dear, how are you?"

"Good. Really good, Mother."

"Oh, I'm so glad." She smiled, and I noticed a sparkle in her eyes.

I hesitated and then took her by the hands. "How are *you*, Mother?"

"Well, I'm just fine. As I told you on the phone, I'm in a good place—really at peace with my decision. Just knowing I wouldn't face more treatment or hospital time seemed to give me a sense of relief and even a burst of energy. I've been getting out and visiting friends, running errands. You know, just little things—very normal things that seem more special to me now. It won't be long before winter's here, and I just don't do well in cold weather any longer."

"I'm glad you're getting out, Mother. And if you're really at peace with your decision, Jack and I are one hundred percent in agreement." I swallowed hard and, hopefully, imperceptibly. As my eyes moistened, I got up and took our empty cups to the sink, washed them, and put them away. *Don't let her see my true feelings.*

"You don't have to do that, dear, but thanks. Oh, I told Tom and Ethel you'd be here this weekend, and they really want to see you. Maybe dinner tonight or lunch tomorrow?"

"I'd love that," I said as I helped her up to go into the living room.

"Ah, much more comfortable than those kitchen chairs," Mother said as she took a seat in one of the wingbacks.

"This room sure brings back a lot of memories, Mother."

"Mostly good, I trust."

"Of course!" I smiled, but my mind, for some reason, went back to the day my dad walked out and the night I was assaulted by Chip Edwards. Both times, Mother and I sat in that very room and talked about it. She was there to comfort me, to calm me down. I didn't consider then how much her heart must have been hurting, but she'd pushed her own feelings aside to make room for mine. I guess that's just what mothers do. Someday, I hoped to be that mother for a child in need of comfort.

"Mother, I didn't tell you I saw Chip's mom when Jack and I were here before the wedding."

She narrowed her eyes. "What on Earth brought that up?"

"Sitting here, like we did that terrible night."

"Well, I see her around, but we keep our distance." Mother looked down and slowly shook her head.

"That's understandable. I know you were put in an impossible situation that night."

"I guess we both did the best we could, didn't we?" She looked up. "Annie, does Jack know about Chip?"

"He does."

"And?"

"He got upset and angry . . . but at Chip, not me."

"I'm glad you told him. Marriages don't do well when there are secrets, you know."

I nodded. *Secrets.*

———

With the difficult discussions behind us, I was able to relax, and we enjoyed each other's company for the rest of the weekend. Tom and Ethel had us over Saturday night for Ethel's famous fried chicken, mashed potatoes, and okra. Her blue-ribbon cooking skills still left nothing to be desired.

"We're so glad to see you, Annie M," Tom said. "Virginia tells me you and Jack are doing well. Staying busy, but I guess that's good."

"It *is* good to be back home, to see you, and especially to be with Mother."

"Doesn't she look great?" Ethel said.

"I'd be less than honest if I didn't say I needed to see that with my own eyes— you know, just to know for sure."

"Ahem. I'm sitting right here, don't forget." Mother laughed.

"Well, you do look great, Virginia, and I'm sure Annie *is* happy to see that," Tom said. "Now, let's get up and move to the den. Ethel, we'll take care of the dishes later."

"Annie, will we see you and Jack next month at Thanksgiving?" Ethel asked as she brought in coffee.

"No. I've got to work that day." I noticed Mother tilting her chin down and frowning. "Mother and I haven't discussed it yet."

"Coffee, Virginia? It's decaf."

"Yes, please. Thank you . . . Eric and the kids will be here then. I was hoping we'd all be together, Annie."

"Actually, both of us are working Thanksgiving, but I'm pretty sure we'll have some time off over Christmas. If so, we'll be here for sure."

Mother smiled. "The kids will be with their mom for Christmas, and Eric is going snow skiing with friends. I'd love to have the two of you here."

"Let me talk to Jack first thing when I get home tomorrow. I'll let you know as soon as possible. I promise."

"Ethel, Tom. I'm getting a little tired. I hate to be a stick in the mud, but I think Annie and I should get back home."

We all stood, and Tom went for our jackets. "So good to see you, Annie M," he said as we hugged. I took Mother's arm in mine, and we walked back next door.

———

Mother and I were having a simple lunch on the porch that Sunday. Pimento cheese sandwiches, chips, and sweet tea. A CD of hymns played quietly in the background, and the air was filled with the cool, sharp aroma of fall. Orange, red, and yellow leaves rained down from the backyard trees.

"Dear, it was a short visit, but I'm so glad you came down for the weekend. And, Annie, I hope I didn't pressure you last night to make you feel obliged to be here over the holidays."

I shook my head. "Not at all, Mother. Anyway, there's no place I'd rather be. I'm happy I came down, too, and I promise I won't be a stranger."

After cleaning up from lunch, I gathered my things to leave. As Mother and I hugged, we both got a little teary.

"I love you, Mother."

"And I'll always love you, dear."

As I climbed into the car, she waved and called out, "Have a good trip, Annie, and drive safely."

Chapter Thirty

Chapel Hill

Annie arrived home late Sunday afternoon. She came in bright-eyed and excited.

"Hi, sweetie!"

"Hey, babe. Good trip? Your mom doing okay?"

"Yes, on both counts. But I need to talk to you about something. I promised Mother I'd ask you first thing about us going to Wilmington for Christmas."

"I'd love to. After all, she's our only family, except Eric and the kids. No place I'd rather be than with you and your mom—my two favorite gals!" *An actual family together at Christmas—something I'd longed for and now would finally have.*

She sighed deeply and then smiled. "Great!"

We easily made arrangements to spend time with Virginia after Christmas. We swapped some shifts and scheduled time off for the entire week. Since we didn't have kids, we both volunteered to work the stretch of Friday, Saturday, and Sunday, Christmas day. Our co-workers were more than happy to cover for us after Christmas if it meant they'd get to be home with family on the big holiday. Work would be busy, as patients would be more likely to come in for almost anything for fear of being sick on Christmas day.

Despite my busyness, something was gnawing at me—I needed to see Pete and not leave things as we did at the restaurant. For over a week, we'd texted each other about trivial matters, dancing around our last conversation.

When I called Pete, he invited me to breakfast the following Saturday at his new apartment. Exemplifying bachelor pad chic, the place was sparsely furnished with a few faux leather easy chairs and a well-worn Goodwill sofa, with a flat-screen strategically placed for optimal viewing. Nothing on the walls. The familiar odor of freshly brewed coffee was as welcoming as Pete's invitation to come in.

"Hi, Jack. Welcome to the new digs! I'll grab you a cup of joe. Got bagels, cream cheese, and muffins too. Take your pick."

"What, no Pop-Tarts? Looks like you stepped up your game and your break-fast options with this place, buddy. You know, I'm embarrassed I haven't been here sooner, and by the recent circumstances that prompted my visit, Pete." Molly padded in from another room for the obligatory head-scratching she always expected.

"*Recent circumstances?*"

"You know, how we left things at the burger joint last time we went out."

"Oh, that. No worries, dude. Ancient history. Far as I'm concerned, the only thing left was your half-eaten food!" He laughed. "I knew you had a lot going on and understood why you got so upset. Outside of family, you're just about the only person who seriously values my opinion, so you've gotta realize when you come to me for advice, I have to do my level best to live up to your faith in me. Otherwise, what good would I be?"

"Man, I'm glad to hear you say that. I was worried I'd lose you as a friend."

"You're making my point, Jack. You're always worried about loss. With your history, I get it. The child in you is still hurting, but you're no longer that child, and you've got to stop living in the past and taking everything personally. That's way too much to shoulder, bro. You're your own worst enemy."

"Meaning?" *Okay, what's coming now?*

Pete's eyes narrowed as he leaned in. "Your goal is to be a practicing physician. Anything less will be considered a failure—at least by you. But you've got these hang-ups about loss and trust that interfere with your other goal: to have someone in your life you can love and depend on. Don't defeat yourself, bro."

I understood Pete's point and appreciated his honesty. I just wasn't in the mood the last time we were together to hear the truth spoken, but now, it all seemed to make sense. I'd work on living in the present. "I'm going to work on it, Pete. But it's just hard to forget things I've experienced—not that I would expect you to understand, especially with your family."

"Actually, I do understand . . . more than you'd know."

"How's that?"

"Jack, there are things about me you don't know. I've never told you my whole story."

"About what?"

"My childhood. It's not something I dwell on or talk about, and I apologize for never sharing it with you. See, I was abandoned by my birth mom or parents—I don't even know which—as a young infant. Since black babies are not easy to place for adoption, I was in foster care for the first four years of my life. I bounced from family to family until, finally, the folks you know as my parents adopted me. They're really the only parents I've ever known; I have very little memory of my time before that. The questions and memories I do have—who my birth parents are and the foster homes I sorta remember—I decided I wouldn't dwell on. My parents have always said that of all the children in the world they could have chosen, they picked me. And you know what? That's good enough for me. Knowing your history and the painful memories you have of your parents just made me uncomfortable telling you my story. I'm only sharing it now so you'll understand I do get what you're dealing with."

All this time and he'd never told me. More secrets. Maybe that explains the premature gray flecks in his hair, his fingernails, and, more importantly, his lapses in self-confidence. For a few seconds, I just stared at Pete, my mouth open but not to speak. Then, I put my hand on his shoulder and lamely offered, "Oh, Pete. I'm so sorry."

"Don't be. Like I said, I choose the memories I cherish and don't dwell on the others. I'm just thankful for the family I do have. Our family's not perfect, but as far as I'm concerned, they're the best parents a guy could ever want."

At first blush, Pete did have the perfect family. I knew, however, that his parents pressured him to take pre-law and follow in his dad's steps by going to law school. And now, these revelations. I needed to do more to boost his self-esteem and confidence.

"Well, thanks for sharing this, buddy. But how do you put those memories aside?"

"I just focus on all the good that's occurred in my life and avoid those dark places in my head where bad thoughts lurk."

"Man, I admire you. This helps me a lot."

"Good to hear. See if you can do the same. But enough about all that. Give me an update, dude—found a practice yet? How's marriage? C'mon, give me the good stuff!"

"Married life with Annie's great, and I'm close to making a practice decision. Pretty sure it'll be someplace around here. What about you, Pete? Any plans?"

"No job offers. Of course, we both knew a major in Art History wasn't going to open a lot of doors. I'll probably opt to stay here and go to grad school. With my master's degree, at least I could teach—maybe even instruct on campus as long as I'm on a Ph.D. track. I've pretty much decided to stay in North Carolina, rather than go back to Virginia. This area sorta grows on you. Right?"

"Agreed. I never thought a Missouri boy like me would love living in the south so much. Hey, speaking of love, how's your love life? The last time I saw you with a girl was when you and Mary were dancing together at the wedding reception. You told me the two of you went out a few times. Still dating?"

"We are! Hard to believe, right?" Pete grinned. "Far as I know, she's not seeing anyone else, and I'm certainly not. We really like each other or, at the very least, she puts up with me. It's been a long time coming, so I don't want to say too much and jinx it."

"Don't sell yourself short, Pete. You're a great guy. Any girl would be lucky to have you." Try as he might to hide it, Pete lacked self-confidence. *Now, I know why.*

"How's Annie?"

"At work, she's doing great. Very happy with her job at the university hospital, and my colleagues in oncology say she's exceptionally good at what she does. You know, not just the clinical stuff, but how well she relates personally to her patients. I'm not surprised. From the moment we started dating and discussing our careers in medicine, I could tell she was going to be one heck of a nurse."

"That must be a hard job, though. I mean, helping patients who have cancer? Especially with her own mom having it."

"Actually, I think that's the main reason she loves what she's doing. She treats her patients the way she would want her mom to be treated."

"That's actually a good approach for anyone in medicine, including doctors. Want another muffin?"

"No, thanks. You know, I suppose you're right. I hadn't really given that much thought."

"I guess that's why it's called the 'art' of medicine. There's a personal touch that's necessary. For me, it means a lot to have a doctor with a personality and really seems to care."

Sometimes, Pete's insight surprised me.

"Hey, Jack, the four of us should really make an effort to get together for a meal or just go out for coffee. We haven't all been together since the wedding. I know Mary would love to get together."

"Let's do that. We'll need to find a time that works for all of us," I answered, knowing that might be a challenge.

"You said Annie is doing well at work. Why the qualifier?" He wiped some butter from the corner of his mouth and reached for his coffee mug.

"It's her mom's cancer. Things are getting worse. She's decided to stop all her treatments, and it's really tearing Annie apart."

"Yeah, I get it. What a shame. She was so nice to me when we were there for the wedding. Made me feel right at home."

"Yep. She's a gem, for sure. And as the saying goes, with Annie, the apple didn't fall far from the tree. I'm a lucky guy to have the wife and the mother-in-law I have. Annie was there last weekend and can't wait to go back, so we're going to visit the week after Christmas."

"Glad you can get there to see her. I'm sure looking forward to being back home for the holidays too."

Having finished our breakfast and drained the coffee pot, we said our good-byes. I could have stayed all day just shooting the breeze, but I had work to do. As I stood to leave, I said, "So we're good, Pete?"

"We'll always be good, bro."

As I headed home, it hit me: I knew it was way past time I talked to Annie about the lost pieces of my childhood. No more excuses. No more delays.

Chapter Thirty-One

Late December 2017

When I got back home from Pete's, I found a note from Annie saying she'd gone to bed early because of a headache. I was worried about her; this wasn't the first time she'd complained of a headache that sent her to bed. Probably migraines, as they ran in her family. But maybe she was just beat from her busy work schedule. Once again, I caught myself trying to diagnose someone's problem when I shouldn't. I planned to suggest she see her doctor, but knowing how nurses are about their own health care, I'd save that discussion for just the right time. Anyway, with Annie asleep, there'd be no discussion tonight about my past.

"The car's packed, Annie," I hollered."

"Okay. Let me grab my bookbag."

"Hey, can you get my thermos from the kitchen, too, please?"

We were on our way to Wilmington after what had been a hectic three-day stretch of work. Both of us were ready for some time off. We were leaving early, anxious to get to the coast. It was a beautiful, crisp morning, with a heavy dew still on the grass and the nearly barren trees allowing streaks of early sunlight to shoot through their branches.

"What a stretch of work," I said. I'd had two admissions: a child who probably ate the wrong thing at a family get-together had to be admitted for dehydration due to either food poisoning or gastroenteritis and an elderly obese man with borderline cardiac function who ate too much Smithfield ham and drank so much water that he threw himself into congestive heart failure. I didn't quite understand it until one of the nurses explained to me that Smithfield ham is a heavily salted Virginia ham—a real treat in the Commonwealth State. Then, it all made sense.

I told Annie about it, and she laughed. "Mother has never served Smithfield ham, but I'm sure Pete knows all about it. You'll have to ask him."

"Well, both patients got tuned up and will be discharged this morning, having paid a heavy price for dietary indiscretions!"

I was stalling. I wanted to talk but not about patients. *Seriously, Wilson. It's Annie. Just talk to her.* "Annie?"

She looked up from her book. "Yeah?"

"I need to talk to you about something."

She marked her book and rested it in her lap. "What's up, sweetie?"

"It's about my childhood." I looked over at her.

"Your childhood? I know that story, Jack. Your parents died when you were young, and you were raised by your grandparents."

"But that's not the *whole* story."

"Go on." She put the book in the bag sitting on the floorboard.

"My parents fought—often, but only when my dad drank. I didn't understand it."

"Understand what?"

"The evil that came out of that bottle. See, he was a good man—and good to Mom and me when he was sober."

"Was he ever violent?"

"He would verbally abuse us, and sometimes, he'd push Mom or take a swing at her."

Annie placed a hand on my forearm. "I'm sorry, Jack."

"Well, that's not all. They died in a car wreck after they drove away with my dad driving drunk. At least, I thought they both died."

"What do you mean?"

I told Annie about the visit from Officer Stanley.

"That's awful, Jack. I can't imagine the impact that must have had on you as just a young child . . . but why didn't you tell me all this sooner?"

"I wanted to, and I tried, but there never seemed to be a good time to—"

"But, Jack. We promised no more secrets, remember?"

"I still don't know how to resolve my issues with my dad. Anyway, that's it—my whole story. I promise. No more secrets." I sighed, relieved to have finally told Annie everything. *That was easier than I'd expected.* "Forgive me, babe?"

"No forgiveness needed. Besides, it's Christmas!"

"Good! Now that that's behind us, we can focus on your mom and on making this Christmas visit really special."

Chapter Thirty-Two

Wilmington

W e were almost to Wilmington. I noticed Annie wringing her hands and taking some deep breaths. Nervous, I assumed, about her mom's medical condition.

"I hope Mother is feeling well and can be up and about to enjoy our visit. I'd love to get her out to see some friends and really enjoy the holidays. She'll be tired and want to just spend time with us, but maybe we can take her to some of her favorite restaurants and visit some folks."

"You know better than me that your mom's a tough woman. I bet she'll will herself into having a good time, even if she's not up to the task."

"I'm just so worried about her, Jack. I don't know why this is so hard—after all, I work in oncology."

"You're your mom's little girl when you're with her. There's a vast difference in how we act with and what we say to our patients and how we handle things when it's our own flesh and blood."

"I guess you're right."

The Monroe house was decorated with a lovely wreath sporting a bright red bow on the front door. A single, electric candle adorned the sill of each of the front windows." I was struck by the memory of Virginia bursting through the front door to greet us on our first visit. She didn't come out this time.

"Guess she doesn't realize we're here," I said.

"Oh, when I texted Mother to tell her we were almost here, she said to just come on in; the door would be unlocked."

We found Annie's mom sitting in one of the wingback chairs in the living room. In one corner of the room was a Christmas tree, decorated in nothing but bird ornaments and filling the room with the smell of fresh spruce. A beautiful poinsettia sat on the coffee table, and a pair of nutcrackers guarded each end of the fireplace mantel. As we walked over, she attempted to get to a standing position with the help of a cane. With both hands, she pushed against the grip, standing partially, and then plopped back down in the chair. I gently grabbed her elbow and helped her up. The sleeves of her blouse sagged from her arms.

"I'm so happy to see you two. You're thoughtful to make time for a visit this week, and I've really looked forward to having your company. I spent Christmas Day alone, pretending it was just another day, but my spirits were buoyed by the thought of you coming soon."

"We'd like to be here much more often, Virginia," I answered. "It's just that we've been so busy with work." It was the truth but perhaps not the best excuse to make for not visiting.

"Oh, I understand. Now, do sit down and fill me in on everything that's been going on in your hectic lives."

Over coffee and hot tea, we brought Virginia up to speed. Annie told her how happy she was with her job. Although the final details had not been worked out, I assured her I would likely join a practice near the university, allowing us to remain in our apartment and Annie in her job.

"Well, selfishly, I'd love for you to move this way, but I'm thrilled things have fallen into place for the two of you. Of course, being near me might not matter . . . oh, never mind. I'm just so happy for you." She smiled briefly and then looked down at her hands, clasped in her lap.

"Oh, Mother, it's so good to be here with you. We do feel terrible that we're not here more often," Annie said, the cracking of her voice suggesting she understood what her mom intimated.

"Don't give it another thought, please. Let's just enjoy being together."

"The house looks and smells just like Christmas, Virginia," I said.

"Tom and Ethel helped me with the decorations. You remember Tom, don't you, Jack?"

"Of course, and I look forward to seeing him again and meeting his wife."

"Mother, how is Ethel doing?"

"She's been fine. Not back to the hospital for months. Said the doctors have finally figured out what she can and can't eat and what medicine to give her to help with her indigestion. Both of them have been so nice to help me with anything I've needed. 'That's what neighbors are for, Virginia,' is pretty much their stock answer. They begged me to come over on Christmas Day, but I would have none of it. I didn't want to impose."

"And how are you feeling, Mother?"

"Well, I can't complain, or if I did, it wouldn't matter." She chuckled. "I have many, many good days and then some where I just don't feel like doing much, so I don't. On those good days, though, I get out and visit with friends and try to run my errands—with Tom as my driver, of course. He calls me his 'Miss Daisy.' Knowing my fate at least allows for a chance to take care of the things that are most important—mostly relationships, I mean." Although she was still smiling, her eyes suggested a certain resolution. "It's been wonderful to reach out to the people in town who mean so much to me. Why, I've even mended a few fences."

"Mother, I didn't realize you had any fences that needed mending."

"Well, nothing earth-shattering, but I've had words at times with some of my neighbors, and I'm just not going to leave it like that. There's something I need to tell you, too. I went to see Nancy Edwards. Oh, dear. Does Jack know—"

"You didn't! How could you? Why would you do that? And yes, I've told Jack all about Chip Edwards. Remember? I told you on my last visit."

"Oh, right. Anyway, I've never felt good about what happened to Chip. Even after what he did to you, he didn't deserve what happened. I wanted his mother to know I pray for her and Chip every day."

"Is that all you told her?"

"Yes. It wouldn't have done any good to tell her more. Well, Annie, while I'm upsetting you, I might as well tell you this too: I've forgiven your father."

"What? Please don't tell me you met with him too!"

I shifted uncomfortably in my seat and looked away, as though I could make myself disappear from this conversation.

"Goodness no, child!" Virginia said. "I didn't even try to find him. I just forgave him in my heart. This is no time for bitterness."

"But Mother, he abandoned us. He walked out on our family and then tried to tear us apart."

"People make mistakes, Annie. Sometimes, terrible mistakes that really hurt the people they love. I've made the decision to forgive him and give up any resentment I still harbor for what he did."

Virginia took a deep breath, reached for a book, and then looked up at Annie. "Let me read you this Martin Luther King, Jr. quote: 'Throughout life, people will make you mad, disrespect you, and treat you badly. Let God deal with the things they do, cause hate in your heart will consume you too.'"

"That's beautiful, Virginia," I said. *She could have been talking about you, Wilson. Are you listening?*

"Let's not talk about him anymore, Mother. Please." Annie sighed and pinched the bridge of her nose.

"So be it, Annie, but I felt I needed to tell you."

Sensing this would be a good time to have Annie catch her breath, I finally spoke up. "Hey, babe, why don't we bring in our things?"

Chapter Thirty-Three

Annie was quiet as we unpacked our bags in her old bedroom. "Is everything okay?" I asked.

"I can't believe she's forgiven my father."

"I get that, Annie, but your mom realizes her days are numbered. She's making amends for things she's said and coming to grips with old hurts—you know, trying to rectify them. It's actually a beautiful thing. In fact, it's something all of us could learn from and try to emulate, long before we think our final days are upon us." *If only I could take my own advice.*

"But . . . to forgive my father—her cheating husband, for crying out loud—for all of the things he did to us. Maybe my faith just isn't as strong as Mother's. I mean, he walked out on us and then tried to destroy what was left of our family, Jack. I'm sorry, but it just doesn't sit well with me."

Annie unpacked her suitcase, put her clothes in the dresser drawer, and then started straightening furniture and pictures in the room.

"Slow down, Annie. Remember, we're here to comfort your mom. You don't have to agree with her, but you have to accept her decisions. I know it's hard, but you've got to try."

"I am trying, Jack. I really am." She put both hands over her face and slowly shook her head as I wrapped my arms around her waist.

The rest of the day went much better. After we exchanged gifts, we had a nice dinner with Tom and Ethel Barnes, who graciously brought over a meal so that none of us had to cook. After dinner, we chatted over hot tea and cookies before calling it a night. The visit from the neighbors had really lifted Annie's spirits. It was a good way to end what had been a long day.

One thing I like about the holidays is the slower pace. That Christmas was no exception. After sleeping in, we caught the news updates on our phone apps, had coffee, and ate breakfast at our leisure. The rest of the week was pretty low-key. Annie wanted it that way—quiet and lots of time with her mom. We were determined that what we feared would be her last Christmas would be a memorable one. Some of Annie's former neighbors and friends dropped by. It was a small community, and word had apparently gotten out that Virginia was sicker now and no longer getting out much. I did hear a lot about Annie's childhood and how she'd been a model child whom everyone loved. Hearing those stories made me long for a childhood I'd never experienced. I was determined that someday, when we had a family, I would be the best dad possible and give our kids the childhood every boy and girl deserves.

All too soon, it was time to leave.

"Annie, I've got to admit I'm sad to be leaving. I thought I would be anxious to get back to my patients, but the time off has been much better than I'd anticipated."

Our departure was an emotional one for Annie and her mom. They hugged each other several times as they voiced their love for one another. Saying goodbye is often difficult with loved ones but impossibly hard when it could be the final goodbye. The ride home was somber and quiet until Annie put her hand on my arm and spoke.

"Thank you, Jack."

"For what?"

"For making this just the kind of Christmas I wanted with Mother. You'll never know what that means to me and how much I'll treasure the memories we made this week."

"I agree, Annie. I'm really glad we came."

Chapter Thirty-Four

Chapel Hill

Is it just me, or does everyone feel like they need another vacation as soon as they return from one? You get home and barely through the front door and then start thinking about all the catching up that's going to be required. Right? Before I could hardly unpack, I was back seeing my clinic patients, handling the residents, and reviewing a boatload of emails, texts, and medical record messages. I also needed time to review my contract offer from the practice I wanted to join. Given the initial testy interview with their senior partner, Dr. August Payne, I was surprised they were still interested in me. He assumed I was a wet-under-the-collar know-it-all with no experience in real-world medicine, and his questions had an edge to them. I hoped he was just testing my composure, but I couldn't help thinking his surname was appropriate.

I knew I had to make time for Pete since I'd ignored him over the hectic holiday season. We met at the Grind for a cup of coffee and snacks.

"How were your holidays, Pete? Your folks doing okay?"

"It's always good to go back to Virginia. Both of my sisters were there, too, and one of them brought home what turned out to be a very serious boyfriend. In fact, my sister got a diamond for Christmas! This guy seems like the real deal, and he treats her well. My parents are thrilled, and I have to admit, I'm pretty pumped to have another guy in the family. We had a great time just sitting around, talking, and eating—a lot!"

Once again, I found myself envying Pete's family life.

"And how's Mary?"

"Good! We went out the first night I got back. I'm starting to understand how you fell head over heels for Annie. Hopefully, Mary feels the same way about me. I guess it's hard to understand all that until you go through it yourself. Even though we're getting more serious, we'll keep it at just dating for now. Not a lot of extra cash for anything more. I'm still a little gun-shy about a serious relationship too. Oh yeah, I meant to tell you I've been accepted into the Art History grad program here. Maybe a Masters in Art History will make my parents proud of me."

I sensed a change in Pete's mood. They had wanted to see him become a lawyer, but they still loved him. "What do you mean, Pete? I've always thought your parents are *very* proud of you."

Pete began to tap the table's surface. "It's the whole law school thing again. That's all they talked about when I was in high school, and they still bring it up. I thought about pre-law, but I had this dream of studying art, and I decided to pursue it. Every time I'm home, they ask me if I've thought any more about switching to law. It gets old, I gotta tell you, but I'm following my dreams—just like you—so I'll be here at least two more years."

He reached for the creamer and a pack of sugar. I noticed his nails were chewed to the quick.

"That's got to be a lot of pressure on you," I said.

"Well, it is. Sometimes, I resent it but, hey, they gave me a family and upbringing I might not otherwise have had, so I cut them some slack."

"Makes sense. Anyway, sounds like the four of us will still be close enough that we really have to make an effort to get together for a night out. Work just seems to get in the way."

"If we let it get in the way, that is."

The simple wisdom of Pete. There was a lot more to him than he'd ever give himself credit for. For his sake, I wished his parents would lay off the pressure about his career choices.

"How was Christmas in Wilmington?" Pete said.

"Really good. Quiet, relaxing. Now, I'm back with an avalanche of work about to come down on me."

"How's Ms. Monroe doing—in layman's terms, that is?"

"She's thinner now because she doesn't have much of an appetite. Some of that is her cancer, but some of it is probably from the pain medicine she's on. She also tires easily. A quick trip out in the car takes about as much energy as she can muster. But she has resolved to handle her fate and control her cancer on her own terms. Since I'm almost always focused on treatment, it probably does me good to see things from a patient's perspective. I think I understand why she's made the decision she has, and I respect her for it."

"Yeah, I had an uncle who died from cancer. The end of his life was spent in a hospital room with doctors trying all sorts of what seemed to me to be heroic treatments. None of them worked, and most of the drugs just made him feel worse. No offense, Jack, but sometimes, medicine can be man's greatest enemy."

I nodded.

"How's Annie handling it?"

"It's hard for her. As a nurse, she wants her mom to do everything the doctors recommend to keep her alive, but, as a daughter, she understands her mom's decision and wants her to live out her days at home as comfortably as possible. There was one difficult moment, however, right after we got there."

"Meaning?"

"She told Annie she's forgiven Annie's father."

Pete shook his head. "Man, I can't even imagine what that must have been like for Annie to hear. It makes me realize how lucky I was to have a stable family growing up. Easy to take that kind of thing for granted."

"I'm sure it is, Pete," I said in a hushed voice, almost to myself.

Chapter Thirty-Five

Annie

"Well, hush my mouth if it isn't Annie Monroe, my personal Flo Nightingale!"

"Good morning, Mrs. Mason. How're you feeling?" I said, smiling as I entered her room to get her up and out of bed. Thin arms protruded from her pajama top, their skin pale and sagging. Thin veins coursed her forearms like highways on a road map.

"Not so hot but a lot better since you're back at work. Honey, where on earth have you been?"

"I was off after Christmas, so I went home to see my mother."

"Well, I guess even nurses get time off, as well they should. Did you have a nice vacation?" She smiled.

"I sure did. Nothing exciting, though. Just lots of family time—what I was hoping for, actually."

"I'm sure your parents enjoyed having you home, Annie."

"It was just my mother, and yes, I do think she enjoyed my company as much as I enjoyed hers."

"Well, I'm just glad you're back. I was worried about you, honey. You *are* my favorite nurse, you know. Now, all I have to do is find out where Dr. Wilson's been."

I wasn't about to respond to that. We had kept our marriage as quiet as anything could be in a hospital full of employees who knew us both, but our mutual patients had no idea. I wanted it to stay that way. I also found it fun, though sometimes annoying, to hear Mrs. Mason refer to "her Dr. Wilson" so often. Other patients talked glowingly of him as well. It made me proud, envious, and irritated—a bunch of jumbled-up emotions I kept below the surface. Jack was a great doctor who loved and really cared for his patients. But I knew his professional dedication had detrimental effects on his personal life. No one else had to know that, though I suspected Pete did.

"The nurses said he had a few days off over the holidays too. They all know how much I like him. I sure hope he's back soon."

"I have a feeling you'll see him soon, Mrs. Mason. Tell me, have you been behaving yourself while I was away?"

"The model patient, Miss Annie, thank you very much. You might be my favorite, but I like all the nurses who work on this unit. The doctors come in and order stuff that usually makes me sick, and then the nurses try their best to keep me comfortable. I reckon at this point, I'd be a whole lot better off to have y'all running the show and leave the doctors out of it. Except for Dr. Wilson, of course."

"Maybe that's because he's not prescribing your chemo. You know, he's here just to be sure you're taken care of and to be certain you understand what's going on with your treatments."

"Yeah, I guess you're right." She paused and looked out the window. "I'm anxious to see him, Annie. I want to talk to him about my future."

"Your future?"

"Sweetheart, I'm weaker than cheap soup and tired of treatments and all these awful hospital stays. I wonder if it's worth it. Maybe I should just let nature take its course. I don't know."

I sat on the edge of her bed and took her wrinkled hand. *I know it's Mrs. Mason, but I see and hear my mom.* "I know you don't mean that, and we both know cancer treatment is hard work, Mrs. Mason, not to mention its side effects."

"I don't know pea turkey about how it all works. All I know is the poisons kill the cancer cells, but they also kill good cells. Collateral damage, I guess. Sorta like when my Jimmy used to go squirrel hunting with a shotgun. Pretty much anything else within about ten feet usually bit the dust too. 'Course, he wasn't the best shot. Jimmy never much swore, but he could cuss the bark off an oak tree when he missed a squirrel!"

"Maybe not the best analogy, but I think you get it." I laughed. "Anyway, you *should* talk to Dr. Wilson. Tell him what you're thinking, but first, give yourself time to recover from this treatment, and then you can make a decision when you're feeling a lot better." I looked down to sneak a peek at my watch.

"I never feel *a lot better*, sweetheart. And I'll tell you this: I'm at peace with my fate and with my maker. I knew my Southern Baptist upbringing would get me through tough times. Had to be some benefit from sitting through those loud fire and brimstone sermons that almost scared a little girl to death! Pointed me on the right road to salvation, though, I'll say for sure."

I have to get to my other patients. "How about this: I'll get a nurse's assistant to change your bed linens, and then I'll call the clinic to make sure Dr. Wilson knows you're here." I opened her blinds to let some sun in. The light might cheer her up.

"Well, I'm sure he isn't back yet, or if he is, he hasn't been told I'm here. He'd have been here by now if he knew. You remember I told you how he looked after my Jimmy, don't you? One thing I've learned: If you can count on your fingers, you can count on Dr. Wilson."

"I do remember, and I'm sure you're right, Mrs. Mason, but I'll check just the same. Is there anything else I can do for you before I go?"

"No, I'm fine. I'll just sit here and be lazy while my body's being hammered by my 'protocol,' as you call it. Sounds very sophisticated for a bunch of poisons, I'll tell you that."

"You may be tired and feeling bad, but I'm glad to hear you still have your sense of humor."

"That's one thing I won't let them take away from me, Miss Annie. Not in a million years."

Chapter Thirty-Six

Annie and I had finished dinner and were cleaning dishes, one of the few times we weren't preoccupied with her writing and my catch-up work. She put down the drying cloth, turned my way, and said she had a couple of things to mention to me. "I know we don't like to talk about mutual patients, what with HIPPA and everything, but you need to know something about Mrs. Mason."

"Oh, yeah. I saw her name on the in-patient list. I plan to go by to see her tomorrow. She's one of my favorite patients—a real spunky old gal."

"Well, that spunky old gal really thinks you're the straw that stirs her drink. But that's not what I wanted to tell you. She told me today she's ready to stop all treatment. It was all I could do to keep my composure, as it reminded me so much of Mother. Her treatments make her sick, and I'm not sure she's really responding the way her oncologist would like. She doesn't look healthy. Anyway, I encouraged her to talk to you before making a decision."

"Good advice." Sometimes I thought Annie should have been the doctor in the family; her instincts were so good. "I'll block out some time so I can sit down with her and just hear her out. I know it's not much, but allowing her to vent seems to lift her spirits."

"Yes, and there aren't any bad side effects to that kind of medicine, right? I know she'll be thrilled to see you. She really does think you hung the moon, you know."

"Good to know. Thanks. Oh, by the way, Pete and I met the other day for coffee. He'll be staying on for grad school this coming year and . . . the big news: he and Mary are still dating! Sounds like it could be pretty serious to me."

"Yeah, I know. Mary and I keep in touch. I'm happy for both of them. I think the world of Mary and, of course, I know how you feel about Pete—the *bromance* thing, you know."

"Well, I don't know if I'd call it that, but we do go back three years, and he was a great soundboard for me when I started seeing you and was confused about my feelings."

"Confused? Really, Jack? What do you mean by that?"

Did I actually say that out loud? "Oh, I meant confused in a good way. You know, at how quickly our relationship blossomed, so to speak. Anyway, he and Mary will be around, and we have to make a point of getting together with them. Now, you said you had a couple of things to discuss. Mrs. Mason and what else?"

"Oh, it's probably nothing, and I feel better now, but at work today, I got another headache. I rested my eyes over my lunch break and took some ibuprofen and then everything seemed to get better. Probably just stress. My worst headache started after I learned that Mother was stopping her treatment. Today, my discussion with Mrs. Mason got me thinking about Mother again, and then I started to feel bad. Weird, huh?"

No way could I objectively assess Annie's health. Most headaches are stress, migraines, or related to poor vision, but it wouldn't hurt for her to get checked. "Why don't you at least schedule an appointment with one of the ophthalmology residents to have an exam?"

"Okay, I'll do that, Jack. Now, back to Pete and Mary."

When it came to changing topics, Annie was all-pro.

"Let's make a point of going to dinner with them—in fact, maybe dinner and a movie. I'll call Mary this evening. It's been so busy that I haven't seen her in a while, and it'll be great to catch up in person, not just by texts or calls. We'll compare calendars and try to come up with a night that suits all of us. It'll be nice to go out with another couple, don't you think?"

"What are you saying, Annie? I'm not enough company for you?" I said, grinning.

"You know what I mean, sweetie. There's more to life than work, coming home, fixing dinner, cleaning up, and then collapsing in front of your computer. If we're not careful, we'll get in a rut—you know, like a couple of old geezers."

"Well, geezer this," I said, as I playfully grabbed Annie around the waist and drew her close. "I'm glad you're feeling better, Annie, but I do want you to get an eye exam."

"Of course, Jack."

Right. When pigs fly. The only people worse than doctors about their own health were nurses.

Later that evening, as I was completing some patient notes, Annie bopped into the bedroom, seemingly in a much perkier mood.

"Just talked to Mary. She and Pete would love to have dinner with us. They're on an even tighter budget than ours, so we'll skip the movie."

"Super, Annie," I said. I went back to finishing my notes.

"For crying out loud, Jack. Can't you put that away? We could watch some TV, just talk, or maybe do something even more romantic." She tilted her head and opened her eyes wide.

"I'm almost finished, but then I've got to look over the in-patient list to plan for tomorrow's rounds." I looked at her over my glasses, raised my hands, and shrugged.

"Always working—and always preparing." She rolled her eyes.

"Maybe that's why patients like Mrs. Mason think I 'hung the moon,' as you put it. You know we've talked about this before. Work takes priority."

"Well, I think you hung the moon, too, but you seem to spend more time either at work or doing more work at home than you spend with me. Why can't I be your priority? Why can't you give me the same attention you give patients like Mrs. Mason?" She moved up against me and began rubbing my back.

"We're both in the same business, Annie, but there are differences." Immediately, I didn't like the direction I was taking this conversation. I looked down and shook my head.

"Like what?"

I looked at her and answered softly, "When you end a shift, you're finished until your next day at work. At the end of my day, there's usually more work to do: finishing notes, cleaning out my in-basket, and answering emails. Also, because I'm senior resident, I'm responsible for the other residents too."

"Will this get better once you're in private practice? I don't mean to sound selfish, but will there be more time for life at home—more time for me, for us?"

"I'm counting on it, Annie. I won't be very busy at first since I'll be new in practice, and I certainly won't have anyone to supervise. Everyone tells me private practice is a nice change from the hours and work that residency requires. Speaking of private practice, I'm meeting with the department's contract attorney the day after tomorrow to review my offer."

"An attorney? Can we afford that?"

"No worries—it's a free service the hospital offers senior residents. If the contract looks good, the last piece of the puzzle will fall into place, and come July 1,

I'll enter private practice. I can't wait! By the way, Annie, do you ever run across a Dr. Payne at the hospital?"

"No, at least not directly. But in nursing school, I remember taking care of a few of his patients who he referred to the hospital. His patients loved him, but he had a reputation as being hard to work with—you know, one of those docs with kind of a hard edge—very demanding and serious. Why?"

"He's actually the senior partner of the practice I'm joining. He's kind of a prick. We didn't get off to such a great start, but all the other partners loved me—I think."

"I'm sure it'll work out. Anyhow, it's been a long day, and I'm going to bed. See you in the morning, sweetie. Oh, by the way, Mrs. Mason thinks I hung the moon too!" She cocked her head, winked, and then kissed me goodnight.

As I listened to Annie get ready for bed, I thought about what she'd said. It wasn't the first time we'd had that conversation. I *was* spending a lot of time on work and not much time with her. But my position demanded it of me. She deserved better, especially given her worries about her mom. Yes, I could be more intentional about managing my professional and personal lives. How hard could that be? I resolved to make more time for her . . . just as soon as I finished my residency.

Chapter Thirty-Seven

After I finished seeing my patients in clinic the following day, I headed over to the hospital to make rounds with the residents on the in-patient service. Pretty routine cases, with nothing terribly serious: a child on the pediatric floor getting breathing treatments and steroids for asthma, a young mom in for post-partum depression manifesting as anorexia, a woman with pneumonia, and a man with a staph infection unresponsive to out-patient antibiotics. Once rounds were over, I headed to the oncology floor to see Mrs. Mason. Maybe I'd see Annie too.

I knocked on the door and walked in. "Hi there, Mrs. Mason," I said. "How's my favorite patient?"

"Well, I'd say a whole heap better now that you're here. Favorite patient? I bet you say that to all of your patients."

"No, I don't, either. Only the sweet ones and you're the sweetest!"

"Then what took you so long to come see me?"

"I just got back to work from some time off. Last night, I saw you'd been admitted, so here I am! How are you feeling?" I asked. I thought about what Annie had said—her pale, thin body blended in with the white sheets of her hospital bed.

"I'm just real tired . . . and real tired of feeling bad. I think you doctors are going to cure me, even if you have to kill me to do it!"

"Still the comedienne, huh?"

"Well, I try. But on a serious note, Dr. Wilson, I *am* glad you're here. I was telling my nurse—Annie, who's a real dear—that I don't want to continue treatment. I'm just tired of always feeling bad . . . you know, kinda drained, like I've really done something when all I've done is simply lie here while others do things to me and for me."

"But your disease is under control, Mrs. Mason. Some of that is due to your strong will, but a lot of it is courtesy of the chemotherapy you've been getting."

"Why does everyone around here love those poisons? All they're doing is making me feel terrible!"

"Now, you know that's not true. They keep your cancer in check. You've only got a few more weeks of chemo, and then you'll just need frequent lab work to make sure your blood count stays normal. I want you to hang in there. You know we're in this together. I'll always be there for you, and it sounds like there's someone else you trust. What's your nurse's name again—Annie?" I said, my curiosity piqued as to Mrs. Mason's take on Annie from a patient's point of view.

"Her name is Annie, and she's a sweetheart. She listens just like you do, and she makes me feel like I'm the only patient she's taking care of, even though I know she's busier than a bee in pollinating season. I can tell her anything without being afraid I'll be judged. I just love her!"

"She does sound like quite a nurse."

"I'm surprised you don't know her, Dr. Wilson. She works up here full-time. She's mighty pretty and, far as I know, she's single. She'd make a great catch for you, Doc."

I caught myself grinning. "Well, you know I just drop in to check on you and make sure you're behaving. I don't really get involved with progress notes, doctor's orders, or the nurses. I leave all that to your oncologist."

"My poison pusher, you mean?" she said as she shook her head.

Seizing what was a good moment, I said, "So you'll get to feeling better, go home, and then call to set up an appointment so we can talk about what we're going to do going forward, right? And I promise, I'll honor and respect whatever decision you make."

"You've got a deal, Doc."

As I turned to leave her room, she placed her wasted, wrinkled hand on my forearm. "Thank you, Dr. Wilson, for all you did for my Jimmy and for what you're doing for me. Also, I hope I didn't step in it by talking about something kinda personal."

"Personal?"

"Talking about my nurse, Annie, and all that blabbering I did."

"Oh, that? No worries. Looking after you is why I'm here—it's my pleasure," I said. "Tell you what: I'll keep my eye out for this Annie." I patted her on the shoulder.

As I left Mrs. Mason's room, I felt a real sense of joy, happy that I'd convinced her to postpone her decision regarding future treatments and grateful for a wife who's so gracious, loving, and caring. Walking down the hall to the elevator, I caught a glimpse of Annie. As our eyes met, we smiled and winked at each other in a way no one else would pick up on but, for me, meant the world.

As I exited the elevator, my pager went off. It was one of the residents on the in-patient team, calling to tell me her patient with pneumonia had spiked a high fever and was transferred to intensive care due to a possible blood infection, what we refer to in medicine as *sepsis*. Just two hours earlier, she seemed stable. Medicine was both frustrating and challenging. It meant we always had to be on our guard for the next complication, but I loved that. Forgoing any notion of getting home early, I shrugged and re-entered the elevator to head for the ICU.

Chapter Thirty-Eight

February 2018

It had been months since that painful encounter with Sydney, and I was worried about her. Typically, she scheduled an appointment to see me every few months, sometimes for trivial issues that didn't deserve a visit. Perhaps, she had decided to change doctors. I really wouldn't fault her for that. On the chance I might find her at home, I stopped by her grandparents' house after clinic on a Friday afternoon. Bea Mitchell, her grandmother, was as affable as she had been the first time I visited.

"Oh, Dr. Wilson. Another house call? Didn't know doctors still did that. But why are we standing in the cold? Come in, please. Coffee?"

"That would be great, thanks. Sorry to show up unannounced and, to your point, we don't typically make house calls. But Sydney hasn't been in, and I was in the area, so I thought I'd try to catch her at home. May I speak to her?"

"I'm sorry, doctor, but she's not here. She's moved home to live with her dad."

"But I thought he was in jail—"

"He went before the judge and got off almost scot-free. Judge showed him leniency and gave him just thirty days in jail. After that, he was released on two conditions: that he re-enters AA and stays out of bars. Once we knew he was committed to staying sober, we thought it best for Sydney to go home and live with him. A child needs her parents, or at least one of them. Don't you agree?"

My jaw dropping, I skirted the question and replied, "May I have their number, please? I'd love to call her."

"I'll have to look that up—it's a memory thing, you know. What can I say? It happens. Tell you what, just head over there, and I'll call and let her know you're coming."

———

Sydney's dad came to the door. He looked healthy but disheveled, with his shirttail partially out and soiled oversized cargo pants. He seemed guarded as he asked me in. "Been a while, Doc. Guess you heard about my backsliding, huh? Bea likes to yak."

"What I heard is you're sober and back in your program, which is great."

"Well, it's a process, as they say. Going to try to walk the straight and narrow, but it's hard. Guess that's why alcoholics are never considered fully recovered."

"I guess that's right," I said as my thoughts flashed back to my dad's demons. "Uh, if Sydney's home, I'd love to see her."

"I'm home, Dr. Wilson," she said, entering from a side door. "Daddy, can you give us a few minutes, please?" Clothes that now seemed too big covered her thin frame, and her hair looked as though it hadn't seen a brush in days. She stared at me, no expression on her gaunt face.

"Well, Syd. It's good to see you. How're you doing?"

"Better now. I love my grandparents and what they did for me, but it's good to be home with my dad."

"I was worried about you—hadn't seen you in quite a while, which is not typical for you."

"The truth . . . you see, the truth is, Dr. Wilson, I'm not coming back to you anymore."

"You're not? I'm sorry to hear that. May I ask why?"

Her eyes narrowed. "Honestly, I feel like you betrayed me. Maybe you did what you had to do, but I don't trust you anymore. You see, the reason I came to see you so often was I loved you—not *loved* loved you, if you know what I mean, but maybe more like I looked up to you, and I knew I could trust you. That wasn't always the case at home, so having you as my doctor meant a lot. That's all changed now, though."

"But, Sydney, I was only—"

She held up her hand, indicating she didn't want to hear what I had to say. "I'm in a good place now with my dad, and I'll be fine. I really need to go help Daddy fix dinner. Thanks for coming by."

"Syd, wait . . ." but I was speaking to her back, as she'd quickly turned and walked away and, presumably, out of my professional life forever.

Her words kept replaying in my head on the drive home. My heart was beating out of my chest and sweat was forming on my forehead. Losing a patient under such circumstances was bad enough, but losing her trust and respect made it so much worse.

Once home and unable to think about anything else, I changed into jogging clothes and went for a run. Running was therapeutic. I still ran with Molly loping along beside me when possible, but that required advanced planning—calling Pete to see if she was available. I pulled my stocking cap down over my ears as I turned into the wind to run up the road. Although the exercise didn't fully relieve my angst, at least I was calmer when I got back home. Knowing Annie would be home soon, I went to take a quick shower.

Chapter Thirty-Nine

"**S**weetie, I'm home," Annie called out as she entered the house.

I walked out of the bedroom, wrapped in a bath towel and drying my hair. "Hey."

"Oh, I'm glad you're getting ready. I was afraid you'd forget we're going out with Mary and Pete tonight."

"How could I forget?" I smiled and gave her a kiss. Okay, true confession: I had forgotten, but I'd been a little busy with everything going on at work.

The last thing I wanted that evening was socializing, but there was no way out. *Wilson, Annie would kill you if you even tried.* We chose a nice little restaurant in town with reasonably priced entrees. The couples were going Dutch, and I didn't want Pete to have to stress about the size of the check.

"Man, I didn't think this evening would ever happen," Pete said.

"Same here," Annie replied. "I'm just glad we could find a night to make it work. Doesn't seem like it would be that hard. Right?"

"Mary, it's been a while. How's everything going?" I asked.

"Things couldn't be better. I'm finishing my last year of school and interning at a local elementary school most of this semester."

"Oh, cool. How's that going? It must be great to finally get in the classroom."

"So far, I've loved it. In fact, I like the school and they must like me, at least enough that the principal has offered me a job! I've already accepted the offer, so I'll still be local next year. Lucky Pete—he gets to keep me around!"

Pete smiled. "Yep. I'm a lucky guy. I've got my two loves—art history and Mary!"

"Hopefully, not in that order, Pete, but that's sweet." Mary took his hand and looked over at me. "You look kind of tired. Is everything okay? Have you found a practice?"

"Sorry, kind of a tough day. And yes, I do plan to sign with a practice near Chapel Hill—Carrboro, actually—so Annie can stay at the hospital, and we won't have to move. It's a great practice, even though the senior partner is a bit of a hard case."

"It's nice to have plans fall into place, isn't it?" Mary said. She turned to Annie. "How's your mom doing?"

Annie recounted how her mom had decided more treatments would serve no purpose and only make her feel worse. She preferred to stay at home and be in control of her own care. "I admit, I'm struggling with it all, but its Mother's decision."

"She's such a dear woman. I hate she's going through all of this. Why do bad things always seem to happen to the nicest people?"

"You know, Mary, that's a question I've asked myself a thousand times in my short nursing career. I'm sure Jack has as well. There are just some things we can't understand, I guess."

"That's true," I said.

"I see it all the time on the oncology floor. It's just harder because it's so personal for me right now. But I'm really happy for you, Mary. Who would've thought we'd all still be together this next year and working—except you, Pete."

Pete shook his head. "I'm working—working at finishing school, that is. But if I'm going to have any chance of making a career out of art history, I've got to at least have my master's. We'll see where that takes me. At least I should be able to teach a few undergrad courses and make a little money, so I actually *will* be working too. Who knows, maybe I'll discover I like teaching."

I sensed that Pete felt like the odd man out. A little encouragement couldn't hurt. I reminded him I had to go through college, med school, and then residency before I got the job I wanted. I knew Pete as well as anyone, and I knew he'd land on his feet doing something he enjoyed.

"Thanks for the vote of confidence. I can always count on you for support, bro. Hey, not to change the subject, but I've been thinking. How 'bout the four of us go to my parents' beach house for a week this summer? Jack and I have gone for three straight spring breaks, but we never get tired of the beach."

"Let's do it!" Annie and Mary said, almost in unison. "Nice thing about teaching—I have the entire summer off before starting," Mary said with a big grin and then added, "There's nothing like a week at the beach."

I nodded, but just quietly listened as the three of them talked excitedly about the beach trip and what we might do while there. These were my best friends and my wife. I needed to do my best to join in their enthusiasm. My tension slowly eased, making me determined to carve out some time to make the trip happen. Maybe I just needed to get away and relax a little.

"This has been a wonderful night," Annie said as we began to wrap up dinner. "We ought to make it a regular event."

"Yep. I agree," Pete said. "I've got to get Mary back to her place but, before we go, Jack, are you sure you're, okay?"

"I'm okay, buddy." It was a lie.

Chapter Forty

"Tonight was so much fun," Annie said as we walked through the front door. Turning to me, she wrapped her arms around my waist and pulled me close. "I hope things work out for Pete and Mary, just like they did for us."

"It would be nice."

"Jack, are you really just tired, or is something wrong?"

I decided to tell Annie about Sydney. "Actually, there was something—"

We were interrupted by Annie's phone. As soon as she answered, her color drained as she sat on the couch and grabbed the armrest. It was the call we had anticipated and dreaded, but it was coming much too soon.

"This is all so sudden, Dr. Parke. Hospice? I didn't even know she was under hospice care." She paused and then began to pace. "Of course, I'll be there just as soon as possible. Thank you for calling me."

As she ended the call, Annie could no longer keep her composure. Her eyes filled with tears that spilled onto her face, running down her cheeks like raindrops on windowpanes.

"It's Mother. She's suddenly taken a turn for the worse, and the hospice staff feels the family should be there." I followed her into the kitchen, where she cleaned the counter and began emptying the dishwasher. "Dr. Parke told me he called in the hospice team about two weeks ago, and when he asked Mother if she wanted him to call me, she said not to bother us because we're so busy . . . why are these glasses still wet? . . . I feel awful. I've got to get there—now. Mother needs me. I'll leave word at the hospital that I need emergency time off. Jack, don't just stand there. Help me straighten the kitchen."

I started putting away dishes. "Slow down, Annie. Listen, you *should* go, but I'm going too."

"But your clinic and your residency responsibilities?"

I knew I could call the clinic and get them to clear my schedule. One of the other senior residents could fill in for me as chief. I could spare a few days—the least I could do for Annie. Nothing trumps family. I took her in my arms and gave her a hug. "Come on, let's throw some things together and hit the road."

She nodded. Annie needed me to be with her for this, just as much as she needed to be with her mom. Telling Annie about Sydney would just have to wait—again.

We hurriedly packed our clothes and toiletries and rushed out the door. I grabbed my thermos of coffee for the late-night drive. With little traffic at such a late hour, I knew we'd make good time, arriving around midnight. Of course, just getting there would be all that mattered to Virginia, and to the two of us.

The darkness weighed heavily on me, matching the gloom I felt for what we might find when we arrived. Annie was silent most of the way, occasionally dozing off. We pulled into the driveway just after midnight and were met at the front door by the nurse's aide, Dorothy, who'd spoken to Annie when she dialed her mom's number just as we got to town.

"Miss Virginia's asleep right now," Dorothy said as she ushered us into the house. "I'd suggest you children try to get a little sleep so you'll be fresh in the morning."

Both of us slept restlessly. When we awoke at dawn, daylight was slowly emerging, but waves of clouds blanketed the sky and stopped the sun from making its usual appearance. We could hear stirring downstairs, so both of us quickly showered, dressed, and went downstairs to confront a situation we suspected would be very difficult. As we entered the living room, a slight opening of her eyes confirmed that Annie's mom was aware of our presence. The blinds were open as if to welcome a morning sun that had yet to arrive, leaving the room illuminated by only a bedside lamp. Virginia's change in appearance struck me. She was but a shell of the woman I had first met less than a year earlier. Thin, frail, and too weak to sit up on her own, she whispered to Dorothy to raise the head of the hospital bed and prop her up with an extra pillow. Her smile was weak but genuine. She reached up to give Annie a hug, her arms thin and coursing with prominent veins and splotched with bruises.

"Hello, children. Dorothy told me you got in late. It's so good to see you, but I'm sorry you had to disrupt your schedules just to be here with me. I hate to be such a bother."

"Mother, we wouldn't dream of being anywhere but here! Don't be silly. Why didn't you let me know you were calling in hospice and home care?"

"Oh, I know how busy both of you are. I didn't want to worry you. I'm fine. I just needed a little more help with things around the house. I'd imposed on Tom and Ethel long enough. Everyone's been so helpful and kind, especially Dorothy. Why, they do everything for me, and I hardly have to lift a finger!"

"But we're family, Mother. You should have called us," Annie said, her voice emphatic. She took her hand and gave her shoulder a squeeze. "Anyway, we're here now, and we'll do anything for you we can."

"I don't know that anything more can be done, dear. Your being here is enough. And Jack, I know how busy you must be. Please update me on your plans."

Feeling guilty for talking about myself, I explained I had finalized an agreement with my new practice and the contract was signed. "I'm scheduled to start in mid-July, but they gave me the option of taking a month off and starting in August."

"That's wonderful, Jack. I'm so happy for you—for both of you, really." She rested her head on her pillow and turned to look out the window.

As Annie grasped my hand tightly, I attempted to lighten the atmosphere by suggesting we grab some breakfast. "Can we get you anything, Virginia?"

"I'd love some English breakfast tea, Jack, but nothing to eat right now, thank you."

"English tea, coming up!" I said, trying to sound chipper. Silently, I wondered how Annie and I could best help her mom over her final days. I'd dealt with many terminal patients but a family member was so different—and so much harder.

Chapter Forty-One

Annie and I excused ourselves and walked to the kitchen, where she couldn't hold back her emotions any longer.

"Jack, Mother is dying," she whispered as she emptied the drying rack and put dishes away. "I can sense it and see it. I've seen it a thousand times at work. Why is this happening so quickly?"

I followed her to the pantry, where she started straightening boxes and re-stacking jars of food. "I've got to call Dr. Parke. I don't know Mother's hospice doctor, and I need to speak to someone I trust," she said, her thoughts working as rapidly as her hands.

"Annie, stop," I said gently. I turned her to me and held her close. "Tell you what. I'll put in a call to Dr. Parke's office and ask to have him call you at his convenience. You put on the coffee, warm some bagels, and heat the water for your mom's tea."

Annie nodded silently. She turned away to throw together some breakfast as I googled Dr. Parke's office and then put in a call.

"His office took a message, babe. They said he'll call back."

"He'll call. Trust me."

We took Annie's mom her tea and sat down near her with our breakfast. Annie spoke first. "Mother, are you in pain?"

"No, dear. They have me on medicine for that. It works, but it sure makes me sleepy. Mostly I'm just tired and short of breath whenever I try to get up. Usually, I just lie here. It gets pretty boring, even with Dorothy or one of the other aides to keep me company. There's only so much we can talk about, and I've listened to about as much music as I can stand for now. I never dreamed I'd get tired of '60s music," she said, smiling weakly.

As I was about to speak, my cell rang, the screen indicating it was Dr. Parke's office. I was surprised to hear a man's voice.

"Jack, this is Dr. Parke. We haven't met, but I know you're Annie's husband. I'm glad you two were able to get to town so quickly. If it's okay with you, I'll stop by Virginia's house at the end of the workday today. I really want to talk to you and Annie face to face."

"That would be great, Dr. Parke, and very much appreciated. I'm certain Annie would love to see you. Thank you so much."

"Please tell her I should be there by about 5:30. See you then."

Annie nodded and sighed when I relayed the information. She didn't seem surprised he was going to drop by instead of handling it over the phone.

"He must be some doctor, Annie."

"As the saying goes, he's the 'doctor's doctor.' The best."

Annie's mom nodded. "He's been our doctor for years, as well as a family friend. He promised me he'd be with me every step of my journey, and he's held true to that promise. I just love that man." She closed her eyes and sighed.

I thought of Mrs. Mason and smiled.

We spent the day at Virginia's side, idly chatting when she was awake and drifting off whenever she fell asleep. It was an overcast, gray day—perfect for cat-naps. Annie and I were both startled awake by Virginia's request.

"Dorothy, get me to the bathroom, please. I want you to help me brush my hair, freshen up, and put on just a hint of lipstick. I want to look my best for Dr. Parke." As they left, Annie and I went to the kitchen, where we re-fueled on coffee.

"Dr. Parke should be here any minute, Annie. Are you ready for this?"

"Yes, I guess I'm as ready as I'll ever be. I know what he's going to say, but I need to hear it from him."

We heard the car door close just before there was a knock at the door. Annie rushed to the door, opened it, and hugged a middle-aged gentleman.

"Come on in, Dr. Parke. Thank you so much for taking the time to come see us."

"Well, Annie, I wanted to talk to you in person, but I also wanted to see you again. It's been so long."

"Oh, Dr. Parke, it's so good to see you. This is my husband, Jack. Jack, this is Dr. Parke."

Shaking his hand, I was struck by the firmness of his grip and the kindness of his face, sculpted in wrinkles and framed with a full head of silver hair.

"Jedediah Parke. My friends and medical colleagues just call me 'Jed.' Please do the same. Virginia has told me you'll be starting in private practice this summer. Congratulations! You know, Virginia is mighty proud of you—and Annie, of course."

Dr. Parke then went into the living room, took Virginia's hand, and asked her how she was feeling. Her hair was neat, and she was now wearing soft pink lipstick. Her elegance defied the ravages of her disease. Shortly thereafter, he excused himself and walked with Annie and me to the kitchen, where we could talk privately.

"Can I get you some coffee, Dr. Parke?" Annie said, before sitting down with us at the table.

"I'm good, thanks. Annie and Jack, I know you're both in the business and speak the language, so please allow me to be straightforward."

"Of course," Annie offered. She took my hand and squeezed tightly.

"Your mother's lung metastases have enlarged, and she now has very limited breathing capacity. When she gets out of bed, she gets winded quickly. As you know, the cancer is also in her bones. The hospice folks are controlling the bone pain, but there's been some infiltration into the marrow, and she's very anemic—another reason she has very little stamina. I know the rapid pace at which her illness has advanced comes as a surprise to the two of you and, to be honest, to me as well. But she's a real trooper. She rarely complains, and she's always grateful for what's done for her."

"How much time do you think she has, Jed?" I said as I caught a glimpse of Annie wiping tears from her eyes.

"Well, all of us, including Virginia, know the end is coming. When that will be is hard to say, but my best guess is just a month or two. Of course, I could be wrong."

"So that's it, Dr. Parke?" Annie asked, biting her lower lip.

He nodded. "Ever since she made the decision to stop all treatment, her mind hasn't changed. I feel duty-bound to honor her decision. All we can do now is be here for her and keep her as comfortable as possible. Seeing the two of you probably did more for her spirits than anything the rest of us could have said or done."

Dr. Parke reached over and took Annie's hand. "This won't be easy, but while you're here you should talk to her about final arrangements—what she wants to be said in her obituary and the funeral home she prefers. Dorothy told me the minister came by the other day to discuss Virginia's preferences for her service. As I said, it won't be easy, but I think you'll be surprised at how forthright she is about these things. In fact, she's told me how much thought she's put into it. It will probably reassure her to know that everything is in order. By the way, Annie, your mother asked me to call Eric, which I did. She actually tried to call both of you, but just couldn't do it—she was afraid she'd break down. Eric asked about coming now, but I told him to wait. It's such a long trip for him, and I'd hate for him to come into town, go back home, and then have to return again shortly thereafter. He fully understands the situation, and he's grateful the two of you dropped everything to get here."

Annie nodded and said she'd call Eric that same night, just to let him know how things looked to her. The plan would be to then call him when their mom seemed to be reaching the end, giving him time to get here.

Turning to Jed, I said, "Annie and I should talk about what we'll do too—you know, how long to stay. I'll have to get back to work soon."

"We'll do that after Dr. Parke leaves, Jack," Annie replied briskly, her eyes narrow and firm. "We really shouldn't keep you any longer, Dr. Parke. Thank you again for coming over tonight, and thanks for being so honest with us. It was hard to hear but helpful." Annie gave the doctor another quick hug before he went back to tell Virginia goodbye.

After Dr. Parke left, I said, "Gee, he's some doctor."

"He's the absolute best, Jack."

"Annie, I think you should stay here to be with your mom as long as you need to and take care of as many details as possible. As much as they love you at work, you should have no problem getting more time off, especially given the circumstances. But I need to get back—I just can't expect the other residents to fill in for me in the clinic and also cover my responsibilities in the department for too long. It doesn't feel right to leave, but I don't think I have a choice. I feel like I'm juggling too many balls. That said, if anything changes, you just say the word, and I'll drop everything and be right back."

"I understand, Jack," she said, her voice cracking. She collapsed in my arms and then stood up straight and began re-arranging things in the kitchen cabinets. There was nothing I could say or do that would be of much comfort.

The next two days were quiet ones, our conversations with Annie's mom frequently lapsing into reminiscing about her family and friends. When her energy allowed, we'd sit on the screened porch for lunch or coffee. She often stared into the distance, as if sizing up the backyard trees still shedding their dried, brown leaves. The birdhouses sat empty, with nesting over until the upcoming spring season.

The second night, as Annie and I prepared for bed, I told her I didn't think there was much more I could do for the moment, so had decided to head back to Chapel Hill the following day.

"Of course, Jack."

"You know I'll just be a phone call or text away."

Annie looked away. "I know."

Saying goodbye to Annie had been hard for me since the first day we met, but this time, it was particularly difficult. In addition, I could barely keep my composure when I went in to say goodbye to her mom. She was the mom I hadn't had in a long time, and now we were losing her.

"Virginia, it's time for me to leave. Annie will be here with you for as long as you need her, and I'll be back soon. You take care of yourself or, better yet, let everyone else take care of you." I gave her hand a squeeze and her cheek a kiss, not knowing when, if ever, I would see her alive again.

Chapter Forty-Two

The rain beat against my front windshield like pebbles against a tarp, the rhythmic motion of the wipers and the growing darkness lulling me into a daze, which I fought off with my thermos of coffee. The ride home was lonely, and my mind raced through thoughts of loss: my parents, Sydney's trust in me, and soon, Annie's mom. With Annie, I'd found love and the family I longed for, and now, we were losing the family matriarch. The only things that remained constant were Annie's love and my career, and I resolved to never lose either of them.

The blinking blue lights were visible before I heard the siren. My car must have been racing as fast as my thoughts. I pulled over. The patrol car stopped behind me.

"Good evening, sir. License and registration, please."

"Hello, officer. What seems to be the problem?"

"You were driving a little fast. I'm going to need that driver's license and registration," he stated again.

Handing over the documents, I said, "I'm really sorry, officer. Just had my mind on other things. I won't let it happen again. Promise."

"Driving distracted is how accidents happen, sir. I see it all the time with drivers, usually when they're on their phones. I'm going to have to cite you for speeding, but I'll put you at ten miles over, instead of the actual eighteen. That'll give you a break on the cost."

"Yes, sir. I appreciate it. I won't let it happen again."

"See that you don't. You have yourself a good rest of the night." He entered the citation into his iPad, walked to his patrol car, and returned with a copy for my records.

I was mad at myself for getting a ticket, but soon, the monotony of the drive calmed me. The rain was relentless. Suddenly, I saw headlights ahead, but something was wrong. They were on my side of the road but eerily illuminating the opposite lane. As I slowed and then came to a stop, I saw two cars—one resting on its hood and the other parked behind it, its engine still running. Someone in the second car, screaming into her cell, was frantically pointing toward a dark shape off the side of the road. A person.

I got out and ran up to her car. The woman yelled, "I've called 911. They said there's a patrolman nearby. The car flipped as it rounded this curve . . . oh my gosh, it was awful!"

The man on the ground must have been thrown when the car flipped. He was still conscious but seriously injured. I noticed a crush injury to his chest, the bloodstain on his shirt and jacket growing. A screaming siren announced the approaching patrol car.

"Sir, my name's Jack. I'm a doctor," I said as calmly as possible. "I'll help you."

Feebly, he answered, "It hurts to breathe, and I'm . . . I'm really lightheaded."

"I'm going to help you," I repeated. "Tell me your name."

"Lehninger—Bill Lehninger," he whispered. "Please help me."

"Medic's on the way," the officer said as he approached. The voice sounded familiar. I looked up and realized it was the same officer who had ticketed me just minutes earlier.

"I'm a doctor," I explained. "I'm going to do what I can until medic arrives."

Mr. Lehninger's color was ghostly pale, and his chest labored for air. I leaned close to his face as he said, "Please . . . tell Marty . . . I'm so sorry."

"Marty? Who's Marty, Bill?"

His eyes rolled back as he drew his last breath. I dropped my chin to my chest, closed my eyes, and slowly shook my head.

Chapter Forty-Three

Chapel Hill

I sometimes lost patients. It came with the job. If a doctor can't handle that, he probably should try another profession. As a family medicine doctor, most of them were older and death was a merciful end to a painful existence. The unexpected death of younger people was different, especially children. While Bill Lehninger was middle-aged and not my patient, I was the physician in attendance when he died. He was my responsibility, and the fact I could do nothing to save him ate at me. I slept fitfully that first night back home but got up early the next morning, had a quick breakfast, and headed for my continuity clinic.

"Good morning, Mr. Baker. Great to see you. What brings you in today?"

"Just not feeling good, Doc. A little more winded than usual and an occasional headache. Plumbing's working good, though," he said, smiling. "In fact, too good during the night," he added and then slapped his thigh.

Seeing my continuity patients always lifted my spirits. We had a relationship that would be unavoidably severed when I moved on to private practice, and they were left to another resident's care. That was the system, however, and the patients, mostly elderly and uninsured or on basic Medicare, had adapted. Or maybe just resigned to it.

"You managing your diabetes and high blood pressure properly, Mr. Baker?"

"Oh yeah, Doc. Never miss a pill—well, almost never." He winked.

After examining him and finding only a little more swelling of his ankles, I realized he just needed a little fine-tuning of his meds. That and watching his diet—especially the salt—should bring him back into control. But, just to be safe, I ordered a few labs and changed his diuretic dose. I stifled a yawn as I finished my assessment.

"Doc, are you okay?"

"Sure. Why do you ask?"

"You look a little tired and don't seem as upbeat as you normally are."

"Lots going on, Mr. Baker, but I'm fine. Thanks for asking. Remember though, I'm the one taking care of you, so you don't have to be concerned about me."

"Just checking, Doc. You can't help me if you're not taking care of yourself and on top of your game, you know." He grinned.

The wisdom of patients.

I slogged through the next few days at work, practicing adequate medicine but not with my *A* game. I hoped no one else noticed like Mr. Baker had. It was good to see Friday evening come, even though I had to carry the pager for backup hospital call for the weekend. I called Annie nightly, but that Friday night, we talked for a long time.

"How's your mom?"

"Nothing much has changed. She sleeps a lot and doesn't eat much. Fortunately, she's still drinking, so she's not getting dehydrated. When she's awake, which seems to be less and less each day, we've had some nice talks—you know, about old times. Of course, we also got through all of the planning that needed to be done."

"I hate I'm not there with you, Annie."

"When do you think you can get away for a few days?" she asked.

"Since I'm on call this weekend, it won't be until next weekend. I can get up really early on Saturday and get to Wilmington by breakfast."

"Another week," Annie said, with what sounded like a sigh.

"Best I can do. Make sure you take care of yourself too. Get your rest, eat properly, and get outside some. I don't want you getting one of those headaches. And what about Eric? Should he be called in now? I hate you're handling this all alone."

"Too soon for Eric to fly in. But don't worry. I'm fine, sweetie. Mr. and Mrs. Barnes come over occasionally and give me a break so I can get away for a while. Don't worry about me. There's enough going on with Mother for both of us to worry about. I actually have had a few minor headaches, but I'm sure they were just from stress."

"Maybe you're right, but when you get back—"

"I know, I know. You want me to see my doctor. I will, but I'm sure I'll be fine."

Chapter Forty-Four

February 2018
Wilmington

The weekend call was relatively quiet. I got some rest and stopped by Pete's to grab Molly for a few runs. As I was catching up on my medical journal reading, the phone rang.

"Hey, bro. Got your note about Molly. How was the run today?

"She was great, and I enjoyed the company!"

"Did she run you to death? You sound really tired."

"Is it *Dr.* Pete, or are you now my mom?"

He laughed. "No way, but my ears work, and I can hear fatigue in your voice. Seriously, is it Annie's mom?"

"Yeah, I guess so. She's not doing well, and Annie's struggling."

"Don't you think you should be there, Jack? I mean, with her mom's health and all. I know your work's important to you, but what's more important than family?"

His oversight annoyed me. "Going back the end of the week, Pete."

"Good decision. Annie needs you. When you go back, give her our love, please."

Monday morning, I was back in clinic but more rested than the prior week. While I was in with my second patient of the morning, my nurse knocked on the exam room door. I knew something had to be wrong, as the staff had strict orders not to interrupt me when I was with a patient unless there was a real emergency.

"Sorry, Dr. Wilson, but there's a Dr. Parke from out-of-town on the phone. He said it's urgent."

I excused myself to take the call. My pulse quickened, and I suddenly felt like I had a golf ball in my throat.

"Jack, this is Jed Parke. Sorry to bother you, but it's Virginia. She took a turn for the worse early this morning, and I think you need to get here as quickly as possible. I've called Eric and he's on his way. I'm with Annie right now. She's so distraught she asked me to make the calls."

"I understand, Jed. Please tell Annie I'm on my way, and thank you for being there with her."

"Well, Annie needs someone with her right now. Virginia's in a coma."

After finishing my patient's visit, I stopped at the front desk to explain the emergency and to ask them to clear my schedule for the rest of the week. After rushing home to quickly pack some things, I grabbed my thermos and left for the coast. I'd been on Interstate 40 only about an hour when my cell rang. Annie.

Between sobs, Annie managed to say, "She's gone, Jack. Mother just passed away."

My heart sank, and that lump reappeared in my throat as I massaged the muscles in my neck. "I'm so sorry, Annie. I'm on my way. Are you okay? Are you there alone?"

"No, Dr. Parke is still here, and Dorothy came in on her day off when she heard what was going on."

"I'll be there as fast as I can." The car accelerated.

The rest of the drive was a blur, with the trees bordering the interstate posing as tall, shadowy statues shaded by a green canopy. Before I knew it, I was instinctively turning into the driveway. As I got out of the car, I set my jaw and took a deep breath.

Dorothy, eyes red and puffy, met me at the door and directed me to the living room where Annie sat with shoulders hunched. Dr. Parke was at her side, his hand gently clasping Annie's. Her face was paler than usual and void of emotion until her eyes met mine. Rushing from her chair, she greeted me as the crying convulsions began.

"Oh, Jack. Mother's . . . she's gone. I just can't believe it."

All I could do was hold her as she melted in my arms. When I sensed her knees buckling, I got her to the couch.

"I'm here now, babe," I said softly. I looked over at Dr. Parke, nodded once and whispered, "Thank you for calling me when you did."

"It's good you're here, Jack. I'll leave for now, but I'll be at work the rest of the day. If you need me, I'm just a phone call away."

"I'll walk you to the door, Jed." Before he left, I asked him to bring me up to speed.

"She just dwindled. She got weaker and weaker, shorter of breath, and required more and more morphine to control her pain. The hospice team was able to keep her comfortable until she finally slipped away. Given the circumstances, it couldn't have been more peaceful, but I'm so sorry to lose her. Our loss is Heaven's gain, for sure."

His last comment gave me pause, coming from a doctor—a scientist who deals in facts and evidence. *And why is he talking about Heaven at a time like this? How could anyone invoke the notion of a God when something like this happens?* My faith wasn't as strong as Annie's, but this ordeal knocked it down a notch or two.

"Oh, Jack. Just so you'll know, Annie asked me to call the funeral home. Someone should be here soon."

"I know how much Virginia thought of you, Jed, and all of us appreciate your being there for her every step of the way. Thank you again." Jed nodded and turned to walk out to his car.

Annie had disappeared from her mom's side.

"She's in Miss Virginia's bedroom," Dorothy said, shaking her head slowly.

Annie was in her mother's closet, straightening clothes and grabbing one dress after another, holding them up to inspect and then returning them to the closet rod. Her movements were short and quick as she went from one dress to the next.

"This closet's a mess. I must straighten it. I need to pick out a dress for Mother . . ."

I gently turned her to me, and we hugged. "Annie, slow down. We'll take care of all this soon enough."

She hugged me tighter, gently crying into my chest. She gathered herself and asked, "Would you like to see Mother?"

"Yes. I'd like to tell her goodbye."

Dorothy was keeping vigil at Virginia's bedside, seemingly protecting her like a mama bear watches over her cub. As we walked in, she slipped away to leave us alone at the foot of the bed.

"I'll be in the kitchen, Dr. Jack. Gonna make you children some coffee."

Virginia looked as though she was just napping. Though her color was ghost white and her face thinned by the cruelty of her disease, she seemed at peace. I walked to the bedside and gently placed a hand on her lifeless forearm and told her goodbye. The tears came unexpectedly. After a few minutes, Annie and I walked to the kitchen.

"Annie, you sit down, and I'll be right back. I'm just going to get my things from the car."

"I'll sit a spell with you, Miss Annie," Dorothy said. "I don't want you here all alone."

I quickly grabbed my bag and the thermos of coffee. Running on adrenaline, I'd ignored it on the way to the coast. When I returned, Dorothy took the thermos from me. She looked at the jar—a green, metal relic given to me when I was in college. It was my constant companion when I traveled.

"That is some kinda antique, Dr. Jack," Dorothy said, grinning and shaking her head.

"It still works, Dorothy. They don't make them like that anymore. It's actually an original Thermos brand. I don't go anywhere without it."

Dorothy's quip was just what Annie needed, as she was now nodding and her face showed a hint of a smile. That thermos had been the subject of many a joke, first with Pete and later with Annie. Now, Dorothy was joining in.

"Well, I'll rinse it out. I've got fresh coffee for you and Miss Annie," she said, as she placed ceramic mugs on the kitchen table. Annie didn't touch hers, but I gratefully gulped mine down as quickly as I could without burning my mouth.

"Annie, I never expected things to happen so quickly."

"If you had, Jack, would you have been . . . oh, never mind. We all know this kind of thing is unpredictable; we live with it every day in our work lives. It's just so hard when it's family."

She went silent, and there were no more tears to shed.

"Impossibly hard," I agreed. "I'm grateful that both Dr. Parke and Dorothy were here with you."

Annie just nodded and then closed her eyes, leaving us to sit in deafening silence. Shortly thereafter, the quiet of the room was interrupted by a discreet knock at the front door. The people from the funeral home. As Dorothy went to let them in, we slowly got up to meet them. Annie said, "Oh, God! Please help me through this."

In the caring and professional way funeral home personnel have mastered better than most, they quietly transferred the body to their gurney and gently wheeled it toward the front door, stopping to let us say a final goodbye. It was the last time Virginia's presence would grace that home.

Chapter Forty-Five

Annie did not make it to church weekly—mostly because she had to work every other weekend. But she faithfully attended a Bible study with her friend, Joni. In fact, church, or other topics pertinent to religion, were deftly side-stepped when Annie tried to bring them up. Thus, I had no way to know Annie was a person of such deep faith. While I was mad that we'd lost Virginia, Annie said things happen for reasons God doesn't make known to us. *Some God.*

Not to suggest that all of this was easy for her. No, it was profoundly difficult. Once she got over the initial shock of her mom's death, however, Annie went into all-business mode, seeing to it that arrangements were carried out to her mom's specifications, meeting Eric and his kids at the airport, and receiving old friends from the neighborhood. The local minister made the requisite visit to extend his personal sympathy, pray for us, and make sure we were all on the same page regarding Virginia's service. Annie weathered the hectic pace of all this with a resolute determination.

We were sitting on her mom's screened porch, alone and sharing afternoon coffee—a welcome lull in all the activity that had ensued following her mom's death. The air was cool but refreshing.

"Annie, I know you're hurting, but I'm so proud of how you're handling all of this," I said.

"I'm leaning on my faith. I know God's got this."

"Your faith?" I cocked my head and narrowed my eyes.

"Yes. It's not something we've discussed as much as a married couple should, but going through grief requires a strength only God can provide. I feel his presence with me, Jack. I really do. You know, faith was so important in Mother's life as well. That's why she was at such peace with her decision to stop all therapy and put every ounce of her trust in God. She never flaunted her religion, but she lived it, and she read her Bible every day. I suppose that's how she got through what happened to her marriage and then the trials and stress of raising two children on her own. I just think it's terrible that it took her death for me to really see how important my faith is. But I know God's okay with it. He's always there, patiently waiting."

I squirmed. I knew what little faith I had was no match for hers. I hadn't attended church often or thought much about religion since I'd lived with my grandparents. To me, faith was an esoteric concept too difficult to explain. I just assumed it was something people fell back on during a crisis. No way could some supernatural being in the sky, looking down on us and pulling strings, square with my scientific training. I'd not shared such skepticism with Annie.

At the visitation and again during the memorial service for Virginia, many who spoke to Annie were her former church members. I'd never heard the words "faith," "trust," and "God bless you" used so often. When so many people spoke to us in glowing terms about Annie's mom, the thought crossed my mind that too often, we neglect to tell people how much they mean to us when they're still with us. We wait until they're gone, and it's too late.

We were pleasantly surprised to see Pete and Mary in the sanctuary as we walked out of the church.

"You came!" Annie said, her voice choking as she reached out to give them each a hug.

"It's so good of you two to make it down for the service," I said.

"We really wanted to be here," Pete said. "As I've said before, Ms. Monroe really struck me like a princess of a woman, and she was so kind to both Mary and me. Of course, we wanted to be here for both of you too."

"Hey, the family is gathering at the Monroe house. Please, join us," I said. "We'd love having you there."

"Wouldn't be anywhere else, Jack. We'll stay as long as we can. Thanks."

Once back at the house, all of us had time to reflect on Virginia's life. It seemed to lift Annie's and Eric's spirits to talk about her. In addition to Pete and Mary, Tom and Ethel Barnes were also there. Once Pete and Mary left to return to Chapel Hill, Annie and Eric talked briefly about things to come—the reading of the will, the decision to keep or sell the house, and a few other relevant issues. They finally decided to table those discussions until the dust had settled and their emotions weren't so raw.

The following morning was ushered in by more of the same dreary, dark weather we had soldiered through all week. After getting Eric and the kids back to the airport, Annie and I returned to pack our things and head home. Tom and Ethel had volunteered to keep a close eye on the house while it lay empty. As Annie and I neared the front door with the last of our luggage, she turned to glance at the house one last time, dropped her head, and wiped a tear from her eye.

Then she stopped, looked up at me, and said, "Let's go home, Jack."

Chapter Forty-Six

March 2018
Chapel Hill

Annie and I went home and threw ourselves back into our work. When off, I liked to go for runs or catch up on work, but Annie preferred to either scurry around, cleaning and straightening up, or retire to a quiet corner to write. She was also working more shifts at the hospital. She never shared her poetry with me, claiming it was amateurish, and she'd just be too embarrassed. We realized our loss was ours and no one else's. It was hard to accept, but the world, including our lives, didn't stop when a loved one died. If we stayed busy, maybe the grief would just ease on its own. I was plenty busy wrapping up my senior resident duties, and that filled the void created by our lack of communication.

Silence was the uninvited guest in our apartment.

One night, several weeks after her mom's death, I decided we needed to talk. I'd come in from a run and showered. Annie was sitting and writing. I asked her to close her tablet and then took her in my arms.

"Death is a savage opponent, and people respond to the painful wound of grief in various ways, not all of which are healthy, Annie."

"Is that what you think we're doing, Jack? Handling Mother's death in an unhealthy way? Are you analyzing us now . . . or maybe just me?"

I held her closer. "Look, I know we're both doing the best we can, and obviously, no one gets to practice managing grief."

I felt her body relax a little.

"I do think we need to talk more and do things together, Jack. I've just been so busy volunteering for extra shifts so we can put away money for a house."

Annie knew she had her inheritance coming once her mom's estate was settled. I suspected the increased workload was just her way of coping with her mother's loss. Somehow, being with cancer patients was therapeutic for her. Annie's co-workers told me her patients raved about how empathetic she seemed after her mom's death—willing to stop what she was doing to take the time to listen to and talk with them. Perhaps selfishly, I thought she spent so much time at work as a way of avoiding being at home. Was she reluctant to share her feelings with me?

"We just aren't seeing enough of each other lately, sweetie."

"But we both know what's going on here, Annie. Staying busy occupies our time and thoughts, and keeps us from talking—"

"I just lost my mother, Jack, and I'm still trying to cope with it in the best way I can. Stop analyzing everything."

"I'm not, babe, and I get it. I really do. I didn't know your mother for very long, but she was like my second mom." We sat on the couch. I took her hand, and we were silent for a moment.

Annie sighed. "We just need time. Everything is still fresh and emotions are so raw. With time, hopefully, some degree of closure will come for both of us."

"Can we at least agree to talk about it with one another?"

"Of course," she said, briskly. Then, apparently sensing the abruptness of her response, she immediately apologized. "I'm sorry, Jack. It's not just losing Mother. I'm also having some trouble sleeping and having more of those headaches I've had before. So much stress, you know?"

"Why didn't you say something? If you're getting headaches that keep you awake, you need to get that checked. I've told you that before."

"When I get time, Jack. I'm not too worried. I think I'm just internalizing my emotions and it's causing the headaches."

Somatization. A psychological problem like stress or anxiety manifests as a physical ailment. But I'd done it again—diagnosing someone who was not only *not* my patient, but someone with whom I was way too close to emotionally to be objective. I decided to change the subject.

"Maybe I can talk to Pete about that week at the beach we'd considered earlier. I saw him the other day, and he asked how you and Eric are doing. I think he's waiting on us to decide about a beach trip."

She agreed that some time away from home to relax and be with friends might be good, but asked if we could talk about it later. "Right now, I don't feel great, and I'm going to bed."

Chapter Forty-Seven

April 2018
Smithfield, North Carolina

Virginia's sudden death and the time and attention it demanded had made it easy for me to put off for months something I should have done much earlier. Recalling the name tag on the officer at the scene, I called the station and asked for Patrolman Taylor.

"Officer Taylor, you probably don't remember me, but you ticketed me for speeding late last year."

"You're right—I don't remember you. I ticket a lot of people. What can I do for you?"

"It was the night of the single-car accident when we both stopped to help a man named Bill Lehninger. I was the physician. Remember?"

"Oh. Yes, of course. Now, I remember. Is that what you're calling about?"

"Yes. You see, Mr. Lehninger's dying words were 'Tell Marty I'm sorry.' I feel obligated to honor his request. Do you happen to know if Marty's a relative?"

"Matter of fact, he's the son. He came to the morgue later that night to identify the body. Pretty upset, but I guess that was to be expected. I've seen it a million times—a tragedy occurs and the loved ones are left to pick up the pieces and move on with their lives. But what exactly are you planning on doing, if I might ask?"

"I'd like to find his address or phone number and contact him. He needs to know what his dad said."

"Well, I'm not authorized to give you his contact information but, just between us, he's local. Now, you didn't hear it from me, understood?"

"Understood . . . and thanks."

I got lucky and found Marty's contact information through social media. I reached him and briefly explained the purpose of the call. He agreed to a visit. On an afternoon off, I drove to his house, a rather plain, old ranch in a very dated community on the outskirts of Smithfield—a town off I-40 just northeast of where it crossed I-95. The landscaping was simple but not well-maintained, and the house begged for a paint job. I knocked on the door, and a young man opened it.

"Hi, I'm Jack Wilson. You must be Marty."

He smiled and said, "No. I'm Cary. I live here too."

"I was at the scene of Bill Lehninger's accident. May I speak to Marty, please?"

"Come on in. Marty said you'd be by sometime today. He's out back. Please, have a seat and I'll get him."

In just a few minutes, another young man came in. He was of medium build and had short, neatly combed hair. He wore jeans and a dirty work shirt, with sweat stains under both arms. The resemblance to his dad was uncanny.

"Hi, Jack. I'm Marty. Sorry for my appearance. Just doing a little work in the yard."

"No problem. I just appreciate your agreeing to see me. I'm really sorry for your loss."

"Thank you. The officer who'd been at the scene and called me about the accident assured me that nothing could have been done for my dad. Said the fella who stopped was a physician, so I figured what he was telling me was true. Made me feel a little better, anyway."

"Well, Marty, I'm here because your dad's last words were to ask me to tell you he was sorry." He looked away as tears welled in his eyes. "It's none of my business what that was all about, but I felt obligated to let you know."

We took a seat as Marty recounted their last moments together. They'd had a big argument that night. Being very old-school, his dad had a hard time accepting Marty's lifestyle choice. A confrontation erupted when he criticized Marty for being gay and accused him of shaming the family. Marty then accused him of trying to deny his identity or possibly disown his son. Things got pretty heated, and his dad went out for some air. Marty figured he'd cool off, come back in, and they'd work things out, just like they'd always done over less complicated issues.

"I never imagined I wouldn't see him again. I should have gone after him. You have no idea how tough it is to live with the memory of my last minutes with him."

I swallowed hard and said, "I'm sure it must be terribly difficult, Marty. I'm so sorry."

"You know, you didn't have to come here. I really appreciate that you did."

"No. I did need to come, and I feel better now that your dad's last request has been honored."

I drove away, grateful I'd made the effort to find Marty. But, once again, the specter of my parents' loss had risen and slapped those ugly memories against my psyche. Pete was right that I couldn't live in the past, but how could I escape it when it continued to re-visit me?

Chapter Forty-Eight

July 2018
Ocean Isle Beach

T he busyness of our lives did nothing to bring closure but did seem to make time pass quickly. The end of June was suddenly near, and my residency was ending. I was excited about an increase in earnings once I was in practice, as both Annie and I thought that would be necessary before we could even consider starting a family. The brief time with the Monroe family had reminded me of all the things I missed out on as a child and made me want a family more than ever. My mood was upbeat, something Pete apparently noticed when we met for coffee at the Grind. We sat at an outdoor umbrella table, shaded from the hot sun. The hustle and bustle of nearby Franklin Street provided uninvited background music.

"Hey, bro! You sure are looking better than the last time we talked. Hope Annie's doing better too."

Just seeing Pete and hearing his voice lifted my spirits. "Well, it's tougher for her. She was very close to her mom. But I'm glad to report she does seem happier lately."

"Jack, I don't want to seem insensitive to your situation, but we'd talked about a beach getaway. Any chance y'all are still interested?"

"Truth be told, I was hoping you'd make the offer. Annie and I actually talked about it not too long ago. We don't think anything could help us more right now than some time away with good friends, especially if it's at the beach."

"How 'bout the weekend after next? My parents are there now, and they've promised the cottage to friends of theirs for all of next month, so we need to grab that weekend, if possible. Mary, of course, is off until the school year starts, and all I'm doing this summer is some part-time work in the department and boning up on my art history before I start grad school. We're free almost anytime, so late summer's fine too. No worries if you can't make it work on such short notice."

I knew Annie could get coverage for her shifts at the hospital, as she'd worked so many extra hours that her co-workers were worried about her and wanted her to take some time off. It would also be my last free weekend before starting practice. I reassured him that I thought that weekend would work, but I'd have to check with Annie.

As we finished our coffee, I felt compelled to mention something to Pete I should have told him a long time ago. "Buddy, I want you to know how much our friendship means to me. You've always been there for me—even more so this past year. You're a great friend, the one person I know I can always count on."

It wasn't like Pete to get choked up, but his voice caught as he answered, "Thanks, Jack. That means a lot to me, and I know you'd go to the mattresses for me, too, bro."

"Okay, enough of this sentimental dribble. You check with Mary, and I'll run it by Annie. Hopefully, we'll be headed to the beach before we know it!"

Arriving at the coast, Annie and I left the mainland to cross over the huge bridge that spanned the Intracoastal Waterway, an aquatic snake that bears the geographical responsibility for the Carolinas' barrier islands and whose slow currents slither imperceptibly along the Eastern Seaboard. As we got closer to the ocean, the air became heavy with the familiar, rich scents of brine and seaweed.

"We finally made it work," Pete said as we got out of our car at the Crab Shack to meet him and Mary. "We dropped off our bags at the cottage and walked down here. I'm starving!"

The Shack was just that—an inauspicious former gas station converted to a diner, painted in blazes of coral, sea green, and ocean blue. It was Pete's and my favorite hangout for a calabash-style affair and was a must as our first stop on this trip. There was little room for indoor seating, but Pete and I always opted for patio seating, if a patch of beaten-down grass populated with weather-damaged picnic tables qualified as a patio.

We polished off a bucket of crab legs, hush puppies, fries, and coleslaw, all washed down with southern sweet tea. Weighted down and sluggish from lunch, we were content to sit back and take in the wide expanse of sand and water and enjoy the ocean's clarion call—the rhythmic sounds of waves cresting and tumbling onto the beach.

"Well, fellas, I've got to hand it to you. Lunch did not disappoint," Annie said. "I don't know about everyone else, but I'm stuffed. I could use a walk."

"The cottage isn't that much farther down the beach road. Why don't we walk, and then Jack and I will come back to pick up the car," Pete suggested.

As we walked down the beach, seagulls squawked their welcome, and we soaked in the luxuriant blue sky seared by an unforgiving summer sun. Suddenly, I noticed Annie lagging a little behind, squinting as she shaded her eyes with the back of her hand.

"Annie, is everything okay?"

"Yeah, Jack. I think I ate too much, and the heat's getting to me. I feel a little dizzy."

"We can stop and get you in the shade while we get the car," Pete offered.

"Don't be silly. I'll be fine," she said as we trudged on.

"Annie, isn't this the cutest beach house?" Mary said as we walked toward the steps to the cottage deck.

"Just as I pictured it! Now, I know why Jack's raved about it."

"I'll give you girls the nickel tour of the cottage before Jack and I go back for the car," Pete said.

As we left the girls and walked back to the diner, Pete said, "Hey bro, is everything okay with Annie?"

"I'm sure she's fine. Just needs to get used to this heat and humidity."

"Okay. You're the doctor. Anyway, I'm glad we're finally all here. The weekend should be a blast!"

"Agreed. Be sure your folks know how much we appreciate their generosity."

We drove back to the house and found Mary sitting alone on the deck.

"Where's Annie?" Pete said.

"She was still a little dizzy after you went back for the car, and then she complained of a headache. Said it was nothing—probably just caused by the glare of the sun. She forgot to grab her sunglasses from your car, Jack. Annie asked me to tell you guys she was going to rest for a while and then she'd re-join us."

Trying not to look concerned, I went in to check on Annie. She was asleep, so I didn't disturb her. About an hour later, she joined us on the deck.

"Babe, are you okay?"

"Yep. Good as new, sweetie. Thanks. But I'm going to stay on the deck the rest of the afternoon. I don't think I need any more sun today."

———

Pete planned to grill out for dinner that night, and on the way, he and Mary had stopped on the mainland to pick up groceries. The grill's smoky aroma stimulated our appetites as he prepared steaks and baked potatoes. After a delicious dinner, we pushed back from the knotty pine table and headed out to the deck to watch the moonlight dance off the breaks in the waves.

"What a day!" Mary said. "I'm sorry that you weren't feeling well, Annie."

"Oh, I'm fine now. Yep, a great day, especially since neither one of us had to lift a finger to help with dinner. These guys are great—I think we should keep them!"

After a couple of hours of lively conversation and card games, Annie and I excused ourselves for the night. I wrapped my arms around Annie and asked if she was really okay.

"I'm fine. You're a dear, Jack, but you really don't have to keep asking."

Climbing into bed, Annie grabbed a *Southern Living* magazine from her tote bag and began to thumb through it, and I opened the latest Vince Flynn novel, anxious to see what international crisis Mitch Rapp was about to solve. The perfect beach novel. Only a chapter or two into the book, I glanced over at Annie as her head bobbed to her chest and the magazine fell to her lap. I quietly got up, put away her magazine, gently kissed her on the cheek, and turned out her light.

With the inexorable tug of sleep coming on, I yielded to my drowsiness, switched off the light, and closed my eyes. I was so happy to be at the beach with Annie and even happier that she finally seemed at peace with her mom's death.

Chapter Forty-Nine

We climbed into the car to go out for our last dinner together before heading home the next day. "My treat tonight, Pete. It's our way of thanking you for sharing the beach house with us."

"You don't have to twist my arm, but don't thank me, thank my parents. They were thrilled that we were able to make time to come down for the weekend. They don't get here that often anymore, and they love to see the cottage get used."

I made a "note to self" to drop them a thank-you card when we returned home. They were gracious people, and once again, I caught myself envious of Pete and his family.

We'd chosen a popular local spot, and tonight was no exception. The tables were covered with paper tablecloths, allowing easy disposal after a party finished a lobster dinner. A candle illuminated each table, but the overhead lights were dimmed, affording better outdoor visibility. We got lucky—our table was close enough to the windows for a good view of the ocean, glistening and quiet in the warm glow of a full moon.

"Okay, everybody. Order anything from the menu you want. The price doesn't matter. I want this to be one to remember."

Pete needed no encouragement; he ordered the surf and turf entrée, preceded by a crab dip appetizer we all shared.

"We need to think about the next time we can all get away," Pete said.

"Whoa, buddy. Slow down. You know I'm starting my new job. No idea when I'll have some time off."

"Well, just remember, Mary and I are always ready for some time away with you two."

"Jack, maybe we can all go to the mountains this fall, at least for a long weekend," Annie said.

"Let's make a point of getting something on the calendar," Mary said. "Sometime in October, maybe."

Back at the house, we returned to our favorite spot, the oceanside deck, and relaxed in the chairs. While Pete poured wine for himself and the girls, I ran in to grab a Coke Zero. As we talked, I noticed Pete biting at his nails again. When the conversation slowed, I sensed we were all growing tired—except for Pete, who was drumming his fingers on the deck rail as he paced.

"Hey, buddy. You alright?"

"I'm fine, thanks. Why do you ask?"

"You just seem nervous."

"Nope. It's all good," Pete said, now biting with renewed vigor.

When Annie and I excused ourselves for the night, Pete said they'd be up a bit longer, as he wanted to talk to Mary.

We'd spent our time on the beach playing cornhole, throwing frisbees, and joining in some group volleyball games, but mostly just sunbathing, reading, and going for swims in the ocean.

On one outing, we were at the putt-putt course by the roundabout. An easterly wind blew the scent of low tide our way, cooling us from the heat of the day. I looked up after a shot and saw Annie with her head cocked and smiling.

"What?" I asked.

"What do you mean, 'what,' sweetie?"

"What are you thinking, and why are you looking at me that way?"

"I'm just enjoying you looking so relaxed—no work, no tablet, no care in the world other than getting that stupid little ball in the hole." She pointed to my ball, a good three yards from the cup, and laughed.

It was a nice moment, and I'll always remember how carefree life seemed that night.

When we got back from playing putt-putt, Annie and I went to bed. As had been the case every night, after all the sun, fresh air, and other beach activities, we were both out before we knew what hit us.

The following morning at breakfast, Pete set his coffee cup down on the kitchen table and stood behind Mary. He put his hands on her shoulders and cleared his throat.

"I have an important announcement. I proposed to Mary last night . . . and she said yes!" Mary sat there beaming. "Just to confirm, you really did say yes, Mary, didn't you?"

Mary lifted her left hand to show us her diamond. "Of course, I said yes!"

Pete was kidding. I think.

"Mary, that's wonderful," Annie said, reaching over to hug her. "I'm thrilled for the two of you. Jack and I have thought from the first time we saw you together, you were right for each other."

"I can't wait to call my folks and give them the news. I think they figured, with my bad luck with girls, I wouldn't just be late for the party, but that I'd never show up, resigned to live my life as a lonesome bachelor with my art slides and books."

"Well, they're going to be thrilled when they meet their future daughter-in-law, buddy. Congratulations to both of you," I added, kissing Mary on the cheek and giving Pete a big hug.

After breakfast, we packed and prepared to leave. Pete walked out on the deck and stared at the ocean and then walked in to ask if we really had to leave.

"Yep. All good things must come to an end. But think of all the vacations we'll have together in our future. That makes it easier to leave, right?"

"Yes, you're right, bro, as usual."

"By the way, buddy, why didn't you tell me you were going to propose to Mary?"

"Wasn't sure she'd say yes, and I didn't want to risk being embarrassed."

I shook my head. "Oh, Pete." I didn't know what it would take to have him gain more self-confidence, but the engagement would have to help.

Annie and I left first, with Pete and Mary staying long enough to make sure everything was turned off and the house was secured and locked. As we headed over the bridge to the mainland, resisting the urge to do a U-turn and just stay on the coast, my thoughts turned to what was ahead for me: a new job in a great practice, doing what I'd set my sights on so many years ago, and a great marriage.

"Jack, you seem deep in thought. Is everything okay?" Annie said.

"Everything's more than okay, Annie. I was just thinking about my new job and how lucky I am to be sharing all of this with you. What could be better? I *am* one lucky guy!"

"I think we're both pretty lucky, sweetie."

Chapter Fifty

E ntering the clinic for my first day in private practice, an air of anticipation
hung over me like a kid walking into a candy store. Karen Hite, the office
manager, greeted me and said, "Dr. Payne would like to see you before you
get started. He's in his office."

"Jack. Welcome to the practice. Have a seat, please," he said, pointing to one
of the chairs facing his desk. "I'm sure you're anxious to get started, but allow me
to go over a few things."

"Sure, Dr. Payne." I gazed around at the art on the walls, with one wall covered with his diplomas. *Mine will be on the wall soon.*

"Please, call me Gus. After all, we are partners—not equals, mind you, but
partners."

Wow, that sounded odd. "I don't follow you."

"Look, Jack. I know you're fresh out of residency . . . and senior resident at
that. Captain of the ship, so to speak. Here, though, you're the new kid on the
block. You've got to start over. People don't know you, and frankly, they don't
care where you trained or how well you did. They just want a doctor who cares
about them. You've got to earn your patients' trust—show them you're a good
doctor. I've been at this for thirty-five years, so take my advice. In fact, I started
the practice. I've earned the trust and respect of my patients, and I expect you to
do the same."

"Of course, I have every intention—"

"Also, it's important to treat our staff with respect. Based on your recommendations, that shouldn't be a problem, but we work hard to recruit and train our employees, so I don't like to lose them."

"Of course, Gus. That makes perfect sense. I've always—"

"That's all for now, Jack. Got to get my day started. Good luck and, again, welcome."

As I walked out of the room shaking my head, I ran into Karen.

"Good talk?" she said.

"Actually, I'm not quite sure what it was. He caught me off-guard."

She laughed. "Oh, don't let Dr. Payne bother you. There's an edge to him at times, but you'll get used to it, just like everyone else has. He just wants you to be successful. We all do. After all, your success is our success."

As the new doctor, I knew work would start slowly for me. While I had to start from scratch to grow my patient volume, I was known locally from my training, and I quickly got referrals from associates. It didn't take long for me to get busy. Before I knew it, my days were nearly full with scheduled patients and work-ins. I loved every minute of it, and the patients seemed to like me, or if they didn't, at least they didn't complain. I was fulfilling my childhood dream—the culmination of all the effort I'd put into achieving my goal. Every night, I shared the events of the day with Annie, who humored me by patiently listening before she recounted her day for me.

As I drove home from work, I called Annie to suggest we celebrate my one-month anniversary in the new practice by going out for dinner and maybe taking in a movie.

"We should do that but for both of us. Not just you, Jack."

"What do you mean?"

"Well, not to rain on your parade, but I also have some exciting news."

"You're pregnant? We've taken the proper precautions—"

"No, silly boy. I'm not pregnant."

"What is it, then?"

"I've been asked to work in quality control at the hospital!"

"That's great, but you love what you do so much. Are you willing to give it up?"

"Nope, don't have to. I'll still work on the floor three days a week and spend two days each week in the new position. It's something I'm really interested in, and of course, it's a huge initiative in hospitals these days. It also means more money, sweetie. We can use that to save toward the down payment on the house out there just waiting to be found."

Her news vindicated how much the hospital administration thought of Annie. I knew she'd do a terrific job, so I was all for it.

"One more thing, though. I may have some evening meetings that will keep me at the hospital a little late. You'll be on your own for dinner those nights."

"Oh, cool! Kind of like being a bachelor again," I said, teasingly. "Actually, just down the street from my office, there's a diner that serves southern comfort food. Some of the staff go there for lunch and say it's pretty good. I could always eat there, or I could actually learn to cook real meals," I replied, laughing. "But seriously, Annie. Don't let your work overwhelm you."

"Yeah, you're one to talk," she said.

She had a good point., and I knew I'd just get busier and busier. In a way, it was a good problem to have, but doctors complain when we're too busy, and we complain even more when it's too slow. In retrospect, it was the busyness of my practice that almost doomed me.

Chapter Fifty-One

Chapel Hill

We were at a nearby Chinese restaurant—a small place whose owners were a gracious husband and wife team. I could always count on top-notch food and excellent service. A buddha statue, mounted over a small fountain that emptied its water into a lily-filled, ceramic basin, watched over us as we ate. Each table was decorated with a lighted candle and a single orchid. The lighting was subdued, as were the patrons' conversations. I assumed they were as busy as we were eating generous portions of our entrees. Is it just me, or does everyone think Chinese rice comes in a bottomless container?

After dinner, as we waited on coffee and dessert, Annie excused herself to go to the ladies' room. I was so busy at work, I'd ignored my phone all day. I noticed a missed call, but no message, from Pete.

"Hey, Petey. I see you called. What's up?"

"Just wanted to let you know Mary and I have our wedding date set for next spring. I'll be near the end of my first year of grad school, and hopefully, I'll have a better idea of what I'm going to do with my life. Anyway, I'd like you to be my best man. It would mean a lot to me."

"Pete, I'd be honored and thrilled to return the favor. Man, I'm so happy for the two of you, and I can't wait to tell Annie about the save-the-date."

"You're the best, Jack. Thanks, bro."

When Annie returned, I told her the good news.

"Oh, yes! Mary called me today and told me the date was set—I forgot to tell you. She didn't mention you being in the wedding, but I assumed you would be.

I'm sure she wanted Pete to talk to you about that. She did ask me to help her with all of the wedding plans. I'm so excited. She's like the sister I never had; it should be a lot of fun. But sweetie, suddenly you don't look so happy."

I shook my head. "It's nothing." *How could she forget to tell me something so important about our friends? Maybe we are too busy.* "Actually, I'm surprised you didn't tell me."

"You know we don't really spend much time together, and when we do, we're usually each doing our own thing or talking about work."

"Well, we need to make more time for each other and talk more. We're just too busy for our own good."

"Isn't that what I always say, Jack?" She glared at me, her lips pressed tightly. "Just get the bill, please. I don't feel like dessert now."

I guessed the movie was out too.

My schedule was getting busier. To keep my patients from waiting too long to see me, I put off charting notes and returning calls until lunch or after hours—either before leaving the office or after I got home at night.

"Dr. Wilson, we're getting very positive feedback from our patients regarding your care," Karen said.

"Well, that's good to know, but you wouldn't think that to be the case from the way Dr. Payne has been acting. I've seen him talking to my nurse several times, and sometimes, he sticks his head in my office, looks at me, and leaves without saying a word. I think he's checking on me."

"Remember . . . sometimes, you just have to ignore him. He means well but often doesn't come off that way. Don't let him get under your skin. One of my jobs is to buffer the rub between Dr. Payne and the other partners. Anyway, as I was saying, we're getting a lot of calls from people who want to come into the practice, most of them requesting you."

I tried not to show how flattered I was, but I couldn't hide my smile. "That's great, Karen. But if you get any negative feedback, I want to know about that as well."

"Of course. Since patient satisfaction is one of the compensation metrics, we must be as transparent with the doctors as possible."

I thought back to my residency and how much I hated those satisfaction surveys. All it took was one disgruntled patient to ruin an otherwise stellar review.

Now, the reports were of greater importance, as doing well and meeting bench-marks meant more take-home pay. With our desire to buy a house and start a family, every little bit helped. Maybe if I made more money, Annie would work fewer hours.

When I got home from work, I found Annie in the kitchen, preparing a salad to go with the grilled chicken sitting on the island. My mouth watered. "Hi, babe. Killed my review today! My practice is growing and patients seem to appreciate my care."

"Well, Jack, no one would be surprised by that, least of all me." She stood at the small, wooden island and chopped red peppers and carrots. "I know what kind of medicine you practice and how you treat your patients. I've heard enough about it, especially from Mrs. Mason." She smiled but then paused. "Of course, I've lived with the time and energy you devote to your work when you're at home too." She was no longer smiling. "You could get your nose out of your tablet for a change and help me with the cleaning and cooking, you know."

Ignoring her last sentence, I asked, "How is Mrs. Mason, by the way?"

Annie looked away and shook her head and then looked back at me. "She hasn't been in the hospital for a few months, which I take as a positive sign. Of course, she's no longer getting treatments, and I guess her counts are stable enough that she hasn't required any transfusions. I kind of miss her, actually, but I'm happy she's been able to stay at home. Hey, not to change the subject, but remember when we talked to Pete and Mary about a long weekend in the mountains?"

"I do remember, but I just don't see it happening anytime soon. I'm working five days a week, or seven when I'm on call. My contract doesn't allow for a scheduled day off in the first four months of practice. And not only am I busy, but you've also got your hands full between your clinical shifts and the quality control work."

"You're doing it again, Jack. So busy you don't have time for me—for us. And, by the way, you don't have to use *my* work as an excuse. Yours is enough."

"Fair point. But I've been thinking. We'll both have some time at Christmas or the week after. How would you like to spend it in Asheville? You remember how much fun we had there, right?"

"Of course."

"We could even ask Pete and Mary to join us for part of the week, at least if it's after Christmas and Pete's back from time with his family."

"Now, you're talking, Jack. That would be great! Let's plan on it." She was beaming.

I took her enthusiasm to mean a getaway like that would mean a lot to her. She deserved it. I'd have to make it work, even if it meant being out of the office at such a busy time of year. Our marriage deserved it too.

Chapter Fifty-Two

Annie

"Well, Miss Annie. You're a sight for sore eyes!"

Mrs. Mason always lit a spark in my day. "Hi, Mrs. Mason. I saw your name on the admission list and requested I be assigned to you. It's been a while. You're looking good."

"Annie, there are four stages in life: young, middle-aged, elderly, and 'you're looking good!' But I know what a sweetheart you are, and I bet you say that to all of your patients, especially a frail old woman like me."

"Don't be silly. You do look good. Matter of fact, so good I'm not certain why you're here. Are you having trouble?"

"Oh, I'm just tired, honey. My doctor says it's 'low blood,' which I think means my red cell count is down."

"I'm impressed! You're learning *doctor speak*. I'm going to have to watch what I say around you! By the way, how do you like your new doctor? I spoke to him last week when he was here checking on another patient. He seems very nice."

"'Wet behind the ears' is what I'd say. He's no Dr. Wilson, that's for sure. But I'll give him a chance. Don't really have much choice, now that Dr. Wilson has finished his training and is out there in the real world, taking care of people. I'm happy for him, but it pains me to know he's gone. I sure do miss him. 'Course, before he left the hospital, I asked him if he'd be back. He said he probably wouldn't, but if he ever got by, he'd check to see if I was in the hospital. Nice of him to say that, but I doubt he meant it, now that he's a big-shot doctor."

You miss him? I miss him, too, and we live together. "Now, you know you don't mean that, Mrs. Mason. I realize it's hard to lose your doctor, but you know as well as anyone that's how the system here works. Doctors come, they train, and then they move on to private practice or subspecialty training."

"I understand that, but I don't have to like it. I really do miss him. I'll never forget his kindness. But enough about all that. How're you doing?"

"Well, since I last saw you, I've taken on other duties at the hospital. I'm—"

"Don't tell me you're leaving me too," she interrupted, her eyes suddenly darts, aimed at mine.

"Oh, no. I'm just working in quality control part-time, but I'm still working on the oncology floor. I'm super busy, but I love it!"

She took a deep breath and smiled. "Now, don't you get to be such a big shot that they promote you right out of your nurse work, young lady. I wouldn't want to lose my favorite doctor *and* my favorite nurse."

"You don't have to worry about that. Taking care of patients like you is what I like best about my job. Now, let's get you comfortable in your bed. They're going to be here soon to type and cross you for a transfusion."

"Oh, I know the drill, sweetie. You can bet your bottom dollar on that. Never have been here that they didn't bleed me like a vampire sucks his victims dry. I don't like getting stuck, but at least I'm not getting those poisons running through me that used to make me so sick . . . by the way, Annie, if you happen to see Dr. Wilson around, please give him my best and tell him I miss him."

"I'll make a point of it, Mrs. Mason. I'm sure I'll run into him; you can be certain of it. Now, c'mon, let's get you into your bed."

Chapter Fifty-Three

Early September 2018

"I've got good news and bad news," I said as we sat down for a quick Saturday breakfast at the Grind, where the air was heavy with the scent of strong coffee. I'd wanted to see Pete and had just enough time to squeeze him in before leaving for weekend hospital rounds. Since Annie had a hospital meeting, it was the perfect opportunity to catch up.

"Uh-oh, Jack. That's never a good thing. What's up?"

"Well, Pete, I just don't see us making that mountain trip this fall. Things are getting crazy busy at work and, as you know, Annie's taken on more responsibilities at the hospital. I remember how excited we were at the beach when we started talking about a fall trip, so I'm really sorry."

"I understand. No worries, bro. We'll make it happen at some point, I'm sure. What's the good news?"

"Annie and I thought it would be nice to use our time off at Christmas to go with you and Mary to the Biltmore—that is if you're interested."

"I'd love to, but Mary and I already have plans to be with my family over Christmas—"

"Which is what I figured," I said. "I'm talking about a trip after Christmas. What do you think?"

"That's really nice of you to offer, bro. Of course, I'll have to check with Mary, but I think we can make it work. I hear it's beautiful there at Christmas."

"A Christmas tree in every room!" I said.

"Cool! Let me get back to you on that."

As our waitress walked up with coffee and juice, I asked Pete how school was going. Sometimes, I worried that he thought his work got lost in all that Mary, Annie, and I were doing, and I didn't want him to feel left out.

"I love the course work, and I'm instructing in some undergrad art classes, which brings in a little money for me as well. I think I like teaching, but the jury's still out, so to speak. With the wedding coming up, I'm saving every penny I can."

"Speaking of the wedding, Annie tells me Mary's over the moon with excitement about all the plans. Sounds like they've had a great time planning and shopping. I think it's really been good for Annie too. You know, with no sister, she considers Mary her surrogate. She never knew she'd have the chance to help plan someone else's wedding."

"That's good to hear. I gotta tell you, I'm still pinching myself over this whole wedding thing. Mary's so amazing! I never thought I'd find a girl like her, much less have her agree to marry me."

"Pete, as I've told you a thousand times, you need to give yourself more credit than that. You're getting exactly what you deserve."

"Thanks for that. By the way, how are Eric and Annie doing?"

"It's tough, of course, but they're managing."

"I can't imagine how tough it would be to lose one of my parents, even though we all know that it's inevitable—we just don't know when. You know that better than most."

"Knowing doesn't make it any easier, though. Even knowing months before she passed away that Virginia was going to die, it was still devastating—not just for her children but for me and all of her close friends too."

"She deserved a better fate, Jack. Such a nice lady."

"Agreed. You know, Pete, she said something odd in her final days."

"What was that?"

"She said she was ready. That she was at peace, and she looked forward to what was coming."

"That was her speaking her faith, Jack."

"But how? And why? After all the bad breaks she had in life—and to be suffering from cancer until she died—how could she be talking about *faith* stuff?"

"She was a Christian. It's hard to explain, but when you need it the most, that's often when your faith will be strongest." Pete smiled and gently nodded. "I'll admit I've gotten away from the church, but I still have my faith."

I shifted in my seat and picked up my coffee cup. "Okay, I'll have to take your word for it. For me, however, that might be too great a leap of faith—no pun intended."

"So, are you working all weekend, dude?"

"Hospital rounds, but it's pretty quiet right now. Hope it'll stay that way. After that, home for a run and then some office busywork. How about you?"

"A little studying and prepping for the next undergrad class I'm teaching. After that, Mary and I plan to go to an exhibit at the Fine Arts Center."

"Well, have fun, and give Mary my best—"

My pager sounded. The hospital. I needed to check on a patient whose condition was deteriorating. "Got to go, Pete," I hollered as I rushed out, forgetting he'd be stuck with the bill. I'd Venmo him later.

I drove to the hospital, excited about plans for a holiday getaway with our friends. It would be a busy time, but I told myself, again, that I'd make it work.

"Hey, Annie. I had breakfast with Pete this morning," I said as she came in from work. "He's gonna talk to Mary about spending some time in Asheville with us over the holidays."

"Okay, good," Annie said. She plopped into a chair, closed her eyes, and massaged her temples.

"Everything okay? You look beat. I'll make you some hot tea."

"That would be great, sweetie. Oh, just a busy day. You know how that goes."

"Yep. But you can relax now that you're here. Be thankful you don't have to bring your work home with you," I said.

"And you do, Jack?" She opened her eyes wide and glared at me.

"Meaning?"

"Do you *really* have work you must do every night, or is it just a way to avoid spending time with me? I'm not asking for much: sitting and holding hands, going to the movies, or a simple dinner out. Do you realize we don't even run together anymore?"

"You know how compulsive I am about work. I have to dot every *i* and cross every *t*, right?"

"Sure, Jack. But I wish you were as compulsive about our marriage. I mean, doesn't it deserve as much or even more attention than work? Do you think I like playing second fiddle to a work computer? Even when we go to bed at the same time, you bring that thing with you and pound away on the keyboard." She was now standing, hands on hips and shaking her head.

"Where's this coming from, Annie? Is something wrong?"

"Yes, something's wrong. Our marriage is wrong, or at least, it's suffering."

"But I thought you understood I would need time to ramp up my practice and get it running like a well-oiled machine. Once I'm better at managing the time I spend with my patients, I'll get more work done at the office and have less to do at home." I paused. *She's right. I talk to Pete and say how lucky I am, and then come home to Annie and often ignore her.* "Know what, babe? You're right. I need to do better, and I will."

"That's what you've promised, Jack. I just haven't seen you live up to it. First, it was finishing residency and then getting started in practice. Now, it's that you're busy at work, and you have to learn how to budget your time. You've always got an excuse."

"Well, you're not exactly sitting around at home doing nothing, either. With your extra hospital work and meetings, you're as tied to your work as I am."

"Enough! I don't feel like arguing. I'll make my own tea, do a little writing, and then go to bed. I've got to work again tomorrow, you know."

"You just made my point, Annie."

Chapter Fifty-Four

Annie

I paced impatiently in front of The Body Shop, waiting for Joni. Suddenly, she rushed out the door in a whirlwind, her short, candy-apple red hair resembling a bird's nest on fire. It wasn't like her to be late.

"Sorry, Annie. I was growing old waiting on my last client's nails to dry."

I had to grin. "I understand. No worries. Wanna try that new café just down the street?"

"Sure, sister," she said, taking my arm. "Let's go."

We took a seat at the bar and ordered our coffee. The place had a new smell to it, not seasoned with the flow of people and the scent of food and caffeine embedded in the walls and furniture of the Grind. Nice enough, but different. Just needed time, I guess.

Joni swiveled toward me and leaned in, her eyes laser-focused on mine. "I read between the lines of your text that this wouldn't just be two friends meeting for chit-chat, right?"

"Right."

"Well? Out with it, girlfriend. What gives?"

"Oh, it's just Jack. Seems like we're arguing a lot."

"All couples argue, Annie. Heck, the last serious boyfriend I had argued with me over who was the more argumentive!"

I nodded. "I know, but he never seems to get it. He's devoted to his work, which is good, but it's not so good for our marriage. When he's home, he keeps working. We spend very little time doing *couple things*: you know, going out, watching Netflix, time together in bed—"

"Whoa, girlfriend. This does sound serious. Have you talked to him?"

"Of course, but it doesn't do any good. He just gets mad and goes back to his work. In fact, he leaves all the work around the house to me. We're both working, so we should share chores at home. Am I right?"

"Absolutely. Why are men such inconsiderate pigs?" She must have noticed my eyes widening. "Just kidding. Well, kind of."

"Seriously, Joni. What would you do?"

"If he was just a boyfriend, I'd tell him to take a hike. Marriage is different, though. I know you, and I know you take your wedding vows seriously."

"I do."

"Watch it, sister. That's what you said at the altar, and look where you are now!" She winked and laughed loudly. Joni could lighten even a serious discussion. "Maybe the two of you just need some time away. No work—just together time."

"Actually, just last week we were talking about going back to Asheville at Christmas. Before I knew it, we were arguing. I don't know, maybe I'm just making a big deal out of nothing. I've been so busy at work, and these headaches—"

"You're still getting headaches?"

"Off and on, but they're just stress headaches. Jack thought I might need glasses, but I went to the eye doctor and my eyesight's fine."

"Yeah, sounds like stress, but what do I know? I do nails and hair."

"You're a smart girl, Joni, and I value your insight. Plus, there's no one else I can talk to about this kind of stuff the way I talk to you."

She put down her coffee and reached over to put her hand on my shoulder. "That means a lot, Annie." Then, she raised her eyebrows as she cocked her head and raised her index finger. "I've got an idea. Why not try meditation or yoga? I do both to help with stress."

"Yeah, maybe. Jack would probably laugh because he's such a traditionalist. But maybe I'll give it a shot. Okay, Joni. Enough about me. How are *you*? Any hot new romances since we last talked?"

"Definitely not. I think I've been looking for love in all the wrong places, so to speak. Thinking about moving closer to home . . . maybe the Asheville area. It's kind of an alternative place that fits my style. Anyway, I've plowed all my fields in Chapel Hill."

"Joni! I'd miss you." I stopped, thought for a few seconds and put my hand on her thigh. "But you know what? You should do it if you think it's right for you. Asheville's not that far from here. We could still see each other, and that would be the perfect excuse for visiting the city. You know you're an important part of my life."

"I do know, and that means everything to me, Annie."

We finished our coffee, paid the bill, and left to go home. As Joni and I hugged, I whispered in her ear, "Girlfriends always. Right?"

"Forever, sister."

Chapter Fifty-Five

Late September 2018

A few weeks later, as my day at the office was ending, my phone chirped. Annie.

> got to stay late tonight. another meeting.
> sorry.

I called her immediately.

"The quality assurance committee has called a meeting about a safety issue. Figure I might as well just grab something for dinner in the hospital cafeteria. There are leftovers in the fridge if you want them," Annie said.

"That's fine. I'm still at the office. I can stay here and get some charting done until it's time to eat. Don't worry about me. I'll be okay," I assured her. "Love you."

"Okay, then. I'll see you when I get home. Love you more, sweetie."

After working a bit longer, my stomach won out, and I decided to try the diner. Just down the street from my office, it was a nice walk in the brisk dusk of an early fall evening. Leaves from the trees of a nearby small park crunched under the weight of my steps. Carrboro was small and homey, much like the little area where Annie was raised. Shop owners were friendly, often standing in their doorways to greet folks walking by.

The smell of grease and coffee jolted my senses when I pulled open the door. *My kind of place.* Seating was booth style, with dated Formica tabletops and Naugahyde upholstered seats, comfortably worn and softened by years of use. Behind a long counter was a pass-through from the kitchen, where ready orders were barked out for the wait staff to retrieve and deliver to customers. The walls were a creamy off-white, with some areas smudged and dirtied by repeated exposures to patrons' dirty hands, spilled beverages, and other unfortunate mishaps.

"Coffee?" the waitress offered before I'd hardly taken a seat.

"Perfect," I said, looking up at Holly, so identified by her name tag. She'd drawn a smiley face inside the "o." *Clever.* She appeared to be about my age, with short brown hair, large blue eyes, and a winsome smile, all suggesting she should be doing something other than waiting tables. I was being judgmental again—just one of my many faults.

As promised by the office staff, my order of fried chicken, fries, and collards with a side of vinegar—quintessential comfort food—was as advertised. It was one of the many reasons I loved living in the Carolinas.

"How about some dessert?" Holly said.

"Well, I was planning on it, but I'm stuffed! Better just bring me the bill now before I'm tempted." She laughed.

The cool air settling in with nightfall brought me out of my comfort food coma. I drove home, only to find the house empty. No Annie.

After fiddling around and then changing into more comfortable clothes, I sat down to finish my charting. An hour later, Annie walked in.

"Long day, huh?"

"You can say that again. Sorry I'm so late."

"Not a problem. I've had my share of late nights too." She sat down beside me and leaned forward. I massaged her shoulders gently. "How was the meeting?"

"A typical hospital meeting. Everyone got to speak their minds without really saying anything, so we didn't resolve any agenda items. The only thing on which we all agreed was that we'd have to meet again," she said. "I started feeling bad during the meeting. Another headache. Probably just from looking at that stupid computer screen for so long."

"You promised you'd get that checked out, sweetheart."

"I know. I did, Jack, but I also know it's just stress. I'm sure of it. Anyway, once I had my vision checked and everything was fine, I felt better. I don't have the time or desire to go to another doctor right now. I'll take some ibuprofen and be good as new, like always. Just need to rest."

"I've seen this movie before, Annie, but suit yourself. Obviously, you're not going to listen to me."

"I'll go later if the headaches don't stop." She leaned into me and looked me in the eye. "Jack, can we talk?"

"About what?"

"About us. We hardly see one another, and when we are together, you're often busy with work that should have been left at the office."

"Seriously, Annie? This again? You knew my work would be time-consuming and take precedence, at least at first. Just hang in there—things will get better later."

"Time-consuming, yes. But, all-consuming, no. I didn't expect that. I'm talking about work again because that's all you seem to do, and I'm tired of hearing *later,* Jack. We'll get a house later, we'll have a family later, and now you won't be as busy later. Really? I'm beginning to think that maybe later doesn't exist."

"Annie, you're being unfair . . . and a bit selfish, if you want my opinion."

"No, I really don't, if that's all you've got to say."

We looked away from each other and were silent.

Finally, Annie said, "My headache's worse. I'm just going to go to bed. Love you. Goodnight."

Frustrated that she would complain to me but not go to the doctor to be checked, I continued my charting and curtly answered, "Well, goodnight then." Without even looking up at her.

Chapter Fifty-Six

I was up early and before Annie, which was unusual. Her workday started much earlier than mine, and she was usually ready to walk out the door just as I was rolling out of bed. When I came out of the shower, she was still asleep. *Must be sick. Maybe a lingering headache?* She needed to wake up and call in sick if she wasn't going to make it to work. When I leaned over to call her name, I saw it. Her beautiful complexion was a sickly gray. I jostled her but got no response. I rolled her from her side to her back, and she still didn't move. Immediately, I noticed her breathing was slow and shallow. I felt her pulse. It was weak. Very slow. My heart sank.

"Oh, dear God," I said out loud as I ran for my phone. I dialed quickly, reaching someone almost immediately.

"911. What is your emergency?"

"It's my wife. Something's terribly wrong. I need an ambulance—now!"

"What seems to be the problem with your wife, sir?"

"She's barely breathing, her pulse is slow, and her color is terrible," I said. "Look, I know. I'm a doctor."

"I'm calling Medic right now, sir. Give me your address, please, and stay with her. Help is on the way."

Despite my hands shaking and my heart pounding, I somehow managed to finish the call. The boulder in my throat made it hard for me to swallow, and my breathing quickened. I quickly played CPR scenarios in my head. A pulse. Breathing, although barely. *Rescue breathing.* I began mouth-to-mouth at ten breaths per minute. No change in color or heart rate. I continued, trembling as my panic grew. My sweat fell in small drops to Annie's face, like dew on a rose, as I continued the resuscitation efforts. Suddenly, I heard it. An ambulance screaming its arrival. A loud knock at the door.

I ran to the door. "Follow me."

"We'll take it from here, sir," one of the medics said, as I attempted to resume my effort to help Annie.

No! This can't be happening. I collapsed in the single chair in our room, tears welling in my eyes as I played out what could be wrong. Sepsis? Meningitis? No, with infection, her heart should be racing, valiantly attempting to maintain adequate circulation despite a lower blood pressure and dilated blood vessels. Some kind of heart problem? Unlikely, given her age and perfect health. Then, it hit me. *Oh, my gosh! It's her brain. Something's wrong with her brain. The headaches weren't just stress.* Now, it was all tragically coming together and starting to make sense. *God, let me be wrong.*

The medics began to bag-mask ventilate Annie, a much more effective way of providing air for her oxygen-starved lungs. They moved her to a gurney, secured her, and wheeled her to the front door. One of them, whom I'd recognized from my work in the Emergency Room, turned to speak to me.

"Doc, I didn't realize it was you when we got the call. Wilson is such a common name, you know. We'll do everything we possibly can for your wife."

"Can I stay with her?"

"We'll be working on her. If you think you can drive, why don't you follow us?" he said as they lifted the gurney to ambulance height and slid her into the back.

"Yeah, I'll do that . . . I'll follow you."

"You sure you're in good enough shape to drive, right?"

I nodded quickly. "I'll be fine," I said, not convinced it was true.

While waiting for the medics to secure Annie's gurney in the ambulance, I called ahead to the ER. A friend and former colleague, one of the residents, came to the phone.

"It looks bad," I said. "Maybe a neurologic insult or possibly a cardiac event. I don't really know. I can't even think straight right now."

"Jack, don't worry. We'll get her into the crash room immediately, assess things, and go from there. I'll call the cardiology and neurology residents, too, just to give them a heads up. Sounds like we might need one of them—or maybe both."

"Thanks. I appreciate that." *It pays to know people.* I raced off to chase the ambulance speeding toward the hospital, its siren blaring.

Chapter Fifty-Seven

By the time I rushed into the ER from the parking lot, Annie had already been transported to the crash room. Despite the fact I was a physician, the staff insisted I remain outside the room until one of the doctors was free to update me. My protests fell on deaf ears.

Not knowing what else to do, I nervously paced back and forth. I needed to talk to someone. I called Pete.

"Pete."

"Oh, hey Jack. It's early. What's up, dude?"

"It's Annie. We're at the hospital—"

"The hospital?" he interrupted. "What's wrong, Jack?"

"I found her in bed this morning, almost lifeless," I blurted out, now sobbing as reality hit me like a ton of bricks. "I don't know what happened. She's being evaluated right now."

"I'm on my way."

A nurse approached. "Pete, I've got to go."

"One of the doctors will be out soon, Dr. Wilson."

"Good. I really need to speak to someone as soon as possible," I said. I began pacing.

She nodded. "We know this is so difficult for you, and we're doing all we can, as fast as we can. It shouldn't be long."

Ten minutes later, a physician emerged from the room. I knew the look on his face. It couldn't be good news.

"We did a quick EKG on your wife, Dr. Wilson, and her heart rhythm is normal—just a slow rate. Given her slow pulse, high blood pressure, and a dilated right pupil, we're pretty sure it's an intracranial event. We're hyperventilating her and giving IV mannitol—you know, to help with increased intracranial pressure.

We've also ordered a STAT brain MRI and, any second, she'll be taken to Radiology. He put his hand on my shoulder and leaned closer, speaking softly. "Dr. Wilson, you know as well as I do that it doesn't look good. I think you should prepare for the worst but hope for the best. I wish I had more encouraging news, but I assure you we'll continue to do everything we can."

A team of ER personnel suddenly rushed out with Annie and wheeled her toward the Radiology Department. A quick glimpse showed her color to have improved, but it was still pallid. That slight improvement brought me a glimmer of encouragement. *Maybe she's improving.* Hope was all I had.

Hearing footsteps drawing near, I turned and saw Pete. I collapsed in his arms. "Thank you for coming," I barely got out as I started shaking.

"I wouldn't be anywhere else. You'd do the same thing for me, and you know it. Have they updated you?"

"They think she had some kind of acute intracranial event."

"What does that mean—in English?"

"Something has happened in her brain—a stroke or bleed? I don't know. She's being taken for a brain MRI. That scan should tell us what's going on."

"Whatever they find, it's not something you should have to deal with by yourself."

We sat in the waiting room, hardly talking, and with Pete's arm draped over my shoulders. He got up only to walk over and grab us coffee from the beverage station. With the lump lingering in my throat, it was all I could do to get down small sips at a time.

"I called Mary on my way over here. She wanted me to tell you she's available if you or Annie need anything, and she'll be here after she's finished teaching."

"That's sweet of her, Pete. Of course, there's nothing we can do right now. Even as a physician, I'm powerless to help her. Here, I'm just her husband. I've worked with most of these doctors, however, and I know she's in good hands."

We were interrupted by Dr. Moore, one of the neuroradiologists.

"Dr. Wilson, I'm Frank Moore—one of the radiologists."

"Yes, sir. I recognize you. And please, call me Jack."

Eyeing Pete, Dr. Moore asked if we could talk privately.

"Anything you need to tell me, sir, you can tell me with Pete here. He's like a brother to me."

"Very well, then. I'm afraid it's not good, Jack. She has a ruptured cerebral aneurysm and has incurred a massive bleed in the right half of her brain."

My heart sank as my mind quickly processed the scenario: an aneurysm, a bleed, the possibility of catastrophe.

He continued. "We're moving her to surgery as I speak, where the neurosurgeon, Bob Forrest, will evacuate as much of the blood as possible, clip the aneurysm, and place an intracranial monitor. As you know, controlling her increased intracranial pressure will go a long way toward determining her outcome."

His words sounded distant—bouncing around somewhere far away. As I looked down, seeing only blurred, painful images, my mind was roiled by thoughts of Annie's recent headaches and now this. *Why hadn't I figured it out? Why didn't I insist that she see her doctor right away?*

"Of course, Bob will update you after surgery," Dr. Moore said before leaving.

As the doctor walked away, Pete said, "Jack, what does all of that mean?"

I explained that Annie had a cerebral aneurysm—a weak area in a brain blood vessel. It's like a ticking time bomb. Sometime during the night, it ruptured, and the bleeding inside her skull increased the pressure on her brain, initiating the cascade of events that brought her to the hospital and surgery.

"A ruptured cerebral aneurysm?"

"It's a brain bleed. Think of it as a weak spot, or bubble, in a water hose. Under pressure, the bubble bursts. Somehow, she survived it, but she's in grave danger of dying or of having devastating neurologic consequences, at best," I said, the tears letting loose. "All we can do, Pete, is wait—and pray." The end of that sentence startled me.

"I'm already praying, Jack. The waiting's the hard part. Tell you what, I'll get us some more coffee and grab some muffins or something from the cafeteria. Better not to deal with all of this on an empty stomach."

"Just coffee for me. I'm not really hungry."

"It's going to be a long day, Jack. You need something to eat."

"It's already been a long day."

Chapter Fifty-Eight

After a seemingly interminable wait, the neurosurgeon came out of the operating room and called me over. As our eyes met, I sensed he recognized me from shared cases we'd had with a few of my neuro patients during my residency.

"Jack, I'm Bob Forrest. We just finished Annie's case." We sat in chairs near the coffee dispenser. He removed his surgical cap and mask and got both of us a cup of coffee. "The surgery went as well as one could expect, but she had an enormous bleed, and we're going to have to take things hour by hour. She's in recovery now and will soon be taken to the Neuro ICU. I wish I could be more positive, but I figured you'd want me to level with you."

"I appreciate that, sir, and I'm grateful for what you've done for us. When can I see her?"

"The nurse will come get you as soon as she's settled in ICU. For now, why don't you move to that unit's waiting room so you'll be easier to find?"

More waiting. I shook his hand and thanked him again. I thought about all those patients of mine who had to wait for lab results, biopsy reports, or, as I was doing now, had to wait outside of an operating room, with a loved one's life hanging in the balance. Now, I understood what they had gone through. Had I been adequately empathetic to their needs? Or had I shielded myself from the emotion of the moment by immersing myself in my clinical duties?

"What'd he say?" Pete asked.

"Just that it'll be touch and go for a while. Come on. Let's go back to the waiting room."

It suddenly dawned on me that I needed to call Eric. How could I forget to call the only other family member Annie had?

"Morning, Jack. This is a nice surprise," he said. "What's up?"

"I'm afraid I've got bad news—Annie's in the hospital. She had a brain bleed at home and was rushed here for evaluation and surgery. She's in recovery now but will soon be moved to the ICU. Honestly, Eric, it's bad. We don't know how bad, but it's bad."

"Oh, my gosh," he responded, his voice cracking. "I'll get a flight as soon as we get off the phone. I'll get there just as soon as possible. I need to be there for Annie—and for you. I'll text you when I have my flight info."

As we hung up, the ICU nurse came out to get me. "You can see her now, Dr. Wilson."

I asked Pete to let me go in alone first but to stay close by. I might need him after I saw Annie.

"You got it, Jack. I'm here for the duration."

What I saw startled me, even though I'd seen my own patients in similar situations. With family, however, it was much different. Annie's head was bandaged, with an intracranial monitor extending through the dressing like a flag mounted in a pile of bloodied snow. Her eyelids, taped closed to keep them from drying out, were puffy, and her skin color was still pale. The bedside monitors created a cacophony of sounds as though they were all competing for attention. As many times as I'd stood with a patient who was similarly monitored, I'd never noticed how distracting and intrusive those machines were. They were necessary to constantly assess her clinical situation and, hopefully, her progress. Once again, I wondered how negligent I'd been about my patients' families' reactions to such noxious stimuli. Would I have thought their complaints to be petty when their loved ones' lives were at risk?

I reached for her hand, its lifeless form incapable of responding to my touch. "I love you, Annie," I whispered. "Please hang in there, babe—please," my eyes filled with tears again and my voice trembled. It was all I could do to maintain any degree of composure. Though it was difficult to speak, I kept talking to her, hoping that something was getting through. The nurse walked in and asked me to step out so she could change Annie into a clean gown and re-dress her blood-stained head bandage.

Pete greeted me in the waiting room. "Well?" he asked.

I sat in the chair next to him. "She looks so pitiful. It breaks my heart to see her like this. I think you'd better wait a bit before you see her."

"I'm fine with that, Jack, and remember, you're here for her. That's all you can do right now." Somehow, Pete knew exactly what to say.

We sat quietly for a few minutes until I realized I hadn't called in to cancel my day's schedule. "Oh, shoot. I need to call the office."

"Already done, Jack. I called for you while you were in with Annie. Figured you hadn't even thought to do so—who would? I hope it's okay I told the office manager a little bit about what's going on. When she heard it, she asked me to hold for your senior partner. A doctor came to the phone and explained that the senior doctor was busy doing a procedure. I filled her in with all the information I could muster as a non-medical person. She asked me to tell you how sorry she is and not to worry at all about work. She reassured me the partners will cover for you as long as you need them to."

It was nice to have one less thing to worry about.

The day dragged on, with my visits to Annie often interrupted so that her nurse could tend to her. It was sad but true that her work was more important to Annie than my being there. I saw no improvement, but it was too soon to hope for much of a change. Pete left to pick up Eric at the airport so I could be near Annie in the event anything happened. With Pete gone, my loneliness suddenly weighed on me. Eric was family, but I'd only met him on two occasions: the week of the wedding and when Virginia died. Nonetheless, when he walked in, I was relieved to see him.

"How's sis?" he said as we embraced.

"She's stable, Eric, but very critical. Right now, I'm just glad she survived the bleed and came through surgery okay. It's hard to know if her unconsciousness is due to her illness or from the medications she's on to keep her pressures as normal as possible."

"What does that mean, Jack?"

"It means we don't know if she'll ever wake up," I said, realizing the truth hit harder when voiced aloud. "We're just going to have to wait and see."

"Can I see her?" Eric said.

"Of course—just as soon as her nurse gives us the okay to go back in."

As if on cue, her nurse came out to the waiting room, acknowledged Eric, and asked if we'd like to see Annie. I warned Eric she would not look like she normally does, but a person is never prepared to see their loved one in a situation like that. As soon as he saw Annie, Eric turned away, buried his face in his hands, and cried.

After a few minutes spent composing himself, he went to Annie's bedside, placed his hand on her forearm, and said, "It's Eric, sis. I love you." Turning to me, he whispered, "Can she hear me?"

Though we don't know how much a comatose patient can hear, it's best to assume they can, so I encouraged him to talk to her. For all we knew, our words might help her brain wake up.

With that encouragement, Eric turned back to Annie and said, "Jack and I are here for you, Annie, and we love you. The kids send their love too. You've just got to hang in there and get better," he said as tears again filled his eyes.

Hearing someone behind me, I turned to find the nurse ushering Pete into the room. Even at a distance, near the corner of the room, he could only look at Annie briefly before gasping and looking away. Pete began to cry. I knew it was time for us to get out of there.

It seemed that with each visit to see Annie I sensed the loss of another little piece of my heart. Her motionless, unresponsive form cast a pall of gloom over me. "Don't worry about work," my partner at work had said. I was sure she meant well, but she had no way to know I couldn't have cared less about work at that point. I finally knew what really mattered in my life—the most important thing: Annie and our love for each other. Would I ever be able to tell her this, show her this, and assure her our time together trumped everything else in my life, including medicine? The room's walls began closing in on me as I motioned to Eric and Pete to leave the room.

"I'm sorry I reacted that way, Jack," Pete said after we returned to the waiting room.

I rested my hand on his forearm. "It's fine, buddy. Hard to prepare to see someone in that condition. Let's go for coffee and catch our breath."

Chapter Fifty-Nine

We went through the hospital cafeteria line, grabbed some food and coffee, and took a seat. No one was hungry. Almost immediately, the emotions spilled out like milk escaping from an overturned glass.

"Jack, I'm so sorry you and Annie are going through this," Pete said. "I know it had to be terribly hard for you, but seeing Annie like that was too much for me to handle."

"I know. Post-op patients never look great. They go through so much and then need time to rest and recover. I'll admit it's much worse, though, when it's your loved one who's lying there."

"It was hard for me too," Eric offered. "I mean, I thought my heart was going to leap out of my chest when I walked into that room. I'm glad I came alone. The kids wanted to come, but I talked to their mom, and we agreed it would be better for them to see Annie after she recovers. There's no way they should see their Aunt Annie like this. They wouldn't understand, and I know I couldn't really explain it to them."

"Same for Mary," Pete offered. "She'd be heartbroken to see Annie right now."

Their comments confirmed what I already knew—Annie's condition was desperate. I mean, if Pete and Eric picked up on the seriousness of her situation, that meant it was pretty obvious, even to someone not in medicine. My thoughts were interrupted when I heard my name paged to the ICU over the intercom. We grabbed our cups and hustled back to the unit.

"Dr. Forrest is in with Annie, Dr. Wilson," the nurse said. "He should be out to speak to you in a few minutes. Please try to make yourselves as comfortable as possible."

It wasn't long before Dr. Forrest walked out. The solemn look on his face betrayed what had to be bad news.

"Jack, may I speak to you alone, or is it okay for your friends to hear what I have to say?" After I properly introduced Eric and Pete, he continued. "Annie's vital signs are stable, but her pressures are higher than I'd like. Although I've reduced her sedative, she hasn't really stirred at all. No response to even painful stimuli, which, honestly, is of concern to me. But neuro patients are hard to figure, and the brain can do unpredictable things. Hopefully, her age and good health are in her favor. We'll see how things look tomorrow. If there's no change in her level of consciousness, we'll need to do an EEG."

"Thank you, Dr. Forrest. Not what I wanted to hear, but I appreciate your candor."

He nodded and walked out of the unit.

"Uh, Jack, what was the doctor talking about when he said, 'do an EEG?'" Eric said. "Isn't that a heart test?"

I explained he was thinking of an EKG, but an EEG is a study that looks at brainwave activity, seizures, or evidence of other abnormal neurologic problems. It was sometimes done when a patient was in a coma and wouldn't wake up.

"But if Annie's unconscious, she's unconscious," Pete said. "We don't need a fancy test to confirm that, do we?"

Just having to explain it triggered more despair for me. I said with a quiet voice, "The EEG is done on a comatose patient to see if there's any brain activity."

"And if there isn't any?" Eric asked.

"That would be a sign of brain death." As I uttered those words, I collapsed back into my chair.

"Well, we're just not going there, Jack," Pete said. "That's way too pessimistic. And speaking of pessimism, Jack, that surgeon seemed too matter-of-fact for my taste."

"He was just being honest, Pete. Plus, he realizes I know full well what's going on. Give him a break—he deals with life and death every day he comes to the hospital."

"Okay. Sorry if I sounded ugly. This is just overwhelming."

As we finished our coffee and headed back to the unit, I decided we would check in on Annie and then go home to get some sleep. I expected the next day would be a long one.

"I think we all need to get some rest and come back to the hospital in the morning when we're a little fresher. Eric, you can stay at our place, of course. Pete, bring Mary up to speed. Try to get some sleep too—even if you aren't planning to come back tomorrow."

"Bro, I'm coming back. Where else do you think I'd be that could be more important than being with you and Annie?"

Pete would go to the mattresses for me. That was just what I needed.

Leaving the hospital, I shoved my hands in my pants pockets and scrunched my shoulders to my neck, surprised by the chill in the air. Somehow, the hours had slipped by and the weather had cooled while we were preoccupied with Annie's condition. The sun dipped into the distant horizon, matching the sinking feeling in my heart.

Chapter Sixty

I tossed and turned, my mind preoccupied with the events of the day and my concern for Annie. Twice, I called the hospital to check on her, both times hearing there had been no change. Without the assistance of an alarm, I was up early. A quick check of the weather app told me it was going to be seasonably cool and overcast. A glance outside confirmed the sun was yet to appear. After shaving and showering, I quietly slipped into the kitchen, only to find Eric sitting at the table, with coffee ready for both of us.

"Couldn't sleep, huh?" he said.

"Not much. You?"

"Up and down all night, just worrying about my sis. I was thinking: It wasn't so long ago that our family grew by one—you—but now, with Mom gone and Annie—"

He stopped, seemingly unable to continue a sentence he didn't want to complete.

"I know, Eric, but we've got to stay positive. I can tell you that strange things happen in medicine. I've seen it with my patients. And let me just say I feel so blessed to be part of your family. That's something I never really had growing up, which makes me appreciate all of you even more."

He managed a smile. He thanked me, got up, and headed for his room. "I'll get cleaned up so we can head to the hospital."

A few minutes later, we were hurrying out the door and on our way. Before leaving, I grabbed my work tablet.

"No change, Dr. Wilson, and Dr. Forrest has already been in to make rounds," the nurse patiently reported.

I walked alone into Annie's room. Her face seemed less swollen, but she certainly didn't look anything close to the way she normally did. Her monitors showed her intracranial pressure was still stubbornly elevated, and she wasn't breathing over her ventilator rate, both ominous signs. Though I was discouraged, when I went out to update Eric, I put the best face on things I could. I told him she was stable with no change, without disclosing the clinical information I'd noticed, but a layperson would completely miss. He nodded his understanding as he took a deep breath, clasped his hands, and steeled himself to see her.

While Eric was with Annie, Pete walked in, carrying a bag of bagels and three cups of coffee. With his shirt only partially tucked and his eyes heavy, I assumed he didn't get much sleep, either.

"Morning, Jack," he said, just above a whisper.

"Hey, Pete. Thanks for coming."

"How's our gal?"

After bringing him up to speed, Pete and I joined Eric at the bedside. Pete suddenly turned and left the room.

"Pete, you okay?" I asked, finding him just outside the room, sitting with his head between his knees.

"I needed some air. I felt woozy standing there looking at Annie. Maybe I just need to eat."

As we sat in the waiting room and munched on our bagels, Pete asked what the plan would be for the day.

"Just more waiting. Hopefully, we'll see some improvement before Dr. Forrest returns for afternoon rounds."

"How do we define improvement?" Eric asked.

"Any spontaneous movement—even a finger or toe wiggle, some breaths on her own, or, at the very least, some drop in her brain pressure."

After a while, Pete left to fetch us more coffee, this time also returning with a newspaper.

"Something to read, fellas," Pete said. "Maybe a nice distraction or at least a way to pass some time."

Before long, I opened my tablet. Although I wasn't working in the office, I figured just handling some messages and questions from my nurse about patient issues would keep me preoccupied and push aside some of my worry about Annie—at least briefly. My nurse had kindly included a message that I was not to think twice about being out of the office. The other doctors were easily handling my patients, and it made them feel like they were contributing something positive to my situation.

A few hours later, before going down to the cafeteria for lunch, I paid a quick visit to Annie's bedside. Her nurse smiled knowingly, apparently realizing I was desperate for some good news or for some sign of hope.

"No change, Dr. Wilson. Believe me, if there's any change, I'll page you immediately. Go on down and get something to eat. I know how to find you if I need you."

At lunch, Pete said, "Jack, I hate to do this, but I have a class to teach this afternoon. I hope it's okay for me to slip away for a couple of hours. I really can't miss—you know, can't give them a reason to fire me!"

"Pete, you've been great to be here so much. By all means, go to your class. You have no obligation to be here all the time. And they're not going to fire you, buddy."

"There's where you're wrong, Jack. Maybe not about getting fired but about my obligation to be here. With our friendship, I wouldn't be anywhere else, so I'll be back later this afternoon."

Eric and I returned to the Neuro ICU after lunch. Its sterile and eerily quiet ambiance stood in sharp contrast to the frenzy in the cubicle where Annie fought for her life. I fired up my tablet to finish some work. Eric retreated to a corner and called his architecture firm to check on a few projects he left hanging when he rushed to Chapel Hill.

Finally, late that afternoon, Dr. Forrest emerged from the elevator and headed toward the unit. "Jack, let me see Annie and check on a few things, and then I'll be out to talk to you." He soon returned with a grim look on his face. "Let's go in and sit down," he suggested, gesturing to one of the family conference rooms. I nodded and followed him into one of the rooms designed for very private and critical conversations between physicians and families.

"Unfortunately, there's been no change—no improvement in her level of consciousness and no spontaneous movements seen by her nurse, who's been watching her like a hawk. She's off sedation now, so none of it can be attributed to medication. To be honest, I'm very concerned. I think it's time to talk about further evaluation."

"Meaning?" I said but already knowing his answer and dreading to hear it.

"If there's no change overnight, I want to do an EEG in the morning to see where things stand. That can give us some guidance regarding next steps." He shook his head. "I'm sorry. There's just nothing easy about this, from your stand-point as her husband or mine as her surgeon. Just keep your fingers crossed."

Eric and I glanced at each other, and then I looked back at Dr. Forrest, nod-ding. My head dropped and my eyes began to tear. I walked a few steps away to gather myself and returned. "I understand, and I appreciate your honesty, as well as everything you've done for Annie. I know you've been extra attentive to her case. I'm grateful for that."

"Anything for a colleague and for a nurse," he said. "It's a special privilege to care for one of our own, you know. Anyway, I've seen how much you care for the patients you refer to me, and they always rave about you. This is the least I can do for you and Annie."

With a handshake and a hand on my shoulder, he got up to leave and then added, "Why don't you and your brother-in-law go home and get some rest? Tomorrow could be a long day. You know the nurses will call you with any change."

As Eric and I climbed into the car to head home, Eric said, "You know, I think Pete misjudged the doctor. He does seem like a caring person." Then he asked, "Jack, explain to me again why the doctor wants to do an EEG. Is he afraid she's having seizures?"

Finding it difficult to put into words, I struggled to explain it to him again. "The EEG is to assess her brain activity. If there isn't any, the hard reality is that she's brain dead, and further prolongation of her support would be useless and even inhumane." I spoke as a doctor, but internally I was without words for what I was feeling.

Eric remained silent for the rest of the ride home.

Chapter Sixty-One

After another futile attempt at sleep—dozing in fits and spurts—morning finally arrived, the sky gray and once again blanketed with heavy cloud cover. It matched my mood perfectly. My stomach did flips as I thought about the EEG's possible findings.

Before leaving the house, Eric and I sat in the kitchen, nursing cups of coffee. A simple breakfast of cereal and juice went untouched.

"Jack, I know this doesn't seem important right now, but I want you to know I haven't done a thing about Mom's house. Nothing's been gone through or disposed of. I just haven't had the time or energy to do it, much less make a decision about selling it."

He was right—it didn't seem important at the moment. It was just nervous small talk, probably his attempt to fill the crater in my heart. "I understand, Eric. Let's head to the hospital."

When we got to the ICU, the overnight nurse informed us nothing had changed. Dr. Forrest then walked in.

"Good morning." He smiled and looked from me to Eric. "Jack, I've ordered the EEG. Maybe we've just been expecting too much too soon. Let's try to be optimistic. I've got two cases in the OR, but I should be back about the time we have a result. You and Annie are my utmost priority today, so I'll get back as soon as possible—hopefully with some good news."

All I could do was offer a simple thanks. I was having a hard time even speaking.

Once the doctor left, Eric and I went in to see Annie. I saw nothing that gave me hope. She lay motionless on her back, maybe with a little less puffiness in her beautiful face. Eric held one hand and I the other.

"More tests this morning, Annie. Just an EEG, though. No needle sticks," I whispered, my voice halting with each word. "Everything is going to be okay, babe. I just know it."

"Jack's right, sis," Eric said. "Everything is going to be okay, and we'll be right here with you." His voice cracked.

When we went back to the waiting room, we met Pete, who'd brought in coffee and Danish.

"Morning, Jack, Eric. How's Annie?"

"An EEG is scheduled. It'll tell us what's going on," I said.

"I'm so sorry. Jack, I know Mary would like to be here. She wants to see Annie, but I just didn't know if it would be okay with you. She got a sub for today so she'd be free. Is it alright if I call her?"

"Of course, Pete. Please do, but ask her to try to come now, before the EEG is done," I said, knowing there was a real possibility that later might be too late, or there might not even be a "later."

Not surprisingly, knowing Mary, she arrived shortly after Pete made the call, giving Eric and me hugs.

"Mary, let Pete take you in to see Annie," I suggested, and both of them nodded. Eric and I took our usual seats and sipped on the coffee, but neither of us touched the pastries.

Before long, Pete and Mary came back out, tears in their eyes.

"Oh, Jack, I can't imagine what this has been like for you, and what you're going through now," Mary said, taking my hand as she sat down beside me. "It's hard to believe that's our fun-loving, sweet Annie lying there like that. This pain is hard to bear."

Our conversation was interrupted as we turned our heads in the direction of a commotion—the technician wheeling the EEG machine across the gleaming tile floor and into the unit. My stomach tightened and my throat seemed to close. My mouth went dry as we waited. About thirty minutes later, the technician averted his eyes as he walked by with his machine. I took that as a bad sign. Time passed slowly as we waited on what could literally be life or death news. When Dr. Forrest finally arrived, his look sent my mind into a tailspin.

"Jack, I have the results. Can I speak to you and Eric privately in one of the family conference rooms, please?"

"Let's sit down for a few minutes, Jack. I'm afraid the results are not what we wanted. The tracing shows no sign of brainwave activity. Of course, this explains why Annie just hasn't shown any signs of improvement . . ." His voice kept droning on, but somehow, my brain took leave from its auditory processing ability. I sat there stoically and tuned back in as he continued. "Jack, I know you realize this means there just isn't any hope for Annie. It's pointless to go on supporting her, and I know it's torture for you to see her like this."

I glanced at Eric, silent and with his chin dropped to his chest, and then looked back at Dr. Forrest. "I understand. I know we'll need to stop her ventilator support. It's just so hard—"

"It is hard, and I do understand," he interrupted. "Why don't the two of you take a private moment to be with her before we stop her support? I'll leave you with her, but I'll be back in just a few minutes."

"Thank you again for all you've done, Dr. Forrest. I know Annie was in good hands, and I'll always be grateful to you for that and for the way you've treated us."

We returned to the waiting room, where I collapsed into the arms of Eric, Pete, and Mary. "Oh no," Mary said. "I can't believe this is happening."

When I composed myself, I said, "Eric, let's go in for a last visit with Annie." We went to her bedside and again both of us took her by the hand, but all we could manage was to stand there, as words wouldn't come. It was impossible for me to wrap my head around the fact that we were saying goodbye. Finally, I leaned over and kissed her precious face, whispering, "I love you, Annie. I'll always love you, but you know that, don't you?"

As we turned to leave, her nurse approached to carry out the order I knew Dr. Forrest had given her, tears welling in her eyes. She gently grasped me by the forearm. "Dr. Wilson, why don't you stay? I know Annie wouldn't want to be alone for this. And, Eric, just as soon as it's over, I'll come out and let you know."

Dr. Forrest returned shortly, nodding to me and managing to force some hint of what seemed to be a compassionate smile. The nurse turned off the intracranial pressure monitor and the ventilator. The beep of the heart monitor steadily slowed and finally stopped. Dr. Forrest listened to Annie's chest, then straightened and removed his stethoscope. He put his hand on my shoulder. "She's gone, Jack. I'm so sorry. We'll step out and let you be alone with Annie. Take as much time as you need."

I nodded and then looked back at my Annie. She looked so peaceful, she could have been lying there asleep. I sat on her bed and kissed her one last time, and then nestled my head against hers. And then it hit me full force: The world as I knew it, and the future Annie and I had planned, had come to a crushing halt. My tears saturated her hospital gown.

Chapter Sixty-Two

October 2018
Wilmington

My head was in a fog as we went about the business of meeting with funeral home personnel to plan a service of remembrance and the burial. The demands placed on me in that situation would have pierced my soul and destroyed me if I wasn't numb to the reality of what was taking place. Maybe Mother Nature orchestrates such a vapid state to protect those left behind. It's not like I was without help. Eric's kids and their mom flew to Wilmington. Annie's former neighbors, Tom and Ethel, insisted that Pete, Mary, and I stay with them. I was grateful for the offer, which I accepted, but it was strangely uncomfortable to be so close to the house where Annie was raised and in which her mom died.

"All of us are diminished when someone dies before their time." The minister's words rang true but did little to heal the hole in my heart.

Our small family, former friends and neighbors of the Monroe family, and some of our friends from Chapel Hill were gathered in Annie's hometown church. The weather was awful, with the overcast, gray sky perfect for the sullen mood in the sanctuary. The minister went on to speak of Annie's attributes and how her desire to go into nursing had benefited so many patients. Had he talked all day about her virtues, he couldn't have been accused of overstating his case. Hearing what he said just confirmed what I already knew about Annie, but it was so disheartening to think that he was talking about a life now gone, and much too soon. But I wanted him to stop so I could get out of that church. If there was a God, I was angry with him and didn't want to be in what was considered *his house*. Whatever faith I had reclaimed with Annie's encouragement was now gone.

I turned to exit the building and noticed her sitting at the aisle end of a pew near the back. Her head was bowed and cradled by her hands, but the silver hair with blue highlights could only be one person.

"Joni?"

She looked up with eyes red and puffy. "Hi, Jack."

"I didn't realize you'd be here. Thank you for coming."

"I wouldn't have been anywhere else today. Annie and I were like sisters. I loved that girl."

"We all did, Joni. You're sweet to be here. Family and friends are gathering after this is all over. Can you join us?"

"Maybe. I'll have to see if I feel like company or would rather be alone. But thanks for the offer."

After leaving the church, we made the short walk to the church cemetery, where Annie's body was interred next to her mom's. And that was it. Annie was gone.

"Very nice service, Jack," Tom Barnes said.

Nice funeral service. I nodded, but it sounded like an oxymoron to me. We were at Tom and Ethel's with Eric, Pete, Mary, and some of Annie's childhood friends, having light refreshments and sharing fond remembrances of Annie. Joni stopped by to give me a final hug but opted not to stay.

"And there was the time when Annie was in junior high . . ." the words faded in my ears as my longing to have Annie back overwhelmed me. When I did tune in, I heard of her silly antics when she was young. How I wished she were here to tease her about those revelations. I was physically and mentally spent from so much time at the hospital and then the three days since Annie's death, but it was comforting to sit in the company of friends and loved ones and quietly reflect on her life.

As Eric got up to head back to the hotel, he said, "Jack, the kids and I love you, man. Even with Annie gone, you know you're still family. Please call if there's anything you need."

"That means a lot, Eric. Thanks for being there for me—and Annie. I've gotta believe she knew you were there."

"I hope so. I really hope so, Jack."

Tom and Ethel insisted that Pete, Mary, and I stay the night rather than drive home so late in the day. It was good to sit, rest, and decompress from the events of the past several days.

"Tom and Ethel, you probably know this, but Annie loved you and thought of you as second parents."

"Annie was one-of-a-kind, Jack, as you well know," Ethel said. "We were blessed to live next door to the Monroe family and have them as part of our lives. We're sure going to miss Annie and Virginia. It's so sad to see that house sitting there empty."

"I'm not sure what Eric's going to do with it," Tom said. "He doesn't even know. Of course, he could just sell it, but it would be real strange seeing anyone other than a Monroe living there. He did say he's considering moving back here. We'd sure love that, but he'd have to work out something—some kind of an agreement, you know—with the kids' mother. Having Sophie and Will running around would remind us so much of when Eric and Annie M were living there."

After eating a light dinner prepared by Ethel, I suddenly realized how exhausted I was. Hoping for an early start home the next morning, I excused myself and went to bed. I had no idea how the future would play out or how I would cope with Annie's loss. It was time to go home, but to what, I wasn't sure.

Chapter Sixty-Three

Chapel Hill

After bringing in my luggage, I wandered aimlessly from room to room, not sure what to do, if anything. I wanted to crawl into bed, fall asleep, and wake up to a new day, absent the events of the past few weeks and having Annie by my side. What my heart longed for was trumped by the implacable reality that what I wanted would never be realized. Two things dominated my life—my love for Annie and my work. Absent one, I would have to turn to the other. I'd force myself to get back to the office.

I hadn't considered, much less prepared for, the harsh impact of walking back into our apartment, now filled with emptiness and the awful noise of silence. My mind played through thoughts of what might have been—the life Annie and I had planned. Reminders of her were everywhere: the pictures of us, her books, her poetry notebooks, and the closet full of her clothes, her smell still clinging to them. I had no distractions from the stark reality of loneliness and the pain of my grief. Solitude was a harsh roommate.

I fired up my tablet to check on messages, results, and anything else I hadn't been able to look at for over a week. Maybe some productive activity would take my mind off of Annie. Seeing messages and lab results, but not focusing on them or processing the information properly, I powered down my tablet, deciding to save it for another day. I knew the office was open so, with a deep breath, I called the private line to check-in. Fortunately, a kind and familiar voice answered.

"Hello, Karen. This is Jack Wilson."

"Dr. Wilson! I didn't expect to hear from you so soon. How *are* you?"

"As well as could be expected, I guess. I just got back home and can't quite figure out what to do with myself, so I thought I'd call and let you know I'm back. We need to talk about when I'll come back to work."

"Now, Dr. Wilson, you know your partners are covering for you, and they want you to take as much time as you need."

That was nice to hear, but I knew I wanted to get back to work. My patients needed me, and I needed them. "I'd like to come back in on Monday, maybe with a lighter schedule than usual. I don't think I'll be moving as quickly as I normally do."

"That's fine, if you think you're ready. Everyone has been thinking about you, and we're all looking forward to having you back."

"Monday it is, then. If I crash and burn between now and then, and I don't think I'm ready, I'll let you know . . . and Karen, the flower arrangement the office sent to the funeral home was beautiful. I know you handle those things. Thanks so much."

Well, it's done. Back to work in five days—the first step back to some semblance of my new normal. Burying myself in work was always my default, sometimes to the detriment of other, more important, things in my life. Work should be good for me. I had to believe that. My thoughts were interrupted by my phone ringing. It was Pete, who'd already texted twice that day to let me know I was in his thoughts.

"Hey, Jack. You doing okay? I wanted to be sure you were safely back home and to tell you that Mary and I are going to bring some carry-out over for dinner."

"Pete, I'm fine. You don't need to do that. I can find something in the freezer that can be thrown together. You've already done so much for me."

"We know this is a tough day for you. We insist. And we'll bring your buddy. I'm sure she's missed you."

"Jack, you're hardly touching your dinner," Mary said, glancing from my plate to me. "I thought quesadillas were one of your favorites."

"They are. I'm sorry. I know you meant well and I appreciate that, but I'm just not hungry." I reached down and scratched Molly's head, which was resting in my lap. She hadn't left my side since Pete and Mary had arrived.

"No problem," Pete said. We'll stick the leftovers in your fridge."

"Before you go tonight, guys, I just want you to know I'm going back to work this coming Monday."

"Jeez, Jack, don't you think that's a little soon?" Pete asked.

"I think Jack knows what's best for him," Mary interjected.

"Pete's right, Mary. I could be rushing it. Nothing feels great right now, but I think busyness will be a good distraction."

"Well, okay, but we're around if you need us, and you know how to reach us—anytime," Pete said.

"You're both great friends," I said as we finished eating. They grabbed their coats to head home. I reached down and gave Molly a final hug.

As they headed to the door, Pete stopped and turned around. "Don't forget I'm here for you, bro," he said.

Once they were gone, the apartment got eerily quiet, forcing me to face my situation and the demons that one day would almost destroy me.

After a restless night's sleep, coffee, and a stale donut I found in the pantry, I decided to go for a run. I needed to clear my head and relieve some tension. My legs felt as heavy as my heart. Annie dominated my thoughts, and running a marathon wouldn't have changed that. After a few miles, I turned around and headed home.

I grabbed some water, cooled off, and then opened my tablet. The menial office work I attempted went at glacial speed. I decided to save call-backs, as I feared patients would know about Annie and bring up a loss I wasn't ready to discuss.

Overcome with fatigue, I fell asleep in the recliner early that evening, only to awaken to the sound of the front door opening. It was Annie, coming in from work. I smiled, relieved to see her. But then I actually woke up and realized I'd been dreaming. Funny how certain stages of sleep set your mind loose to work in ways that are never allowed when you're fully awake and coherent. Hope turned to despair as I realized Annie would never walk through that door again.

It was early morning. I'd slept fairly well in the recliner overnight, at least until my dream about Annie startled me awake. I stared out the window, peppered with the first drops of the morning rain. Nearly barren trees, their gray-brown limbs rapidly dropping leaves, seemed to be giving up on life. I unfolded from the recliner and went to the kitchen to make a pot of coffee—and face another dreary day.

Later that day, feeling more rested, I was able to make some calls to patients. All of them were kind to me, either saying nothing about Annie or expressing heartfelt sympathy. It went better than I'd expected, buoying my hopes that getting back to work was the right decision. I grew more and more confident that staying busy was the answer, as whenever I stopped working, Annie's absence filled my head.

Surely, that would improve. Right?

Chapter Sixty-Four

Carrboro

I walked through the private entrance to the clinic on Monday morning, apprehensive and missing the confidence I usually possessed. Some of my concern was allayed by the warm reception everyone gave me. My nurse, Jen, beamed when she saw me and gave me a quick hug. *Is it me, or is she just relieved she can stop working for a different doctor every day?* Nurses don't like getting moved around. I had my faults, but at least Jen knew how to work around them. Any surge in confidence abated when I ran into Gus Payne.

"Wilson, you're back," he said and then guided me into an empty exam room. "Listen, it's going to be important that you keep your head in the game. Stay focused on your patients and what you're doing. We can't afford any screw-ups here, no matter the reason. Understood?"

"Understood, Gus," I said.

"Okay, then. Good talk."

What an insensitive jerk. Okay, maybe that was too harsh. After all, he had sent a nice sympathy note to me.

Karen had lightened my schedule, with most of my appointments either follow-up visits or physicals. Patients were more than gracious with their comments and seemed to understand—maybe even appreciate—my slower pace. By the end of the day, I was spent, too tired to even finish my notes efficiently. All I wanted was to close my eyes and sleep, but I thought I'd handled my schedule reasonably well.

Paul Scott, one of my partners and also a good friend, stopped me as I was about to leave. "Jack, can I see you for a minute? Let's talk in my office."

"Sure, Paul."

"Jack, I know it's been a long day for you, so I won't keep you long." He paused. "It's . . . it's just that I want you to know we're so glad to have you back. None of us can imagine what you've gone through. But all of the partners want to be sure you haven't come back too soon. How'd it go today?"

"I appreciate that, Paul. I really do. Actually, today was a good day. It got me out of the apartment and took my mind off of Annie. I'll be fine, I promise. But I have to admit I was caught off-guard by my conversation with Gus. He told me—"

"Yeah, I overheard most of it," Paul said. "Don't let him get under your skin. That's just Gus being Gus. There's a reason he . . . oh, never mind. Just remember, Jack, if you ever need to talk, I'm here for you, as are all the other partners—even Gus."

My cell interrupted my thoughts as I drove home. Pete.

"Hey, Jack. Just checking in to see how things went today."

"Okay, I think. No real problems. Just a little tired."

"Want to meet for dinner?"

"No, but thanks, buddy. I'm really beat. I think I'll go home, throw something together for dinner, and go over tomorrow's patients before I go to bed."

"No worries, bro. I'm just glad you had a good day. Call me if you need anything or just want to hang out."

"Will do." My guy Pete.

Chapter Sixty-Five

Chapel Hill

W hatever confidence I gained from a fairly successful first day back at work, I lost when I got home and entered the apartment. Annie's absence was palpable, immediately deflating my spirit.

I grabbed something to eat, tackled the day's notes, and checked my in-basket one final time before shutting down for the night. I was spent, in every sense of the word. When pleasure reading didn't help, I went to bed.

The last thing I thought about before falling asleep and the first thing on my mind every morning was Annie. Her loss cut deeper than I could have ever imagined. I couldn't get her off my mind, but why should that be a surprise? To remember someone we've lost is to honor that person, I told myself. But a balance would need to be achieved so I could continue to function, both at work and personally. I wasn't sure I could do that.

The rest of that first week, and the weeks that followed, went pretty much the same, each day's routine a replay of the preceding one. The apartment grew smaller each day, with the walls closing in and the ceiling hanging over me like a cloud of doom. Somehow, I got through it, claustrophobic though it was. Nothing came easily, but I told myself things would get better if I just persisted.

During one weekend at home, I decided to go through Annie's things. At some point, I had to do something with all of her clothes and personal items. One look in her closet overwhelmed me with the enormity of the task—not because she had a closet full of clothes, but because many of them served as painful reminders: her nurse's uniform, her jogging clothes, her nice dresses she'd often wear when we went to a fancier restaurant, and her dress casual church clothes. I finally closed the doors, accomplishing nothing. I made a futile attempt to look through the items in her chest of drawers. Walking over to the bedside table, I opened the single drawer where she kept her private collection of poetry. As I lifted the notebook out of the drawer, beneath it I saw a simple white envelope with *Jack* written on it. Inside was a note, which read as follows:

My dearest Jack,

If you're reading this, sweetie, it means I'm gone, and what I feared the most and tried to deny was confirmed. We disagreed on my health issues, even though I understood your insistence that I see my doctor. As a nurse, I knew you were right, but as a wife and a daughter who had just dealt with her mother's death, I couldn't face the possibility something could be wrong with me. A diagnosis would have forced me to make decisions regarding treatment and confront my own mortality. I wasn't emotionally ready to do either, so I chose denial, explaining away my symptoms as representative of a much simpler cause. I was hopeful but quite wrong to choose the course I did.

Not that long ago, Jack, we were newly in love and had the world by its tail, with plans to live happily forever. Remember how we let ourselves dream about a house and family? Somehow, both of us let our plans play second fiddle to the busyness in our work lives. Oh, I knew from your reputation and from what I'd witnessed first-hand that I would always take a back seat to your career. I do not begrudge you for that, as I know your dedication is what makes you the doctor you are. Unfortunately, I also let myself get too busy, perhaps trying to fill my time so as not to miss you as much. We both made mistakes. While I can never atone for mine, I trust you will learn from yours and that your life will someday become newly balanced and joyful.

You know I have always kept my poetry private. Embarrassed by its amateurish quality, I chose to keep it to myself. You have my permission to go through my notebooks and read my work if that's something you want to do. I've included in this note my last poem, written in an attempt to put into words what I failed to express to you verbally.

"What Might Have Been"

Our paths crossed just the other day,
you didn't see me from so far away.
But memories flashed and thoughts replayed,
from times we had back in the day.
What we know now, had we known then,

we could have lived what might have been.
But we were young and didn't know
where life would lead, or we would go.

Our lives diverged, we drifted apart,
our busyness trumping matters of the heart.
Time seemed forever, no rush was needed
until it was too late, our time exceeded.
Too late to save what we thought then
was our chance to enjoy what might have been.

I felt so alone but made my way,
Desperately hoping for that day
When our lives would intersect and again be joined,
taking back our time so sadly purloined.

Yet that day never came, you never returned,
promises not kept, bridges burned.
Now, I must be content to dream my dreams
and see you in my imaginary schemes.
And to think until I see you, I know not when,
those four sad words "what might have been."

Jack, you are an amazing doctor and a loving, kind person. Honor my memory by moving on. Find contentment in your work and joy in your life. After all, we both know better than most that life is precious, and we aren't even promised tomorrow, so live it to the fullest. Please do that for me.
  All my love,
  Annie

Tears fell from my eyes to Annie's note, blurring both my vision and her words. I was devastated by the melancholic resignation in Annie's voice, and once again, I felt a pain deep in my core over not just her absence, but our shared loss of opportunity. Beyond that, I could process it no further. Could I ever rise to meet her challenge to me? As I folded the letter and returned it to its envelope, I suspected I'd never be the man Annie always thought I could be.

I had to get out of the apartment. With no route or plan in mind, I got in the car and just drove, hoping my rapid breathing would not trigger dizziness. I noticed a non-descript white stucco building not far from home, the cross rising from the roof the only evidence it was some kind of church. I felt compelled to pull into the empty lot and park. I hung my head, as my mind flashed back to Annie's church, the funeral, her friends' expressions of sympathy, and the minister's words. *Could God be real?* If He was, how could an all-powerful, ethereal being let such an awful thing happen to Annie? If believing in God meant accepting Annie's death as His will, I wanted no part of it. But God or no God, she was gone. We'd never discussed her faith in the detail it deserved, even though she tried. Such a discussion might have enlightened me. That possibility was now gone, and I was in an existential crisis from which I saw no escape.

Chapter Sixty-Six

Late October 2018

As winter approached, the days shortened and, more often than not, were cloudy and gloomy, mirroring my temperament. At work, I maintained the nicest front I could muster, trying to seem as upbeat as I could. I knew it wasn't the old Jack Wilson. As the weeks wore on, patients either no longer commented on Annie or perhaps didn't even know my story. I guess we all live with grief, but the world moves on, even if we don't. It was fine by me, as the last thing I needed were reminders of her absence. My ability to focus on patients and their problems grew more strained. I knew that dwelling on Annie's loss was unhealthy, but I didn't know how to stop it. I considered getting professional help but then decided against it. Was I just like Annie all those times she argued she didn't need to see a doctor? *Why do healthcare professionals ignore their own health?* I wasn't much more functional at home, often making just a token effort to eat something. My dress shirts looked baggy, and I found myself frequently hitching up my pants.

Leaving work one evening, I decided to go to the nearby diner.

"Well, hi there, stranger!"

"Hi, Holly. It's been a while," I said, with a weak smile.

She tried to make small talk, but I just wasn't in the mood. I avoided eye contact with her—and everyone else in the diner. *Coming here was a mistake, Wilson. No more trips to the diner.* No use in wasting money on food I didn't want. I threw a twenty on the table and left the diner abruptly.

Most nights, I sat and thought or, more accurately, obsessed over Annie's loss. Sometimes, I would open Annie's letter and read it again, often nodding off as

216

the day's fatigue set in. On one lonely night, I was startled by my phone's chirp. It was Pete.

> call me when you're free

Reluctantly, I dialed his number.

"Hey, Jack. Haven't heard from you lately. How're you doing?"

"Okay. You know, just busy at work and everything."

"Define *everything*," he said.

Even in my fugue state, Pete's well-established persistence annoyed me, though I knew he meant well.

"Really just work, I guess. Keeps me busy."

"You know what they say about all work and no play. Why don't we get together? There's an art exhibit on campus this week. I'd love for you to go with me so I can expose you to some culture. It would be good for you to get out of the house for something other than work. And hey, you never know: you might even enjoy the exhibit."

"I don't know. Thanks, but maybe next time. Once I get home from work, I like to just stay here and rest."

"No worries. I understand. How 'bout meeting for breakfast, then? We could do it Saturday morning if you're free."

Not feeling I could keep putting him off, I consented.

"Okay then, it's a date, bro. Let's meet at the Grind. I'm looking forward to seeing you. It's been weeks."

"Sounds good." I lied, but sometimes, it seems like the best option. "See you then, and thanks for the call. You're a good friend." I did mean that part.

"Jack!" Pete greeted me, as I walked into the Grind. "Good to see you, bro."

"Hey, Pete," I offered as we hugged. I draped my jacket and scarf over an empty chair.

"We've got a carafe of coffee and the usual coming soon—should shake the chill off. Figured I'd order for both of us since I got here a little early."

Halfway through breakfast, Pete stared at me with eyes narrowed. "Jack, I'm gonna level with you. I'm worried. Your clothes are hanging off of you; you've got dark circles under your eyes . . . I mean, I get it. Losing Annie was hard even for me, so I can't fathom what it was like for you. Now, level with me—how are things really going at the office?"

Pete always could read me like a book. "I don't know. I'm just down. Not much energy and no enthusiasm for doing anything more than just enough to get by. I'm not sleeping or eating properly, work's busier, and the days are getting shorter. It's dark when I go to work and dark again when I get home in the evening. I don't even see much sunlight when I look out of my office window. Seems like the sun has taken the season off."

"Dude, you've got to get out some. You can't just work, go home, mope around, go to bed, and then do it all again the next day. How 'bout if you, Mary, and I go out for dinner soon?"

"I don't know. I don't like the feeling of being the odd man out."

"The last thing you'd be is the odd man out. I consider you family, dude. But I could ask Mary to bring along a friend, if that would help."

I felt my face heating up. Setting my coffee down and fixing my eyes on him and moving closer, I whispered, "That's out of the question. The last thing I'm interested in or need is a new relationship. Thanks, but no thanks."

"Maybe relationships are exactly what you need, Jack."

The conversation was upsetting me. I wanted to ask him why he wasn't the doctor if he was so smart about such things. *A psychiatrist, maybe?* Luckily, I held my tongue. Pete dropped the subject, and there wasn't much else said as we worked on our breakfast.

Wilson, you over-reacted. Pete's your best friend. What's wrong with you?

I reached out and grabbed Pete's forearm. "I snapped, buddy. I'm sorry. I know you're trying to help. I just need to go home, Pete."

He smiled. "It's fine, Jack. I totally understand."

"Thanks. Good to see you," I said as I got up and headed for the register. "I'll cover the check."

"Okay, Jack. Thanks. But please think about what we discussed this morning, and don't be a stranger."

"Sure thing, Pete." Another lie.

Chapter Sixty-Seven

Carrboro

The Post-it was prominently displayed on my desk. *A Mrs. Mason called. She said you'd know who she is and asked for you to call her back.* A phone number was penciled in at the bottom.

I put off the request all day, convincing myself I was too busy to take time for a personal call. After seeing my slate of patients, I was sitting in my office, finishing my notes. The day was already darkening outside my office window as the setting sun hid behind the large cloud cover. Once again, the weather seemed to match my mood. After exhausting all of my mental excuses, I dialed the number.

"Hello, Mrs. Mason. This is Jack Wilson."

"Dr. Wilson! Well, knock me over with a feather! I wasn't sure you'd holler back at me. I'm sure you're busier than a church fan on an August Sunday, so thanks for calling."

"Of course. How have you been?"

"Oh, the usual, you know. But that's not why I'm calling. This is so hard for me, Dr. Wilson, so bear with me, please. I am so sorry about Annie. I loved that girl—as my nurse but also as a person—a friend, really. She had the soul of an angel, bless her heart. I used to sing your praises to her, too, having no idea that the two of you were married. Now, I kind of feel foolish."

"No, please. Nothing foolish about it. You had no way to know. Annie kept her maiden name at work to keep from blurring the lines or risk making patients uncomfortable. And, I agree, she was a wonderful person."

"Well, we're rockin' on the same back porch on that one, Doc."

For the first time in weeks, I felt a smile crease my face.

"Anything new with you, Mrs. Mason, if I may ask?"

"Well, I'm still here, right? Can't complain about that or I would, but no one would understand. Wouldn't mind being with my Jimmy again, you know. I'm still in and out of the hospital. You know the drill. But I'll tell you one thing—I haven't found another Dr. Wilson. You can hang your hat on that!"

"You're much too kind, but thank you."

"Doc, if you don't mind me asking, what happened to Annie? Was she in an accident or something? Don't mean to be nosey, but I just loved that girl so much. No one at the hospital would tell me anything—that Hippo thing, you know."

"HIPPA," I corrected her, another smile appearing. "Well, a blood vessel in her brain had a weak spot, and it ruptured. That caused pressure on her brain, and by the time we got her to the hospital, it was too late. She never woke up."

"Oh, Lord have mercy. I am so sorry. I don't mean to make you re-live the whole thing. I remember how hard it was to lose my Jimmy, but he was an older man. Annie was so young! You'd have thought she would live forever."

"It's okay, Mrs. Mason. I re-live it every day."

"Well, I can tell you that's normal, or at least it was for me—for a long time too. People always goin' on about *closure*. That's just a word people who haven't been through something like this use to make *themselves* feel better. There's never closure when you lose your life partner. I'll swear to that on a stack of Bibles, that's for sure. I'm just a simple-minded country gal, but the way I see it, we honor those we love by never forgetting them once they're gone. Leastways, that's what I think."

"You may be a country gal, but there's nothing simple-minded about you. Thank you for those words and for your sweet thoughts about Annie, Mrs. Mason. They mean a lot."

"'Course it helps to know my Jimmy—and Annie, for sure—are in a better place and completely healed. Right?"

I didn't respond.

"Well, that's what I believe. But another thing, Doc, and not to put you on the spot or nothin', but I know your practice is pretty close by. Any chance I could leave the clinic and start seeing you again?"

"I'm flattered, Mrs. Mason, and there's nothing I'd like more than to have you back as a patient, but the practice has policies for when it's open to new patients, and as the new kid on the block, so to speak, I really can't override them. It's probably better for you to stay at the clinic. Easier to coordinate your care, especially when you have to be admitted."

"I was 'fraid you'd say something like that."

I could hear the disappointment in her voice. *I wish I could tell her it's all Gus Payne's fault. His policy, not mine.*

"But I get it. I sure do. Well, I've kept you long enough, Dr. Wilson. Thank you for your time and for all you did for me when you were at the hospital. And again, I'm so sorry about Miss Annie."

I could tell I'd let her down. I couldn't control who the practice does or doesn't accept as new patients, I rationalized. I thought about what Mrs. Mason had said. Maybe I wasn't crazy or so abnormal to be dwelling on Annie like I was. Maybe I'd find that place for her in my head where I would remember her every day, but the memories wouldn't dominate my thinking. I felt a nudge of encouragement—at least until the next morning.

Chapter Sixty-Eight

"**N**o way, Wilson. We're not opening *that* flood gate."

After a night of tossing and turning, I'd decided to confront Gus Payne regarding the office policy on new patients and the possibility of an exception. It did not go well.

"You've got to understand, this woman was one of my favorite patients—one of Annie's too, for that matter. She's a fighter and has been all her life. She probably doesn't have a lot of time left, and I thought it would be nice to have her under my care rather than in the clinic system."

"You know our policy. We made that clear when you joined us. If we let one clinic patient leave the system and join our practice, word will get out and there'll be no end to it. We couldn't handle all that extra work, even if we wanted to. There'd be no room for our privately insured patients."

I stared at Payne with my arms crossed. "Honestly, I'm not really concerned about how patients are insured. I just want to do what's right for this lady."

"Then do what's best for her—leave her in the university system's care, where she's been all along. I told you things are different here—the patient clientele and the way we practice. Enough said. I've got patients to see."

He walked away before I could respond. I was frustrated and angry. Apparently, I let it show.

The day's first patient asked me, "Doc, is there something wrong with your neck? You're constantly rubbing it."

"Sorry. Just a little crick, I guess."

"Something else, Doc, if you don't mind me asking. Are you okay? I mean, I heard about your wife, and I can't imagine what it must be like to go through that, but you just don't seem yourself."

I explained I just wasn't quite back to full speed. I needed more time to deal with my loss and get over it.

"Well, with all due respect, I don't think you'll ever get over it, Dr. Wilson. When my mom lost my dad, it almost ruined her. She never was the same again. She gave up her hobbies, quit seeing her friends, and just existed—like, almost in a vacuum. It was awful. Now, I'm not saying that will happen to you, but maybe you ought to find a hobby, take a long vacation, or do something to get your mind off things. But, listen to me . . . giving my doctor advice." He shook his head and smiled.

"No, I appreciate your honest concern," I said. "I just heard something similar from a former patient of mine. Guess there's a lot of truth to it, huh?"

"What do I know, Doc? If I was so smart, *I'd* be the doctor, right?" He laughed. "You take care of yourself. I want you around for a long time. It's not easy finding young, dedicated doctors these days."

The fact that people could see right through my veil unnerved me. It was my job to worry about my patients, not theirs to worry about me. If they suspected I wasn't at full strength mentally, they'd lose faith in my ability to provide their care. I had my share of shortcomings, but I'd never lacked for confidence in the care I provided for people. Maybe that confidence was undeserved.

———

It was hard getting used to leaving work at dusk. Crossing the parking lot, I hunched my shoulders and jammed my hands into my coat pockets, each step marked by the crunch of leaves underfoot. I was sure the day couldn't get any worse until my cell rang. Mary's number. Pete must have misplaced his phone again.

"Hi, Pete. Lose your phone?"

"No, Jack. It's Mary. I'm calling about Pete." Her voice trembled.

"Mary, what's going on?"

"Pete's been hurt."

"Pete? Hurt?"

"It all happened so fast. We were out for a bike ride, on a road just off Franklin Street. I was ahead of Pete when I heard a scream and a crash. I looked back to see Pete lying on the side of the road with his bike on top of him. I don't know what happened, but he was knocked unconscious. Oh my word, it's terrible," she said, her voice shaky but rising.

"Where are you now, Mary?"

"We're at the hospital. This was my first chance to call you. He went from the Emergency Room to Radiology and then straight to a special place, the trauma something—"

"The Trauma ICU."

"Yes, I think that's right. Oh, Jack, I don't know what's going on. I can't even think straight, and no one has told me anything yet."

"They'll tell you as soon as they know something, I'm sure. Listen, wait right there. I'm on my way," I said.

This was my first trip back to the hospital since losing Annie. Using my physician's badge, I parked in the doctors' lot and cleared security. As I walked into the hospital, it hit me. What had been my sanctuary for all those years of med school and residency was now more like a house of horrors. Medical personnel scurrying about, machines beeping, and the familiar sterile odor sent my thoughts spinning back to Annie's ordeal. Exiting the elevator on the ICU wing, I had to walk past the Neuro unit to get to Trauma. I wanted to turn and walk away—to just escape—but I knew I had to be there for my friends. I found Mary in the waiting room.

Mary jumped up and gave me a hug and then collapsed into my arms, sobbing. "Jack, I still don't know anything, and I haven't even been allowed to see Pete."

I left her to go to the nurses' station, where I explained the situation to a nurse. She assured me she'd get one of the trauma residents out to us as quickly as possible.

As I was assuring Mary we'd know something soon, one of the physicians came out to speak to us. I recognized him from my residency days when he was completing his general surgery training.

"I'm Mark Miller, one of the trauma fellows. Jack Wilson, right?"

"That's right, Mark. Pete's my best friend, and this is Mary, his fiancée. Can you update us on his condition?"

"Good news, actually. The scans show no broken bones or serious organ damage, as far as we can tell. His right kidney is bruised, probably from the way he landed, as he's got some nasty abrasions and bruises on his right flank. His urine is bloody, but that's to be expected. Fortunately, the head CT is normal. Thank goodness for bike helmets. He's lightly sedated, just to make him comfortable."

"So . . . are you saying he's going to be . . . okay?" Mary said.

"I think he's going to be just fine—very sore, of course, but just fine," he added, with a reassuring smile.

"Can I—we—see him?" She turned to me, her eyes pleading. "Please, go with me, Jack. I can't go into that room alone."

"Of course, you can see him. Follow me," Dr. Miller said.

I was not prepared for the effect seeing Pete would have on me. Seeing him lying there and under sedation sent me reeling back to Annie. I was reliving a horrible nightmare. As Mary gently grasped Pete's forearm, I felt dizzy, and my hands began to tingle. Anxiety. Hyperventilation. I grabbed the footboard of his bed to avoid falling. I knew I had to get out of that room.

"Mary, I'm sorry, but I can't stay in here. I'm lightheaded and nauseated. I need some air."

"Jack, you look terrible," she said. "Go. Go get some fresh air. Now that I've seen Pete and I know he's going to be okay, I'll be fine."

I took the elevator to the first floor and exited as quickly as possible. Stepping outside, the jolt of cold night air steadied my breathing and calmed me.

Entering my apartment, I collapsed in the first chair I reached. Although I was feeling better physically, emotionally I was a mess. I had failed my best friends. When Mary most needed me, I walked out on her. After all he had done for me throughout Annie's ordeal, Pete would wake up, and I wouldn't be there. *What's wrong with you, Wilson?*

I was falling apart, with each passing day seemingly more difficult to navigate than the prior one. My abject failure to be the friend Pete and Mary deserved during a crisis was the last straw. I'd let Annie down, and now, I'd let my friends down too. And medicine was no longer the joy it always had been in my life. Maybe I should toss in the proverbial towel and give up—on my career *and* on life.

Chapter Sixty-Nine

Pete recovered quickly. He was in the hospital for two days, long enough for him to demonstrate the ability to eat and drink normally and for the blood in his urine to clear. The day after his accident, I called Mary, who rejected any notion of me failing to be there for them. Pete got on the phone, sounding tired, but otherwise the same old Pete. I apologized for not being there for him, but anxiety had forced me to walk out—something I hadn't planned on.

"Understandable," he said. "What'd you expect, Jack, when you came into the hospital unit like that for the first time since Annie was here? Once again, bro, you just demand too much of yourself. Mary and I are both grateful that you rushed to the hospital when she needed you."

He was being gracious, but I wasn't buying it. "Well, just take it easy, and I'll see you after you get home," I said. I wouldn't try visiting again.

"Sounds good. Can't wait to see you. I've got some beautiful bruises I know you're going to love and a great story about what can happen to a bike when it hits a rut filled with loose gravel!"

Wilson, you really don't deserve such a good friend.

I didn't visit. I called but said I was busy at work, explaining that with Thanksgiving and Christmas approaching and the predictable winter illnesses kicking in, the patient load nearly overwhelmed me each day. The latter was true, but I knew it was just an excuse. Once again, I'd let down my two best friends. I knew they wouldn't hold a grudge, but could I forgive myself?

In retrospect, I shouldn't have gone to work that day. My practice had devolved into drudgery. I forced myself to go in and, at the end of the day, to go home to an empty, joyless existence. I was always relieved to get home, where I could isolate myself from other people, even though the apartment, the couch, the bed we'd shared, and all the pictures of Annie and me were painful reminders of her absence. My life had become a continuous loop of forced effort, just trying to get through patient visits without caring about anything else. My patients' problems paled in comparison to what I was going through. That day—*the* day—went very badly.

"Hey, Jack. Good to see you." Joe was not just a patient but a friend from my undergrad days.

"Morning, Joe. Looks like you're here for a follow-up visit, right? That is unless something's wrong. You look worried, my friend."

"You tell me. Honestly, I've been concerned about my lab result. Figured it couldn't be good if you waited until I was here to discuss it."

"Your PSA? It was great—completely normal. My nurse, Jen, did call you with the result, right?"

"No one called me. I've been worried sick that, with my symptoms and then no news from you, it was going to be cancer. Remember, I told you my dad died of prostate cancer?"

"I'm so sorry. You should have been called, and I apologize you weren't. That's on me, Joe."

"No problem. Stuff happens. Anyway, now that I know it's normal, I'm more relieved than anything else."

The rest of the visit went well, but I could hardly contain my dismay that a patient didn't receive notice of a lab result and, because of that, worried unnecessarily. That sometimes happened in the residency clinic, but it shouldn't happen in a small private practice. I found Jen at the nurses' station.

"I need to see you, Jen."

"Yes, sir, Dr. Wilson. What is it?"

"Mr. Saunders—the patient who just left—had a normal PSA level but never got a call. He's been worried sick."

"Oh! I'm sorry. Somehow, it must've slipped through the cracks."

"Being sorry doesn't help, Jen—and doesn't change what he went through waiting on a call. Besides, we don't let things 'slip through the cracks,' as you put it."

"Again, it was my mistake. I won't let it happen again, Dr. Wilson."

"No, it won't happen again or, if it does, I'll let you go, Jen. I can't work with someone who I can't trust to do her job. There are plenty of medical assistants looking for work. You can be easily replaced." I noticed tears welling into her eyes. *I think she gets my message.*

"Of course, Dr. Wilson. If there's nothing else, I'll get your next patient roomed." She dabbed at her eyes and stiffened her back as she walked away.

As I turned to go back to my office, I passed one of the other assistants, who looked away from me and shook her head.

The rest of the day went okay, at least until late afternoon. I noticed two patients were booked for the same appointment time. I made it a practice to never double-book patients.

I went to the front desk, confronting my scheduler, sitting with other clerical staff and in full view of patients in the waiting room. "What's going on with my schedule, Lindsay? Why am I double-booked?"

"I was going to come and explain that to you or to Jen, but I got busy. Dr. Payne's having a terrible afternoon, and he asked me to move one of his patients to another provider's schedule."

"Lindsay, you know better than that. I don't care if it was Dr. Payne or Hippocrates who asked, you work for me, and I count on you to control my schedule . . . or at least I thought I did."

"I'm sorry, Dr. Wilson. I should have asked," she said, her voice trembling.

"Just don't ever do that again. And I mean it," I said as I turned and stormed back to my work area.

Mercifully, the day's schedule ended with no more snafus. I felt staff members' eyes on me and noticed they went out of their way to give me space. It was while I was charting, exhausted and half-asleep, that I heard Gus Payne's booming voice.

"Wilson. Got a minute?"

Stunned by the ultimatum Payne gave me, I drove home, my grip on the steering wheel as tight as the strap muscles in my neck. I'd almost lost my job, and that possibility still existed if I didn't take some time off and get my "head straight," as Payne had put it. Once home, and too tense to do anything else, I went for a run. It was cold and dark, but I didn't care. I'd run the streets so often, I could do it in my sleep. As I ran, my thoughts became more organized. Much as I hated to admit it, the old grouch might be right. After all, he'd been at this a lot longer than I. Clearly, I hadn't been myself at work, and today, it culminated with me treating two staff members badly, with ugly comments made in front of their co-workers. I blew it; I let my emotions get the best of me, and I'd acted unprofessionally. Yeah, I had my reasons, but the line between my personal life and the office had blurred. *Unacceptable, Wilson.* I knew better. The old Jack would have never let that happen. Maybe I did need to take some time off and figure things out. I didn't want to, but the other options were far less desirable. I didn't like Payne, but he was the boss, and I had to comply.

I needed to get away. I debated hot versus cold. Maybe a trip to the Caribbean, or should I try something closer and more seasonable? Maybe West Virginia's Greenbrier? No. Both places seemed too silly and too expensive for someone traveling alone, and alone is what I wanted. By the time I got home, I had an idea. Still longing to put my life in reverse and go back in time, I thought about the plans Annie and I had made to go to Asheville for the holidays. Maybe that was the answer. I couldn't be with Annie, but I could try to fulfill our plans. I needed to call Pete.

"Dude! What's up?"

"Just checking in. How're you doing?"

"Things are going well in school. I'm loving it! Looking forward to some time off at Christmas."

"Yeah, I know you're headed home for the holidays, and we'd talked about all going to the Biltmore. Of course, everything changed when Annie died. I've decided to go alone—you know, just to relax and think things over. Kind of a re-set." No way could I tell Pete it would be a forced vacation.

"Great idea, bro."

"Yeah, I think being in Asheville will somehow make me feel closer to Annie, and the change in scenery can't hurt, either. I'm kind of in a rut."

"Sounds good. Hope it's peaceful for you."

As I clicked off the call, I was convinced I'd made the right decision. I needed something to look forward to, even if it was with mixed and uncertain emotions.

Chapter Seventy

December 2018
Asheville

I packed the warmest clothes I owned and made a pot of coffee, filling my thermos for the trip. After an awkward month at work, I was actually looking forward to some time away from the office, and I could tell the staff was glad to see me go. I figured they wouldn't forget my behavior, but I hoped I could return in a better frame of mind—the Dr. Wilson they knew.

As I traveled across the state, bare trees below gloomy skies testified to winter's stark nature, the sun partially hidden in a shroud of cloud cover as it slowly surrendered to the horizon ahead of me. I wondered if my winter of discontent would ever end. *Maybe the Caribbean would have been better.* I held out hope that the coming spring season, dressed in warm sunshine, blooming flowers, and the leafing out of the trees, would brighten my mood. That notion seemed a long way off, like a distant mirage for a lost traveler crawling over sunbaked, parched earth. Preoccupied as I was by my thoughts and memories, I arrived in the town Annie and I loved so much. It all seemed different now. Was it me, or was it Annie's absence? Nothing seemed as inviting or appealing now, as it had been when we were here together. The extraordinary now seemed mundane. Hopelessly romantic then, now I just felt desperately lost.

I checked into a small lodge near the Biltmore Village District that allowed for walking access to the local breweries, restaurants, and the eclectic array of artisans' shops. What had seemed like a good idea earlier had no appeal now. *Give it time, Wilson.*

Once inside my hotel room, I collapsed on the bed, not sure of what to do or if I would even do anything. The all-powerful inertia of depression was winning the battle for my soul, rendering me incapable of entertaining any notion of enjoyment. Maybe a nap would help. Sleep came stubbornly and proved fitful. Fully awake, I gave up. I showered, dressed, and willed myself to leave the room, convinced that I must eat, even if it was a forced effort.

Spotting a pizza joint close by, I walked across the street and went in. The aroma of pepperoni and cheddar saturated the air, thick with Christmas music blaring from wall-mounted speakers. The standard red and white checkered tablecloths rested on maple tables with matching chairs, currently hardly occupied. An artificial Christmas tree with blinking multi-colored lights sat on a table by the cash register. A pizza joint—the old standby for Pete and me. I almost smiled.

"Give me a couple of slices with cheese and onions and a Coke Zero, please," I said to the waiter, then I took a seat. He was a freckle-faced kid who couldn't have been out of high school.

"Two slices and a Coke Zero coming right up!" My mood was no match for his cheerfulness. I picked at my food, occasionally sipping my drink. Fortunately, there was no one at the tables closest to mine, and once again, I could lose myself in my thoughts without fear of interruption. Eating enough just to dull my hunger pangs, I paid the bill and donned my coat and stocking hat, hoping to stave off some of the bitter cold outside. I held on tightly as the wind grabbed the exit door, with noticeably colder temperatures now that the gray, cloudy day had surrendered to nighttime. I scrunched my shoulders against my neck, shoved my hands into my pants pockets, and returned to my room. Maybe the promise of sunshine the following day would lift my mood. Maybe I'd even go for a run. Was I being too optimistic?

I slumped into a chair, my mind ruminating through thoughts, doubts, and memories. Was it a bad idea to come here? I thought this area would help me rediscover a modicum of the joy I'd lost, but that didn't seem to be in the cards. I drifted off, waking frequently. Whenever awake, I thought back to the good times we'd experienced in this grand old southern town—a town that now assumed an alternative personality not nearly as hospitable as previously. I thought of times spent with Annie on the deck of Pete's beach house, watching the waves rhythmically slapping the wet, firm sand of the beach and then disappearing into sand much drier and accommodating. Was life like that? Do we simply slip from the reach of all that we use to define our lives, sinking out of sight, like water into sand?

I accepted the inevitability of death. But the timing of it, that was a different story altogether. Why had Annie been taken from me—from all of us—so suddenly and at such a young age? She had so much to live for: her career, our marriage, and our plans for a family. *Why?* My mind went to God, a being I'd rarely thought about since the funeral.

Annie had such faith, proven and displayed in how bravely she handled her mom's death. But on what did she base her faith? Where was the fairness of it all? In my training, I'd witnessed innocent children die from accidents or horrible illnesses, while drunks and members of the local "Friday night knife and gun club," who frequented the emergency room, somehow always skirted death. Where was God in that? I'd wanted to give Annie some distance from her mom's death before talking to her about such issues, much less challenge them. Now, of course, that discussion would never occur. Had I asked and listened, maybe she could have taught me how to trust such a nebulous concept as faith in a God I couldn't feel, see, or touch.

I crawled into bed and cobbled together several hours of sleep, none of it restorative. I woke up once, the lights still on and the blinds open. A street lamp emitted just enough light to discourage mischief in the parking lot. I closed the blinds and turned off the lights, hoping the darkness would lead to sleep. It was not to be. Giving up on any notion of sleep, I sat up in bed and did something I probably should have done months earlier.

I cried.

Finally calm enough to function, I threw on some clothes and went to the lobby to get a cup of coffee. I'd left my thermos in the car, any remaining coffee likely freezing cold, if not frozen. Even though daylight wouldn't come for a few more hours, I knew sleep was hopeless. I couldn't just sit in my room, so I decided to go for a drive. The cold night air might clear my head. Maybe I'd drive down to the French Broad, back to that beautiful river where Annie and I had spent such wonderful times together.

I pulled my jacket collar high and close to my neck as I walked to my car. The engine reluctantly started, its uneven idling an indication of its displeasure with my decision to go for a drive on such a cold morning. I took Biltmore Avenue toward I-240, planning to work my way over to Riverside Drive, which paralleled the river. With just a sliver of moon peeping out from cloud cover and fog shrouding the landscape, visibility wasn't good. At least there was no other traffic at such a ridiculous hour. My mind continued to stew over Annie's fate, my current situation, and the unfairness of it all. Without properly focusing on my driving, I began to accelerate, first without realizing it, and then, when I did, without caring. *No one else is out here, including the police, I'm sure.* Speeding wouldn't be an issue. But it would.

I noticed the turbulent, dark waters of the river, blanketed in dense fog—a perfect metaphor for how I felt. I decided to turn off Riverside and cross over one of the few bridges that allowed access to the less touristy part of the city. The car skidded slightly as I made the turn onto the bridge. What I didn't see until it was too late was the black ice. *Of course, the signs warn us that bridges freeze before the rest of the road.* I pumped the brakes. The car swerved. I crashed through the low, wooden guard rail, its strength no match for a two-ton, soon-to-be oversized casket. The deafening cracking of the wood disrupted the solitude of the morning and jolted me to the realization of what was happening: an unwitnessed accident, submersion, no escape, death. My heart raced. My panic grew. I braced myself by pushing against the steering wheel.

In a split second, I'd gone from the safety of the bridge to the deadly waters of the river, my car slowly sinking from view. The car died first—no power, no noise, total darkness. I beat the window with my fists as cold water seeped through the damaged glass. My mind raced through the steps one should take when in a drowning car, but I couldn't think straight. I was distracted by the icy water filling the car and soaking my clothes. Now, the car was completely submerged. I lifted my head to stay in the shrinking air pocket as the water level rose, its icy grip of death slowly consuming me. I leaned back against the driver's door and kicked the passenger's door as hard as I could. Nothing. I was enveloped in darkness, descending to what would be my final and inglorious resting place—the river bottom.

Suddenly, a moment of clarity. Just before my life went to black, I blindly felt for my thermos on the passenger seat.

Chapter Seventy-One

The bright white light had an intensity and radiance unmatched by anything I'd ever experienced. *Where was it coming from?* I felt inadequate standing there, so I dropped to my knees. Squinting and using my hand to help me adjust to the brightness, I tried to look up, but the light overwhelmed me. Then, I heard it—the voice.

"John, my son, you are here far too early." The voice was deep and authoritative but somehow comforting.

"Where am I?"

"Where you are not yet needed. You still have much work to do."

"What happened?" I asked, my mind a confused blur. "And who are you?"

"It will all begin to make sense, and then you will remember and understand."

Slowly, my head cleared, allowing some recollection of what had happened. The crash. Drowning. Wait! *Did that mean I was in Heaven, or at least at its gate? Oh c'mon, Wilson—that's impossible. Think rationally.*

"I was driving too fast. I knew it, but I couldn't make myself slow down. The potential for an accident didn't seem to matter to me. All I wanted was to be with Annie. That's why I was in Asheville." Pausing, I then gasped at the next thought I blurted out. "Could it have been intentional? Was I trying to get to Annie?'

"That doesn't really matter, John," said the voice.

"It matters to me."

"No. What matters is what you do now. What happened and why are not as important as your understanding of what it all means for you."

"But I *don't* understand," I said feebly.

"Understanding will come, John. It takes time. Be patient with yourself."

"But what if the accident *was* intentional? What if I was attempting—"

"If it was, you must forgive yourself," the voice interrupted. "Forgiving one's self is even harder than forgiving others. You will not be judged for why it happened, John. My only concern is that you be made whole again. You must also believe no sin or act is greater than my ability to forgive you. That's called *grace*."

I was still confused. "If you are who I think you are, can we talk about Annie, please?"

"Of course. Do you have questions?"

"I have many questions . . . and doubts. My voice rose. And I'm angry—maybe at you."

"Now we're getting somewhere," the voice said patiently. "Your questions?"

"Why is life so unfair? Annie didn't deserve what happened to her. And why was I so stupid and self-centered to spend so much time at work that I lost out on time with Annie? And how could you let Annie be taken from me—from all of us she touched? She was so young and had so much to live for. She was a great nurse, a devoted daughter, and a loving wife. Everything she did was done beautifully. People felt better when they were in her presence. I loved her—like no one I'd ever loved before. We had so many plans."

"I know, but I have plans for you, too, John. My plans, however, are not necessarily your plans, and my ways are not your ways. It's in the Book. You should read and study it, by the way."

"Book? What book and which part?"

"The whole Book, John. You need it. You've been living in a very dark place. The world as you knew it changed drastically and irrevocably, making you angry and depressed. Think, John. It wasn't just Annie's death. You've had issues with loss and mistrust since you were a boy, starting with your parents' deaths. You thought you could fix that by focusing on your career, but you were mistaken."

"I realize that now," I said, "but it's too late. What I'd like is just one more day with Annie. One day to try to make it all up to her."

"I can't allow that, John, but if you're interested in being with her for eternity, I've got a plan for that."

That thought was comforting, but no way was I buying it. "But how can I believe what is written or what you're saying? How can I believe in something I can't see, touch, measure? I'm a doctor, a scientist."

"As was one of my earliest and most ardent followers. Yet, he believed. It's called faith, John. Faith is believing in what you hope for, even if you can't see it. That's also in my Book, by the way. And John, you speak of Annie being dead.

She is dead to you and your world, but she's very much alive to me. Matter of fact, she's living with me."

"This is all so hard to understand and accept." I shook my head.

"Don't be concerned, my son. Some of my most loyal followers talked about how confused and uncertain they were at times, but they believed that, someday, the truth would be revealed, as it will be for you too. You must trust me and have faith."

He spoke with quiet compassion. He called me "my son." I don't know if I'd ever been referred to that way.

A sense of peace came over me, and then I brought up one final issue. "I miss Annie so much. It's hard to be alone."

The reply was startling in its simplicity: "If you truly believe, John, you may get lonely at times, but I promise, you will never be alone. You've been given a second chance. Now, believe, have faith, and live in the light of my promises."

The voice faded. I sank back into darkness.

Chapter Seventy-Two

I opened my eyes and once again saw a bright light. Not as intense as before, to be sure, but bright nonetheless. As it was moved from one of my eyes to the other, I realized it was the beam of a penlight someone was using to check my pupils. I'd done the same to my patients a thousand times. The encounter I'd just had was crystal clear in my mind but different from anything I'd ever experienced. Now, however, I noticed familiar sights—a long, rectangular fluorescent light mounted in standard drop-ceiling, beeping monitors, a ventilator, and two people in scrubs—one likely a nurse and the other a physician, based on the snippets of conversation I could make out. My attempt to talk was futile; there was a tube in my windpipe, preventing me from making any sound. I was intubated and on a ventilator. I motioned for a whiteboard and marker sitting on the bedside table.

Where am I?

"You're in the critical care unit at Mission Hospital, Dr. Wilson," the nurse answered. "You were in a very bad accident."

"What happened?"

This time, the doctor answered. "John, I'm Nate Spaulding, one of the intensivists. You ran off a bridge and into the French Broad. It's a miracle you survived."

Events of that morning began to flash through my memory. Depression, anger, speed, black ice, spinning—all searing my brain in painful flashes of imagery.

How did I survive? And, please, call me Jack. No one on Earth calls me John.

"Yesterday morning, after the accident, your car was located in the river and pulled ashore. The driver's side window was nearly gone, with just bits of glass framing a large hole. A thermos was found in the floorboard, and from the looks of it, you apparently used it to shatter the window, allowing you to escape. That explains the cuts, scratches, and abrasions covering you from head to toe. The nearly freezing temperature of the water caused your larynx to spasm, protecting your lungs from aspirating the river water. What we call *dry drowning*, as I'm sure you know. The water temperature was so low, it probably caused instant hypothermia, slowing your body's metabolism and protecting your vital organs from the fatal effects of oxygen deprivation. At least, that's the best theory we have for why you're still with us," the doctor added, grinning. "It's a miracle, Jack. No other word for it."

But, how did I survive? How did I get out of the river?

"Another miracle. A Boy Scout troop camping nearby was out early foraging for firewood and spotted you near the shoreline. The scoutmaster knew enough about the effects of hypothermia that he left you in the water until the medics arrived. You were immediately intubated and bag-mask ventilated until they got you here. Once we got you on the ventilator, we allowed your body temperature to slowly increase. Your heart seems fine and your chest x-ray shows no signs of aspiration or any other damage. In fact, we've already begun to wean your ventilator settings as you've started to wake up. You're breathing over the vent rate nicely, and we expect to extubate you soon."

I was aware of the discomfort from the tube and couldn't wait for it to come out. My mouth and throat were parched. I was trying to wrap my head around what I'd just been told. Dry drowning, hypothermia, and almost no metabolism? I'd studied all of it but never expected to see it in my practice lifetime, let alone survive it personally. My thoughts suddenly turned back to my conversation with the voice. What I'd been told was beginning to make sense. I was starting to believe.

"That's enough information for now, Jack," the doctor said, interrupting my thoughts. He glanced at the ventilator and then looked back at me. "We're going to let you rest, but we'll keep dialing down the settings as long as your respiratory gases continue to look good. When we're ready to pull the tube, we'll wake you up."

As promised, when I awoke the next time, the respiratory therapist and nurse were at my bedside, preparing to extubate me. The doctor came back into my cubicle to let me know I was stable, my blood gas numbers were good, and they were ready to proceed.

He warned me to expect some discomfort, but only momentarily. Once the tube was out, I'd realize how thirsty I was. "We'll give you a sip of water just to see how you do, but go slowly, please. We don't want you choking on water or aspirating now, especially since you managed to avoid that in the river." He chuckled.

I already knew how thirsty I was—thirstier than after a long run on a hot, humid day. Once extubated, and after a few sips of water, I said somewhat feebly, "Thank you, all . . . for everything."

"It's our pleasure," Dr. Spaulding said. "Now, we'll give you supplemental oxygen by nasal cannula and watch you here overnight, just to make sure your lungs remain stable. I don't anticipate any problems, but you've been through a lot, and a more conservative approach is warranted. Just try to rest. First, though, there's someone who wants to see you."

"Hey, bro. You've had quite a day or two," Pete said, smiling as he entered the cubicle. "How're you feeling?"

"You're here? Thank you! Lucky, buddy—I feel very lucky to be alive, that is. But how did you know I was here?"

He explained how he saw the television coverage of my accident and the miraculous recovery effort. When he saw the video of my car, he knew it had to be me. "I called your cell, but it was out of order—no big surprise after being submerged in freezing water!" He laughed. "I contacted the hospital and was connected to someone in this unit. She explained the HIPPA regs, but after a little pleading, she told me you were awake but unable to take a call. Of course, I immediately drove out here."

"Pete, you're unbelievable. I haven't been the best—"

"Jack, please stop. Let's not get into that right now. There's no need for you to apologize. You need some rest, and your nurse told me I could only stay a few minutes. I'm leaving, but I'll be out in the family waiting room. I'm not going anywhere until we can leave this place together." Then, he winked and added, "But make it fast. You know hospitals are out of my lane, dude. I'm more of an artsy guy, and the art in this place is just awful."

Even though it hurt my throat, I couldn't keep from laughing. *I'm blessed to have Pete as a friend* was my last thought before I drifted off to sleep.

"And who said coffee's bad for you?" Pete said after I recounted the details of my escape from the sinking car. Classic Pete, spoken in a light-hearted moment—something I'd missed since Annie's death.

I was now in a private room. Sunlight filtered through the miniblinds and reflected off of the mountain print on the wall, brightening the traditional, drab hospital décor.

"Jack, you seem different," Pete said.

"Different? What do you mean?"

"The way you're acting. Lighter and, you know, happier."

I quickly weighed the merits of telling Pete about my encounter with the voice. For someone who hadn't experienced it, the story might seem too unconventional to understand—even for a believer like Pete. I was afraid people would think I was delusional. But Pete had noticed a difference in me, and for that, I was grateful.

"Well, by all rights I should be dead," I explained. "I realize how fortunate I am, Pete, and my attitude about life needs some adjustment."

"Meaning?"

"Pete, you know how much I loved Annie, and I know you and Mary loved her too. After we lost her, I dwelled on that loss, to the point that it became very unhealthy for me. I went through the workday like a robot, just trying to get to the last name on my schedule. You, of all people, know I let my friendships suffer. I turned inward, to a very dark place, and didn't want any company there—or at least, that's the way I see it now. I was so focused on Annie that I lost all perspective."

"But like you said, you loved her."

"More than anything," I said, "And I always will. That will never change, but to lose someone and dwell on it to such a degree that it's unhealthy does me no good. In fact, to some extent, it dishonors the person I so desperately miss. Now, I see the best way I can pay tribute to Annie's life is to live *my* life to the fullest—in the same way she would have lived. That doesn't change her absence—that profound void in my life—or how much I'll always love her, but it does challenge me to channel that loss into something positive, something she would have been proud of." My mind flashed back to her letter.

"But this change—it's all happened so fast, Jack."

"I guess you could say a light turned on for me, Pete. I just feel like I've been given the gift of a second chance at life, and it's time for me to seize it."

"Geez, bro. No disrespect intended, but it sounds like you had a 'come to Jesus' moment."

I could only smile.

"Anyway," he continued, "it's great to have you back, both physically and emotionally."

I told him how much it meant to me for him to be there when I work up, and how it showed me the importance of friendships. "I can't tell you how much I appreciate it."

"Well, dude, I figured you'd need a ride home," he said, with a wink and a smile, as tears formed in my eyes and fell to the bedsheet.

Chapter Seventy-Three

Late December 2018
Chapel Hill

O nce home, I had several days to recuperate before going back to work. I needed time to recover, but I was anxious to get on with my life. I'd lost so much time just existing after Annie died and wanted to make up for it. On some leisurely walks through my neighborhood, I saw and greeted many of my neighbors whom I either hadn't seen or maybe hadn't noticed for quite some time. It was great to be outdoors, and the exertion helped clear my head. The sun burned high in the cloudless, blue skies but did little to warm the invigorating chill in the air. I didn't mind.

On my second night home, Pete and Mary invited me to meet them for dinner at a local restaurant. They probably knew how important it was for me to eat something not heated in a microwave.

"Jack, it's so good to see you," Mary said, giving me a hug. "And thrilled you're okay."

"Thanks, Mary, and thanks for sharing Pete with me while I was in the hospital. It would have been pretty lonely if I'd been there without a familiar face."

"I was happy he could get away to be with you, and there was no way I could have stopped him, even if I'd wanted to. You know Pete."

"Hey, guys, I'm sitting here, you know!" he said. "Any plans for returning to work, Jack?"

"Going back next Monday."

"Dude, you've just been through quite an ordeal. I know you're the doctor, but do you think that's a good idea? At least, so soon?"

"I've called the office and asked them to lighten my schedule until I see how my stamina holds up. I'll be fine. I'm actually looking forward to getting back to work. I miss the staff and my patients. It'll be a great way to start the new year."

"I think that's great . . . and Pete, let Jack be the doctor," Mary said.

"Just looking out for my guy."

"I know, Pete, and I appreciate it," I said. "Now, enough of that. Let's order. I'm starved."

Dinner with friends was just what I needed. We talked a lot about Annie, which I handled without losing control of my emotions. In fact, it was good to hear her name spoken. Actually, it was good just to be enjoying life again, with a new perspective not tainted by gloom. As we finished dinner and prepared to leave, Pete asked if I had plans for the weekend.

"No, not really. I'm going to sleep a lot, do some reading, and look over my charts for Monday."

"You could join us for an art exhibit on campus this weekend," he offered.

"I'd love to. Count me in! Even if I don't like it, I'll pretend like I do," I said. We all laughed.

Chapter Seventy-Four

"**J**ack, can I see you in my office, please?"

It was Payne. The last thing I needed on my first day back was a confrontation with him.

"Have a seat, please," he said, his tone sounding more conciliatory than usual. "I know what you've been through, Jack, and just want you to know I'm glad you're back. You need to ease back into work, though. We're more than capable of covering for you, so no need to overtax yourself."

"Thanks, Dr. Payne. I really appreciate that," I said, trying not to sound or look surprised. "And I'm grateful to you and the partners for covering for me while I was out."

"Of course. That's what partners are for. And please, Jack, call me Gus."

"Well, I'll try! I do want you to know that if I start having trouble again, I'll come to you immediately."

"Good plan. I'll count on it. Anything else?"

"Nope."

"Okay, then. Let's get to our patients," Gus said as we turned to leave his office.

It was good to be back at work. I was happy again—not giddy happy but just content in what I was doing and feeling fortunate to be there. Annie's memory was still a dominant part of my thinking, but I somehow kept it in its proper place, allowing me to focus on taking care of my patients. Although my station in life hadn't changed, my attitude had. I could only attribute it to the accident and what

I'd learned from that experience. If one could be grateful for nearly drowning, I truly was. Our office manager Karen, the staff, and my partners noticed, but more importantly, my patients did too. One of them said I must have had one heck of a Christmas. Clearly, he was oblivious of what I'd been through, which was fine with me.

"What makes you say that?" I asked.

"You just seem different today than the last time I saw you. You were kind of dour, to be honest, and seemed to just go about your business, sort of like a robot. Not the usual bantering back and forth that I always look forward to. I mean, I understood it—you'd lost your wife, God rest her soul, so I attributed it to that. Now, you're like a new person or, at least, the Dr. Wilson I first met when you were new to the practice."

"Well, to your point, I did have a somewhat different holiday break, to say the least. I'll spare you the details, but I went through some stuff that made me appreciate what I get out of bed to do every day. I'm glad you noticed, and I'm sorry for my affect the last time you were here."

"Not a problem, Doc. I understand. Glad you're feeling better."

I realized some patient interactions are about much more than just making a diagnosis and prescribing treatment. A patient honestly talking with me, and comfortable enough to give me feedback that would help me be a better provider, was invaluable. I loved it.

As my appetite returned and my stamina improved, I began running again. The exercise improved my appetite. Late in my first week back at work, one of my partners, Jim Davis, a self-avowed bachelor for life, asked me to join him at the nearby diner for dinner. I happily agreed.

As we sat down in the diner, Jim said, "Jack, I know you've heard this from Karen and I'm sure from your patients, too, but speaking for all the partners, we're so glad you're back and doing well. You know, it wasn't easy for us to make you take some time off over the holidays, but we felt that was a better option than Gus's idea of reporting you to the medical board."

"Grateful for that, Jim, to be sure. Speaking of Gus, this past Monday he welcomed me back in a very kind way. Totally unexpected."

"Jack, there are a few things you need to know about Gus. I know he was hard on you when you started with us, but that was intentional."

"Why? What was the point?"

He explained that Gus started the practice when he was fresh out of residency, after he'd been chief resident—just like me. He now acknowledges he was much too cocky and self-assured. One day, he saw a man in his forties who came in with chest pain. The guy had no risk factors, and his exam was negative. Gus reassured him that his heart was fine, and he was just experiencing heartburn and sent him home with an antacid prescription.

"What's wrong with that? I've done it a hundred times," I said.

"Yeah, me too. Well, early the next morning, Gus got a call from the ER. Seems the patient had presented to the hospital dead on arrival. The prescription signed by Gus was found in his shirt pocket. The autopsy showed a massive myocardial infarction."

"Oh, no. A doctor's worst nightmare!"

Jim nodded and raised his eyebrows. "I know, right? Gus never forgave himself; you and I both know that's not something a doctor can ever forget. He resolved to never let it happen again—not to him or to any of his partners. When we joined the practice, all of us were put through the same conversations you've had with him. He just doesn't want any of us to drop our guard and experience what he did."

"So he's doing this for our own good?"

"Exactly. He cares about the patients in this practice and all of us who care for them. His gruff nature is just a front."

"Wow." I shook my head.

"There's another thing you need to know."

Jim went on to say Payne has a classmate from med school who's a hospitalist at the Asheville hospital. Payne had called him daily to get updates on my progress.

"Then, Jack, he'd report your progress to the partners. But remember—you didn't hear this from me!"

Our conversation was interrupted by our waitress. It was "Holly with a smiley face," looking at me with a glance that suggested she remembered me. *Maybe not a good thing, Wilson. You were kind of a jerk last time.*

"Hi, Holly," Jim said. "This is Dr. Jack Wilson, one of my partners."

"Oh, we've met," she said, smiling.

"Holly, it's good to see you back at work. I've missed you. How are things?" Jim said.

"I'm doing okay, Doc. Thanks for asking."

"And Travis?"

"Travis is *so* much better. That's why I'm back at work. Again, appreciate you asking."

After she took our orders and headed to the kitchen, I asked, Jim about Holly's story. He seemed to know her personally.

"Well, Jack, you're probably learning bachelor life means cooking for yourself. I took a stab at it, but my dog wouldn't even eat what I cooked. Most nights now, I just come here. And to answer your question, Holly has been out with her son, Travis. He suffers from poorly controlled asthma and sometimes has flare-ups that land him in the hospital."

"It's always the mom who has to miss work to tend to a sick child," I said as I shook my head.

"In her case, there's no option." He then lowered his voice and leaned toward me. "Holly's a single mom now. She was barely out of high school when she married an immature jerk, at least in my opinion. He walked out on her when Travis was just a baby. He rarely sees Travis, which is just as well since he's a smoker and that just aggravates Travis's asthma. Only reason I know all this is her ex was my patient when he was a teenager. Not sure where he is now, though, and I don't really care. Hard to understand how a father could desert his child."

His statement gave me pause. Having lost my wife, it escaped me how a man could just walk out on his, much less with a baby involved. But there was something else about it that troubled me.

Shaking my head, I said, "Now, Jim, I feel even worse."

"About what?"

"Before my accident, when I was really down in the dumps, I tried coming here to eat. I really couldn't eat, but I also barely communicated with Holly and then I walked out without ordering. I had my reasons, but she had no way to know what I'd been through. I'm sure she thought I was a jerk."

"She probably didn't give it a second thought, given all she was dealing with."

Holly soon returned with our orders. "My, my," she said, smiling. "Two doctors in our little greasy spoon. Who would've thought it?"

Her good-natured mocking made us laugh.

"Holly, it's good to see you again," I said. "My buddy here filled me in on what you've been going through. I'm really sorry, but I'm glad things are looking up for you and your son."

"Only way to look, if you ask me, Doc," she said, smiling again, as she placed our meals on the table. "*Up* is where God lives, you know. Now, y'all enjoy your dinner, and let me know if you need anything."

Her response gave me pause and sent my thoughts back to Annie. Both she and Holly—two young women who'd been dealt a bad hand in life—had still professed such confidence in their faith in God. I had experienced more than my share of loss and disappointment, but I'd not put it all in God's hands as they had. Until now.

Jim and I ate every bite of our orders—southern fried chicken and potatoes and gravy, with a side of collard greens. Not the healthiest of choices, but life is short, I thought, and then regretted how true that really was. As we got up to leave, Holly walked by one last time.

"Thanks for coming in this evening. Y'all don't be strangers, hear?"

I smiled back at her and nodded as we turned to leave. *You can count on it, Holly.*

Chapter Seventy-Five

April 2019
Southport, North Carolina

Winter slowly released its icy grip and reluctantly gave way to spring. As the temperatures warmed, the sun shone brighter, and bulbs and blossoms began to make their annual debut. The practice was rolling along, and I was back to a busy, yet controlled, schedule. Although my focus was back, there was something gnawing at me that I honestly didn't want to face but knew I had to do. Having unsuccessfully tried to push it out of my head, I finally relented and called Tom Barnes, who gave me the information I needed to move forward with my plan.

On a day off, I drove to Southport, a little coastal town south of Wilmington. The mixed aroma of coffee and pastries struck me as I entered the café, the pre-arranged site for our meeting. I spotted a middle-aged man sitting alone at a table, cradling a cup of coffee and rapidly tapping one foot. He looked just as I'd pictured him from Tom's description, and he certainly didn't fit my preconceived image of some version of a despicable monster. He had thinning, gray hair, wrinkles that spoke to a life not without its hardships, and languid eyes. His clothes were clean but disheveled. As I approached, he seemed to sense who I was and stood to greet me.

"Mr. Monroe?" I asked.

He nodded.

"I'm Jack Wilson. Thanks for agreeing to meet with me."

"Hello, Dr. Wilson. Tom Barnes called me to get my permission for him to share my location and contact information. He described you to me so I'd know who to expect."

We took a seat as a waiter brought me a cup of coffee.

"Please, call me Jack. As you know, Mr. Monroe, I married into your family—"

"My former family," he interrupted.

"Yes, I guess that's right. Anyway, Annie and I were married for far too short a time before I lost her—not long after she lost her mom."

"I know. Even though I was out of her life, she was still my daughter. Annie's passing devastated me."

"Well, I'm actually not here just to talk about her, sir. I'm here to talk about you and Virginia."

Lowering his gaze to his cup, he shook his head and said, "Virginia hated me for what I did to her and the kids. Looking back now, I can't really blame her. I was a fool. I fell for a younger woman who I thought had feelings for me, but I later learned she was just chasing the next fat wallet. It cost me everything, personally and financially. But it was all my fault. Like I said, I was a fool."

"I'm not here to judge you, Mr. Monroe, but I do want to talk about something Virginia told Annie and me in one of our many conversations." I noticed his face reddening as he gripped his cup tighter, as though steeling himself for what he was about to hear. The foot-tapping increased.

"Well, I'm sure it wasn't good, but I can't really fault her after the way I walked out on the family."

I then explained that Virginia had told us she'd forgiven him. This was in the last months of her life, when she knew she was dying, and she was trying to see people she knew and mend broken fences. "She told us she didn't want to go to her grave with ill feelings toward the father of her children, so she'd chosen to forgive you."

"I sure didn't expect to hear that," he said, stroking his stubble beard and slowly shaking his head. "I know Virginia was a person of great faith, but I still find it hard to believe she would forgive me." His chin and lower lip began to quiver.

Nodding, I offered, "Well, she was a remarkable woman with an endless capacity for love, kindness, and forgiveness."

Tears formed in his eyes. "All this just makes the choices I made and actions I took seem even more stupid. After all of that, and the years I left her alone to raise our children, she forgave me? How is that even possible? I've lived with regret over what I did to my family and how it impacted my career. Now, I'm just a bitter old man, all on my own. Forgiveness is not something I ever expected or deserved."

"To be forgiven when you don't deserve it is called *grace*. I was once told by a very wise source that forgiving someone can be difficult, but to forgive yourself can seem like an impossible task. But you need to do it so you can move on with your life in a more positive way."

"Jack, I really don't know what to say, but I really appreciate you meeting me here and telling me this. Maybe I *can* somehow forgive myself. But what about Annie? Did she forgive me too?"

I couldn't bring myself to tell him the things Annie had said. Thinking quickly, I came up with a statement that, while true, didn't actually reveal the whole truth.

"My time with Annie was so short that we never got into an in-depth discussion about her capacity to forgive. From what she said, I could tell it was a very sensitive and difficult subject, so I didn't push it. Unfortunately, like so many other discussions we never made time for, I lost her, and things were left unsaid. That's actually something I had to forgive myself for as well. Anyway, I felt you had the right to know about Virginia's decision."

He thanked me again and explained that he'd need to try to wrap his head around all of this, but it could end up being life-changing for him.

As I got up to leave, he grabbed my right hand and shook it firmly, his face dissolving into a river of tears, making any further conversation almost impossible. *Well, that went better than I'd anticipated*, I thought.

As I got to the front door, I turned to look back at him—a lonely figure sobbing, with his face now buried in his hands. I actually felt sympathy for him and hoped he knew he didn't have to handle the rest of his life all alone.

Chapter Seventy-Six

May 2019
Ocean Isle Beach

P ete and I were hanging out at the Grind and enjoying our coffee. It was great to be back at our favorite haunt. Just to walk into such a place, with its old, familiar sights, smells, and sounds brought me a feeling of comfort. "Nothing like inviting myself, Pete, but what about a weekend at the beach?"

He laughed. "Funny you should mention that, Jack. Mary and I've been itching to get back."

"Thanks, but I don't want to intrude on your plans. Maybe just the two of us some time—you know, for old times' sake."

"Don't be silly. She'd love for you to join us. Won't be the same without Annie, of course, but at least it'll be the beach."

Pete didn't have to twist my arm. I knew I could handle time at the coast with them, even as memories of our time there with Annie would come flooding back. While I was now sure I could make a difference in people's lives, I was struggling with something else I needed to do. The beach would be the perfect place to think things over.

We arrived at the coast on a beautiful, "Chamber of Commerce ad" spring morning. The air blowing off the shore was warmed by a sun slowly separating itself

251

from the horizon, the distance marked by beautiful, blue skies dotted with cotton candy clouds. *If only Annie were here.* I kept that thought to myself.

"This was a great idea, fellas," Mary said, excitedly. "I don't know about you two, but I'm changing into my suit and going out to lounge on the beach."

"I think we'll stay up here for now," Pete said. "We both need more coffee."

"Suit yourself. Just holler when it's time to get some lunch."

As Mary walked off, I said, "This is great, buddy. Sort of like the good old days, right?"

"Copy that, bro. Coffee?"

"Have I ever said no?"

As we sat on the deck, Pete looked at me like he wanted to discuss something serious.

"Jack, I can't tell you how great it is to see you back. I mean, not only back here, but also happy again. I know life's far from perfect, but for me, it's a lot better when you're in it and you're doing well."

"Actually, life does seem better. It's hard for me to explain it to anyone—even you—but I feel like I have a new lease on life and faith that everything will work out as it should."

"*Faith,* Jack? You mean, as in religious faith?"

"Well, yes. I've even gone to church a few times, just to try it out."

"Church? You? How'd that go?"

"Let's just say it's a work in progress, Pete."

"I never knew you to be a church guy, dude. In fact, the only time I've seen you in church is at weddings and funerals . . . I'm sorry, Jack. That came out wrong."

"It's fine," I said, smiling. "In fact, you're right. I wasn't a regular churchgoer, and I didn't understand why Annie went. I really had no idea of the depth of her faith. But I've discovered it for myself." Well, *not all by myself,* but I wasn't going to go into that with Pete.

Pete said, "You know I grew up in a religious home, but I kinda got away from it when I left for college. I started questioning things I'd been taught as a child, and I just couldn't square some circles. Just another way I disappointed my parents, I guess." He set down his cup and shook his head. "But for me, the notion of faith is something I have trouble wrapping my head around, especially when I see awful things happen to good people like Annie and her mom. Can you explain it?"

"No, not really. But I did read somewhere that faith is something you know in your heart to be true, but you can't explain it with your brain. I guess that's about as good a definition as I could ever come up with. I came awfully close to death's doorstep, and it woke me up, almost as though someone flipped a light switch. I realized I had a choice: I could dwell on my losses or focus on my future—on all God's given me—you know, being a doctor and having the gift of healing."

"I've always envied that about you, Jack."

"Oh, don't get me wrong. We all have our gifts, and we've got to use them to the best of our abilities. You're gifted with a love for art and the beauty found in the world. Nothing wrong with that, buddy."

"You might be right. I don't know. Anyway, I'll give some thought to what you're saying. It's not like I lost my faith; it's just weaker these days than it should be . . . hey, this is pretty deep stuff, especially on a beautiful spring weekend at the beach!"

Just then, Mary came up the porch steps. "I'm starving, boys. Let me put on a wrap so we can get an early lunch."

As we walked down the beach, mesmerized by the waves, I sensed Pete was deep in thought. Mary noticed too.

"Honey, you alright?" she asked. "You seem distracted."

"I'm fine. Just thinking."

"About?"

"Just thinking. That's all." He looked out at the ocean.

Over the weekend, when Pete and I were alone, he asked more questions about the changes in my life and my newfound faith. He didn't seem all in, but at least, he was asking questions. Why I thought I could be talking to anyone about faith and religion did enter my mind. When self-doubt crept in, I could hear the voice talking in my head, repeating what had been said, and encouraging me.

Our last morning at the coast, I got up early, made a cup of coffee, and went out on the deck. I needed to think, and I figured looking out at the ocean was as good a place as any to do that. To further fulfill my sense of purpose at work, I knew there was something else I needed to do—something simple that was bothering me, and I had thought about it a lot, especially leading up to the weekend. Being at the coast cleared my head and confirmed my intentions. When we left to head back home, I was sure of what I would do and how I would go about it.

Chapter Seventy-Seven

June 2019
Chapel Hill

At the end of my first day back at work after the beach weekend, I called Mrs. Mason on my drive home. It was good to hear her voice.

"Dr. Wilson! What a nice surprise."

"Hi, Mrs. Mason. I haven't spoken to you in a while and just wanted to know how you're doing."

"Oh, same as ever, I'd say. Reckon I'll know more when I see the clinic doctor tomorrow afternoon. I've got one of those follow-up visits. But how are you doin', Doc?"

"I'm fine. Staying busy. You know, same as always."

"Well, you take care of yourself . . . oh, listen to me giving a doctor advice!"

"I'll listen to your advice anytime, Mrs. Mason. We'll talk again soon." *Sooner than she thinks.*

The following morning, I went into Mrs. Mason's electronic record, just to find her appointment time for her clinic visit that afternoon. I knew it was a HIPPA violation, but I also knew it wouldn't matter if things worked out as I hoped they would. I finished my schedule early and headed to Chapel Hill.

I guess some things never change. The drab, eclectic hospital furnishings, medicinal odors, and the chatter of many people talking all at once took me back to the many days I'd spent here as a Family Practice resident. Notwithstanding the spartan surroundings, this clinic held a special place in my heart. This is where I honed my craft and learned to take care of not just a disease, but the person with the disease. I slid inconspicuously into a chair in the corner of the waiting room, picked up a worn and outdated magazine, and prepared to wait as long as it took for her to emerge from her appointment. After some time, she walked out of the clinical area and headed for the checkout desk, failing to see me sitting in the corner until she turned to leave.

"Well, praise the Lord and pass the mustard, if it isn't Dr. Wilson!" Mrs. Mason said.

"Hi, Mrs. Mason. Great to see you. You're looking good as ever," I said. I stood and gave her a hug.

"And your compliments are still as smooth as a baby's butt," she said, squeezing me gently. "What on earth are you doing here? Is one of your patients here for some reason?"

"Well, maybe. That's what I wanted to talk to you about. Do you have a few minutes to walk over to the café for a chat?"

"Let me see . . . a cup of coffee with a handsome young doctor who happens to be one of my favorite people? I think I can clear my busy schedule," she said, her wide smile bringing a sparkle to her tired eyes.

We picked up our coffee order and took seats at a corner table that gave us privacy.

"It *is* so good to see you, Mrs. Mason. Are you still giving your doctors a hard time?"

"Every last one of them, 'cept you, of course. But I can't complain. When I do, nobody listens, so what does it matter? Nothing's changed, I'd have to say."

"Well, no matter what you say, your doctors must be taking good care of you."

"I reckon they're doin' an alright job. It's just that as soon as I get comfortable with one, they move on and are replaced by a younger doctor. Why, I've got Tupperware older than some of those doctors!"

Same old Mrs. Mason. "Still have your sense of humor, I see. That's good. But there's something I want to talk to you about. I have a proposition for you."

"Oh, my, Dr. Wilson, I do declare you make me blush."

"Not that kind of proposition," I said, breaking out in a laugh. "I want to be your doctor again and take over your care—at my office, that is. We're on the same electronic record as the hospital's system, so the transfer of your care would be as seamless as it gets. Of course, the sub-specialists would still provide your in-patient care, but at least, I'd be around to explain things to you. It would be just like old times."

"But when I asked you about that some time back, you said it wasn't allowed by your practice. What changed?"

"*I* changed. I felt terrible when I refused your request that I be your doctor again. I've talked to my partners and explained our relationship. They were all fine with you becoming a patient in the practice, so the senior partner signed off on it. Heck, you'd probably liven things up around there."

"Well, you don't have to twist my arm, Doc. I don't know what to say, 'cept thank you. You know I love you—uh, *love* in the plutonic sense if you get my drift."

Platonic. But I decided not to correct her and risk the sweetness of the moment.

"Okay, it's a done deal then," I said, smiling.

"Thanks again, Dr. Wilson. Now, I have a question for you."

"Shoot."

"How are *you* doing? You seem so much happier now."

"I'm doing well. Thanks for asking."

"Well, we both know what a sweetie Miss Annie was and how awful it is to believe she's gone. It can't be easy for you."

"You're right. It hasn't been easy, but I'm learning how to let go and live . . . or at least put my life with Annie in the proper place in my head. I'm sure you went through that when Mr. Mason died."

"If you can count on your fingers, you can count on that, for sure. I didn't think I'd ever get over not having my Jimmy around. It's still tough at times. Some little thing will trigger a memory and then all kinds of silly, sentimental notions start banging 'round in my brain. That's when I turn into a blubbering fool, I reckon," she said as the gleam in her eyes moistened.

"Yes, ma'am. I've experienced that too. It can be so difficult. Anyway, enough of that. Let's start planning how we're going to take care of you. Once you've requested a transfer to my practice and I'm granted access to your records, I'll get up to speed on what's been happening with you. Then, I'll decide on a time to see you at the office. Sound good?"

"Sounds peachy, Doc. I really don't know what to say."

"You don't have to say a thing. Now, let's get you out to the bus stop so you can get home. You must be exhausted after spending half the day at the clinic."

"You going to escort me to the bus stop, young man?"

"Absolutely! I wouldn't have it any other way," I answered as I finished my coffee and tossed the cup in the trash. "Let's go."

We walked out of the coffee shop, her arm in mine. I'm sure she needed it for stability, but I wanted to think it also represented some amount of affection—or at least appreciation.

As we walked, I looked up. The sky was a brilliant robin's egg blue, with a few cumulus clouds lazily drifting by. The sun was just beginning to descend, its radiance still illuminating the world below. It was a good day to be alive, outside, and walking in the light.

Epilogue

June 2020 (One year later)

Mrs. Mason was my patient again for the last year of her life. We enjoyed many visits, but my presence was mostly one of emotional support, as medically there wasn't anything I could do for her. Her aged body and exhausted bone marrow finally just gave out. She died peacefully at home, just as she'd wanted. Unlike Annie, where death came like a thief in the night, leaving in its wake loss and despair, for Mrs. Mason, it came as an angel of mercy, gently ending what had been a valiant battle. I'm convinced I'll never have another patient quite like her. She had grit and courage, and she lived her life joyfully and to the fullest, setting an example for the rest of us. I was grateful to be there as she drew her last breath. I will miss her terribly.

"Are you comfortable, Mrs. Mason? We can give you more medication," I said, as I took her hand in mine. I'd rushed to her home from the office after getting a call from her hospice nurse. She wasn't expected to make it through the night.

"I'm fine," she whispered. Then, with a little more effort and a slight smile, she said, "Some things just don't change. You doctors are just bound and determined to fill me up with one poison or another."

"Guilty as charged. It's what we do, I guess. I just want you to be comfortable."

"Just sit here with me for a spell, Doc."

"You know I'm here as long as you need me."

"Here for me just like you were for my Jimmy. I'm grateful."

"It's always good to be with one of my favorite people."

"You always know the right thing to say, Doc. Smooth as Tennessee whiskey, I'd have to say."

"Why don't you try to get some rest?"

"Well, I am tired, sure 'nough . . . Oh my, it's beautiful," she said as she looked toward the ceiling and her half-closed eyes opened wide. "Now, I get to see my Jimmy again."

Those were the last words she said, and her eyes slowly closed for the last time.

My interactions with other patients changed as well, as I relied on my faith when I felt it was appropriate. My experiences of personal loss, depression, and near-death strengthened my response to others going through similar trials. It became the most fulfilling aspect of my medical practice. To be with people in their greatest time of need is a rare privilege, primarily reserved for the medical profession and the clergy. Relationships outside of my professional life changed as well, but that's a story for another day.

"Hi, Jack. Thanks for coming," Pete said as we took a seat in the Grind.

"Of course. Always happy to meet you, especially here—just like old times, right? How've you been, buddy?"

"I'm okay. But I need to talk to you about something," he said quietly, leaning forward with eyes focused on me.

"Pete, what's going on?"

"I've decided to switch directions in my life."

"But I thought you loved art history."

"I do, bro. That's not what I'm talking about."

"So what *are* you talking about?"

"I'm talking about my personal life: getting back to church, living my beliefs, and practicing the faith I was brought up in."

"That's great, but why the sudden change?"

"Not really sudden. Mary going to church has influenced me, and seeing you go through what you did and coming out on the other side. That doesn't just happen by chance. It's practically a miracle."

"Yeah, Pete. A miracle, for sure." We both smiled.

———

I've often thought back on my life and wondered if, were it possible, I would change the way things played out. I suppose that's a normal process we all go through as we age and accumulate more life experiences. I've decided it's a rhetorical point, as we're not really in charge of our lives. Many things happen over which we have no control. That doesn't make life easier, to be sure, but through those experiences, we gain wisdom and insight, and when taken in the context of a higher power, we grow stronger.

Do I miss Annie? Terribly, and I always will. I have no answer for why she was taken so young. But I do know this: she lost her life but saved mine. Through her death, I discovered God's grace. What greater gift could a wife give her husband?

Someday, the truth will be revealed, and I'll finally understand everything that still confuses me. That strengthens me when doubts creep in and I wrestle with hard questions. I also know this: In life, especially when we go through dark times, we either have nothing to fall back on or we have faith.

As for me, I choose faith.

Acknowledgments

As the saying goes, "If you see a turtle on a fence post, you know it didn't get there by itself." And so it is with bringing a book to life. I have many people to thank.

Betsy Thorpe, my developmental editor, was the first to read my manuscript. Her suggestions made the final iteration so much better. Kimmery Martin, my physician colleague and a novelist, encouraged me from the start and was always generous with her advice when I had questions.

Terry Whalin, my acquisitions editor at Morgan James Publishing, took a look at a rookie writer's work and then graciously asked for more. Terry, without you, this book likely wouldn't exist.

Cortney Donelson, Heidi Nickerson, Emily Madison, Jim Howard, David Hancock, and all the good people at Morgan James have my utmost respect and profound appreciation. "Thank you" seems so inadequate.

I want to thank my spiritual mentors: the Rev. Dr. Thomas Kort, the Rev. Dr. David McKechnie, and Mrs. Jan Rosser. You will recognize some of the thoughts and lines in the book as your own. I only hope I did them justice. At least, you know I was listening!

A big thank you goes to my (unpaid) technical advisor, Dr. Stephanie Vanderford. My gratitude for your assistance pales in comparison to my gratitude to God that I get to call you my daughter.

Finally, the biggest thank you is for my wife, Carolyn. Writing a book is a solitary journey, and you endured years of me alone in my study and never complained. Your encouragement and support mean everything to me. Also, thanks for not laughing when I first told you I planned to write a book!

About the Author

Tim Eichenbrenner was born and raised in southeastern Virginia. He now lives with his wife, Carolyn, in Charlotte, North Carolina, where he practiced pediatrics for thirty-eight years. He used his experiences as a physician and his own faith crisis after a tragic personal loss as guides in the writing of this book. *To Live in the Light* is his first novel.

You can also find Tim on Facebook, Instagram, and at his website, timeichenbrenner.com.

A free ebook edition is available with the purchase of this book.

To claim your free ebook edition:

1. Visit MorganJamesBOGO.com
2. Sign your name CLEARLY in the space
3. Complete the form and submit a photo of the entire copyright page
4. You or your friend can download the ebook to your preferred device

Morgan James
BOGO™

A **FREE** ebook edition is available for you or a friend with the purchase of this print book.

CLEARLY SIGN YOUR NAME ABOVE

Instructions to claim your free ebook edition:
1. Visit MorganJamesBOGO.com
2. Sign your name CLEARLY in the space above
3. Complete the form and submit a photo of this entire page
4. You or your friend can download the ebook to your preferred device

Print & Digital Together Forever.

Snap a photo

Free ebook

Read anywhere

CPSIA information can be obtained
at www.ICGtesting.com
Printed in the USA
JSHW061750250822
29762JS00004B/6

9 781631 958588